THE TRIPLEHORN BRAND, BOOKS 1-3

DELILAH DEVLIN

LAYING DOWN THE LAW

THE TRIPLEHORN BRAND, BOOK 1

New York Times and *USA Today* Bestselling Author
Delilah Devlin

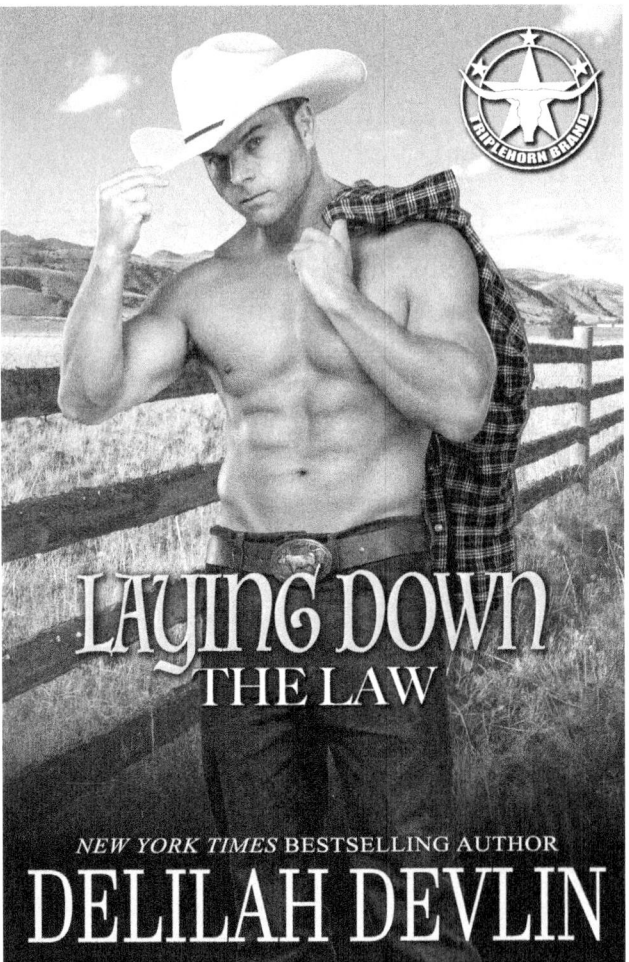

ABOUT THE BOOK

A teller implicated in a bank robbery seeks sanctuary from small-town sweetheart she left behind — who happens to be the new sheriff in town...

A lifetime ago, Zuri Prescott kicked the dirt off her boots and fled her small-time, small town, but lived to regret choosing a glam city life over her high school sweetheart. When she's framed for a bank robbery, she flees to her home town, seeking refuge with her old flame while she figures out her next steps–only to discover he's the last man she can confide in.

Sheriff Colt Triplehorn knows trouble when he sees it, especially when it's one familiar naked trespasser, caught between an angry bull and her underwear. Sure she's up to her usual no good, he grants her sanctuary at his ranch where he can keep an eye on her while he purges her from his system once and for all. When he realizes she's involved with a robbery, he has to make a career-compromising choice between following the letter of the law and his heart...

CHAPTER 1

Rain fell in sheets, so heavy and fast that it wasn't long before Zuri Prescott's hands ached from her death grip on the steering wheel. The darkness muted her headlights so that she couldn't see farther than twenty yards in front of her, but the beams still glossed the highway's surface to a bright glare, which left her wondering whether she was inside the lines or sailing down the middle.

She'd been driving for hours, numbed to the worsening conditions, her mind caught in an endless loop, reliving the horrors of the day.

Her panic hadn't lessened for even a moment since she'd first felt a gun pressed against her temple early that morning as she'd begun unlocking the side door of the branch bank, and a harsh voice whispered in her ear to get it open fast.

A heated body had moved close to her back and

crisp, spicy cologne drifted over her. With her hands shaking, she'd unlocked the door, and then let him shove her through.

She'd landed on her knees, her pantyhose shredding on impact—the long, fat ladder that rippled up her thigh as strangely upsetting as the masked man behind her who grabbed her by the hair and pulled her up to face the security alarm.

She'd pressed the buttons on the key pad, disarming the premises alarm, and dropped her hands. But another nudge of hard steel against her back, and his hushed, "The vault alarm, too, sweetheart," had her punching a second set of numbers before he hustled her around the corner toward the vault, out of sight of her manager who waited in the parking lot for the all-clear signal.

The vault operated on a timer. At any other time of day, she wouldn't have been able to open it—a fact that didn't register until later. She'd spun the two combination locks, heard the inner mechanisms clang as they released, and he'd reached around her to grab the lever and push it down. The large steel door swung open.

The thief had shoved her through the anteroom with security deposit boxes lining both side walls, heading straight for the locked door at the rear. Again, he'd waited while she'd found the key and opened the door, then shoved the mesh interior gate inward.

Forcing her to her knees, he'd wrapped her wrists and ankles in duct tape, and pulled a hood over her head.

Then she'd been left to shiver on the floor, listening to the sounds he made as she followed him in her mind through the gate while he scooped stacks of cash into a bag. One side only. Later, the assistant manager pointed out that the thief must have been timing himself, a real pro, because he'd skipped the temptation of pausing to finish the sweep.

Less than five minutes had passed since they'd entered. Another two and the manager would call the police.

The thief had walked back to her and knelt, his knee touching hers as he leaned close.

She'd stayed silent, afraid as she'd never been before, because she knew he was going to kill her.

But the sound of keys rattling against glass had him scrambling to his feet and rushing out of the vault. A muffled shout and a single piercing shot was followed by the soft swoosh of the door closing.

For several interminable moments, she'd sat frozen, afraid he'd come back. But when he hadn't, she'd crawled on her belly across the floor, inching her way toward the first desk in the lobby to hit a panic button, but she needn't have bothered. Already, sirens screamed in the distance, and she slumped on the floor, shivering and beginning to cry.

When the police arrived, her hood was pulled off,

and a grim-faced police officer helped her sit while he cut the tape binding her.

Her head swiveled toward the door where the shot had sounded, and she saw another officer bent over Sam McWherter, her boss, whose rotund body lay spread-eagle on the floor, blood seeping outward to soak into the carpet.

The officer beside her moved to cut off her view. "You're okay. Don't look. We've got this place secured."

Everyone had been solicitous. A hot cup of tea was pressed between her cold hands. She'd been herded into McWherter's office, away from the body and the team beginning to comb the lobby and vault for evidence. They'd been kind, gently but firmly asking her to go over the chain of events that had transpired.

She'd given them a step-by-step description—of the robber's actions and her sketchy knowledge of his height, weight, and gruff voice. The second time through, she swayed in her chair from melting exhaustion.

"Ma'am, did anyone know your routine?"

That one question from the first FBI agent to arrive on scene sparked a dawning horror, and she froze, noting the glance he shared with the pair of detectives flanking her in leather-upholstered chairs. Someone did know her routine—and wore a crisp cologne that smelled like cinnamon and sandalwood.

She swallowed hard, realizing in a split second that she'd been set up. That she might even be implicated because the robber wasn't a fool. No, he'd been incredibly, devastatingly clever.

While the agent waited for her to respond to the questions, she'd shook her head, giving him a tight smile. How could she tell them they were looking for a cop? Who would believe her side of the story? Especially after they did a little digging into her background. She'd lied about her affiliations with known felons when she'd applied for this job.

When she'd pleaded illness, they'd escorted her to her desk where she'd filled out the bank's incident reports and made arrangements to meet later with the detectives and the FBI agent assigned the case at the station house to sign a statement, but her mind was already racing ahead.

She couldn't go back to the apartment and risk meeting *him*. He'd have to finish what he'd started.

Gathering the handbag they'd already searched, she'd palmed her keys, nodded her agreement to see them later, and walked sedately out the front door of the bank.

Since the moment she'd slid behind the wheel, she'd been on autopilot, navigating out of her Houston suburb and heading northwest. Once, she'd stopped briefly for gas, but there, she'd received another shock when she'd opened her glove compartment to retrieve her SpeedGas key.

Now, she drove with just one thought, just one image burned into her mind. An isolated cabin, deep in cattle country. Somewhere no one would think of looking for her. Then she could take a breath and consider what to do next.

She didn't see the city-limit sign when she passed it, but she knew where she was when she reached the highway crossroad. She turned left, away from the little town she'd once been so eager to escape, and toward the Triplehorn Ranch.

Lights flared behind her as another car took the turn. For just a moment, the rain relented, and she saw the model of the vehicle. Her panic surged again.

How had he found her? She'd driven backroads in case the police were already alerted that she'd fled.

The headlights of the car behind her switched off. Not knowing how close behind her he was, she gunned the gas pedal. Her car surged forward, tires losing traction in standing water. The rear of her vehicle wagged in a wicked fishtail, but she steered through it, not easing up on the gas. If she could outrun him, make it to the cabin, and hide her car beneath the lean-to...

She'd forgotten about the low-water crossing until she saw the yellow warning sign. With only a moment to make a decision, she kept her foot on the accelerator, hoping the water wasn't too deep, that momentum would propel her through if it was, and held tight to the steering wheel.

The road dipped, her car hit the water, jerking

her against her seatbelt, spray coating the windshield, too thick for the wipers to clear. Then she felt the subtle shift beneath her as her car was lifted and floated sideways, off the low bridge, tilting as it slid into the swiftly moving water.

CHAPTER 2

Colt Triplehorn pushed back his cowboy hat and wiped away the sweat gathering above his brow with his shirtsleeve. The blue sky was clear of clouds, the sun rising hot and fast and turning the moisture soaked in the ground into steam. The air was thick, humid, hard to breathe.

Even his dog Scout felt the aftereffects of the previous night's storm. His gray-and-white Australian Shepherd kept pace with his horse. But the dog's tongue lolled from one side of his mouth, and he wasn't as quick to dart toward the herd and nip at the heels of the cows who wandered too far from the main body.

They'd been moving cattle since dawn—shifting them from a parched and overgrazed pasture to this one. Here, the buffalo grass was longer and greening up fast after the downpour. Maybe they'd even be able to put off buying another load of hay for a week or so, if the sun didn't scorch the grass too quickly.

Colt's gaze lifted to the tall elm trees lining the banks of the creek that bordered the pasture, and he stifled a grimace. Past the tall trees stood the ramshackle hunting cabin he hadn't had the heart to enter in years. His brothers kept it stocked, heading there each fall during the short deer-hunting season. Maybe this year, he'd join them.

Maybe this year, he'd get past the memories the little cedar-log cabin evoked. Twelve years was a long time to hold onto a dream.

There in that little cabin, he'd secretly met with his girl, Zuri. There, they'd cuddled after school and explored each other's bodies. There, he'd taken her virginity. It was also there that he'd planned to propose.

The ring had burned a hole in his pocket for weeks, waiting for graduation day. He'd bought new bedding for the twin mattresses of the two bunk beds, replaced the yellowed curtains in the windows with pretty white lace. A white linen tablecloth had covered the plank table, and he'd smuggled china and crystal from the house for the meal he'd planned. Everything had been perfect. Waiting for her.

But she'd never known, because as soon as the graduation ceremony ended, she'd walked over to him as everyone else headed to the parking lot outside the high school gym, gave him a kiss and told him goodbye.

He'd stood there like a stump, not saying a word. Every warning his brothers had given him about not trusting her, about her being bad news, searing his mind.

"What were you gonna tell me?" she'd asked, gazing up at him with her deceptively soft brown eyes.

"Never mind," he'd mumbled, pulling himself together for his own pride's sake and walking her to her car. It had been the last time he'd seen or talked to her. Not that he'd ever expected to again. Once she'd passed the city-limit sign, he'd been history.

He hoped like hell she'd found what she'd been looking for, because he'd been lost after she left.

Sure, he'd gone through the motions—even did a stint in the Army, enlisting that summer because he had to get away. When he'd come back, he wasn't the same person he'd been. He'd worked on the ranch between semesters at Texas A&M and entered the police academy in San Antonio afterward, before heading home to work in the small town's sheriff's department. But he hadn't felt as connected to Destiny, Texas as he had before. He'd stayed because he had a job and a duty to help maintain the family ranch. He certainly hadn't stayed because he'd found everything he ever wanted here.

More selective than his horn-dog brothers, he'd kept his affairs few and far between. Perhaps he needed a little of what the younger Triplehorn brothers were famous for. He needed to let loose, have a couple of drinks, and find a willing woman.

She didn't have to be pretty or slim. Didn't have to be young. Or nice. He wouldn't be choosy. After all, his goal wasn't a relationship.

He needed the kind of arrangement he'd had with Maggie Pounders...until the day she'd up and got married. Last time he'd showed up at her door, she'd lifted her left hand to show him the ring. He hadn't known she'd been seeing anyone else, or that she was even interested in marriage. Not that they'd ever done a whole lot of talking.

One thing was certain, Colt needed some relief to get rid of the edgy, restless energy that had made him a bear to be around lately—more likely to snap than smile. He needed release from the pressure of all the responsibilities he'd taken on in the last year. Hell, he just needed release. Plain and simple.

This morning, as he'd eaten dust churned up by five hundred sets of hooves, Colt had made up his mind. Tonight, he'd take off the badge, head into Destiny, find a willing partner, and get laid. For his brothers' sake.

They'd been tip-toeing around him for days, making sly comments about the source of his bad temper. They'd even offered to hook him up, but the last thing Colt wanted was those two finding him a woman. Gabe's and Tommy's idea of the perfect playmate didn't square with his. Never had.

They'd both warned him about Zuri Prescott

when he'd seemed hell-bent to marry her into the family. Zuri was a different sort of trouble from the kind they wanted for their big brother. And in the end, they'd been right. Still, their preferences for big-chested blondes with easy smiles and easier morals didn't stir his interest. He'd find his own playmate, thank you very much.

Scout's sharp bark pulled him from his thoughts. The dog ran ahead of him, his ears pricking forward, so Colt peeled away and headed toward the creek. Maybe Scout had found Old Mule, the ornery bull who was always one step away from being hamburger due to his contentious nature and independent streak.

Colt lifted his hand to send a signal to his brother, Gabe, and laid his reins over the neck of his horse to turn him toward the trees and the creek. Then he looked for a firm, gentle slope for his horse to maneuver.

From the corner of his eye, something white floating on the surface of the water caught his attention. He pulled back on the reins. A woman's bra.

Finding odd items floating on a river after a storm wasn't all that unusual, and the station hadn't gotten any calls for missing persons caught in the river. Still, he had to check it out.

Colt clucked at his horse, his curiosity and professional instinct kicking into gear. The creek had risen fast the previous night, but had just as quickly receded, leaving the sides of the embankment muddy and soft. His horse's hind legs slipped, but the old paint caught himself and scrambled down to the graveled bank.

Colt dismounted, dropped his reins, and followed the edge of the water.

"Shoo, cow! Shoo!" came a breathy, feminine shout from just beyond the bend of the river, accompanied by Scout's excited barks.

Rounding the bend, he spotted a twelve-hundred-pound bull, the Triplehorn brand standing in stark relief against the animal's dun-colored rump. Scout stood next to him, barking ferociously, but the bull's attention seemed glued to something on the other side of him.

Colt slipped closer and a flash of pale, creamy legs was visible beneath the creature's belly. He crept along the edge of the water, taking cover behind a tree to get a better look. His eyes widened at the sight in front of him.

A naked woman stood in the center of the creek, waving her arms at the bull.

Colt paused, taking in the long, sleek curves and pale skin. Her chin-length hair was slicked back. His cock stirred instantly. His heart hammered fast, stricken by the resemblance...but it couldn't be...

Then Old Mule ambled toward the edge of the water, his head down, snorting. Not a good sign.

"Lady," he said, stepping out from behind the tree, "you need to hold real still."

The woman whipped her head toward him, her brown eyes rounding.

Her shock wasn't any greater than his. For a long moment, they both stood still.

But Old Mule snorted again, pawing his hooves into a pile of folded fabric on the ground beneath him, which Scout was tugging to free.

"Scout, heel!" he shouted and waited until his dog raced to his side. "Don't move," he repeated softly to the woman, reluctantly pulling his gaze from her and turning to the bull.

Old Mule lowered his head, scraping a horn into the dirt at his feet. When he lifted his head, something shiny and pink came up, snagged on the tip of one horn. The bull snorted again, a moist huff, his gaze on the woman standing frozen in front of him.

The woman's gaze darted to the right, toward a rocky ledge overhanging the water.

The bull huffed and stomped his front legs.

Cursing, Colt took off his hat and strode forward, waving the straw hat at the bull. "Get on back. Ha! Ha!"

The bull gave a plaintive moo, all his bluster gone. He headed up the creek, pink panties stuck to the tip of his horn, but taking his time to stop and pluck at grass on the creek bank.

"Get on!" Colt shouted, slapping the bull on the rear to get him moving faster, funneling him up an arroyo and toward the herd, Scout right behind him.

After the bull and the dog clambered up the side,

Colt dropped his hat back on his head and turned slowly toward Zuri.

She dropped into the water, crossing her arms over her chest.

Colt stalked toward the bank, whistling softly—but finding it hard because his lips were beginning to stretch into a smile, anger and lust swirling into a heady mixture of revenge. "Well, well, well," he said quietly. "Mind telling me what you're doin' skinny-dippin' on my property?"

Zuri opened her mouth to speak, but she clamped her lips closed and lifted her chin. "I was at the cabin and decided I needed a bath. There's no runnin' water."

He didn't bother reminding her that her efforts to shield herself from his gaze were too little and too late. His blood had already surged, fueled by a spike of adrenaline and lust. "Sure, there is," he growled. "There's a pump next to the sink."

"It doesn't work."

"You have to prime it with water first." At her blank stare, he muttered, "Never mind. I guess the better question to ask is what the hell are you doin' back here, Zuri-girl?"

CHAPTER 3

Zuri bit her lip. Colt didn't look happy to see her. But why should he? It wasn't like she'd been any more than a convenience for him in high school. The girl from the wrong side of the tracks with the scandalous family—she'd never really stood a chance at being anything other than his little bit on the side.

She could still remember standing in the gym, her heart pounding as she'd stared up at him, telling him she had her bags packed, and she was heading east to start her life. Her stepfather had shown her the door that morning, his duty done. She didn't have any place to go but away—unless Colt offered her another option.

But his face had hardened, his jaw sawing closed, a muscle rippling along the strong, square edge.

"What were you gonna tell me?" she'd asked past the lump lodged at the back of her throat.

"Never mind," he'd said, pulling on a tight smile and walking her to her car.

With that, she'd had the answer to the question that had lingered between them their entire senior year. He hadn't loved her enough to ask her to stay. And besides, she'd had big plans. Plans that didn't include staying in this one-horse town, no matter how handsome her boyfriend was. Or how sweet his lovemaking.

Staring back at him now, she didn't know why she hadn't fought harder to hold onto him. The promise his lean, rangy body had held had been fulfilled. His broad shoulders and thickly muscled arms stretched the pale blue cotton of his work shirt. His waist tapered to well-hewn hips and thighs. His face, however, had undergone the most changes, losing its youthful softness. It was now honed to sharp, masculine edges. Lord, he made her mouth water.

She wondered if he'd been disappointed in the lack of change in her own body. She was still long and skinny, her breasts unimpressive swells that hardly needed the bra that had floated down the center of the river when she'd confronted the angry bull.

Colt knelt beside her clothing, tucked a finger under her skirt and raised it. "This all you have to wear?"

Light shone through a large jagged tear where the

bull's sharp hooves had ground the navy, summer-weight wool skirt. Zuri's shoulders slumped.

"Do you have something else to put on?"

She shook her head, and Colt stared for a long moment. Then he dropped the ruined skirt to the ground and picked up the blouse. It was grayed from her time in the floodwaters and smudged by the bull's abuse. Colt shook his head. He dropped the blouse too, heaved a sigh, then stood and began to unbutton his shirt.

"Where are your shoes, Zuri?" he asked, his voice rough as gravel.

"Guess I lost them," she said, feeling like her mouth was stuffed with cotton.

"You gonna tell me what's goin' on?"

She sucked her bottom lip between her teeth because it had started to tremble, but managed a nod, even though she knew she'd have to wait and see whether she could trust him with all her woes.

"Here," he said, holding his shirt out for her to take.

Only problem was, she'd have to stand and walk out of the water to get it.

Shouldn't matter that much, anyway, she told herself. Nothing he hadn't already seen…or tasted… and caressed. "Um…I don't suppose you'd turn around?"

His steely gaze narrowed. "Not a chance."

"When did you get so mean?"

One dark brow rose, and Zuri felt a flush of heat paint her cheeks and chest.

"You do know you're bathin' downstream from a herd of cattle..." he drawled.

Zuri popped out of the water, her hands curling at her sides. "Ugh! And you just stood there?"

His soft chuckle held a note of bitterness and not a hint of amusement. Zuri began to think she'd run into the wrong man.

Slowly, she stood, barely resisting the urge to cover her "important parts" with her hands. With her head held high, she walked out of the water and snatched at the shirt, but he drew back his arm at the last second and held it just out of reach.

"Colt, this isn't funny," she said tightly.

"No, it's not. Guess I'm just seein' how much you want it."

Zuri dropped her hands at her sides and slowly curled her hands into fists. "What's it gonna take?"

"I don't know," he said, his gaze dropping down her body, lingering over her nipples, which tautened with embarrassing speed, then sweeping downward to the ruff of dark hair cloaking her sex. "How 'bout a kiss? For old time's sake."

Zuri sucked in a breath, startled at how quickly the tension coiled around them. "Just a kiss?"

"Yes, ma'am," he said, his gaze at last meeting hers again, and narrowing.

She stepped closer, knowing she was flirting with

fire. They'd never stopped at just one kiss. Not once they'd gotten past the hurdle of her virginity.

Swallowing hard, she pressed a hand against his naked chest to steady her weakening knees and lifted on her toes. Her mouth grazed briefly over his, and she dropped down and took a step back. "The shirt?"

"Call that a kiss?"

"Colt...don't..." she said, all bravado seeping away as she noted that anger rather than attraction glinted in his storm-cloud eyes.

"Forget how I like it?" he said softly.

Hell, no. She still had lush, wet dreams about his wicked kisses.

The temptation to give him what he wanted was too much to resist. Pretending she didn't feel a thing, not the liquefying heat that curled deep in her core or the hummingbird-fast flutter of her heartbeats, she gave him a blistering glare and rose again, gliding the tips of her nipples across his bare chest.

He sucked in a deep breath. She reached up and thrust her fingertips into his short, black-brown hair and tugged to bring his mouth down.

When their lips met this time, they both gasped at the intensity of the heat twining around them. His arms closed around her. She clung to his neck, her knees weakening, her entire body trembling against him.

Skin-to-skin, she was reminded why any other man had fallen short in comparison. His muscled frame held hers easily, tensing everywhere their bodies met. He dug his fingers into her bottom and pulled her hips flush with his. His cock jerked beneath the zipper of his jeans, filling swiftly and rutting into her belly.

Their mouths didn't move at first. Both breathed deeply, sharing their breaths as their hips ground together. And then he groaned, locked his lips over hers, and softly sucked, moving her lips beneath his in drugging circles.

When their tongues made tentative forays, touching tips, then stroking deeply alongside each other, Zuri grew lightheaded, overcome with the sheer sensuality of their embrace. His silky-slick tongue rimmed the edges of her teeth then slowly stroked over the roof of her mouth. His lips suctioned softly, reminding her how tenderly he'd once suckled her breasts.

She pulled her mouth away, struggling to breathe. Reluctantly, she met his gaze, knowing she'd given him more than he'd asked for because she hadn't been able to stop.

His hands dropped from her skin. His expression hardened. "Guess you didn't forget after all."

Zuri's lips parted as air rushed out of her lungs, and she dropped her gaze from his coldly, assessing stare. The shirt entered her line of vision, and this time he didn't dart it away when she stuck out her hand.

She turned away to put it on, taking her time buttoning the front and rolling up the sleeves to just above her wrists while she pulled herself together. It was just a kiss. The world hadn't stopped spinning.

"Got anything at the cabin we need to retrieve?" he bit out.

She shook her head. Her purse and car were somewhere downstream. Her navy pumps had been pulled from her feet by the force of the rushing water. She'd been lucky to keep the rest of her clothing on, lucky not to drown. She'd have told him that, but his stony presence kept her silent.

"Let's get you someplace where you can clean up. Then we're gonna have a little talk."

Off the hook for an explanation, for now, she hid her relief, forcing a neutral expression, and slowly faced him again.

He stood so close she had to look a long way up to meet his steady gaze and was swamped again with memories that left her belly trembling.

Colt thrust two fingers into his mouth and issued a piercing whistle, never taking his stormy gray glance from hers.

Hooves pounded on the creek bank, and his horse, Diego, galloped into view. The black-and-white Appaloosa pulled up in front of them, lifting his head and snuffling his nostrils.

He must have remembered something about her, because he ducked his head and butted it under her tightly clenched fist. She'd always had a carrot or an apple for him in the old days.

Colt stepped past her, climbed into the saddle

and bent low to gather the reins. Then he pulled the horse up beside her and held out his hand, kicking a boot free from the stirrup.

Just like the old days, she gave him her left hand, placed her left foot atop his dusty boot, and let him haul her up behind his saddle.

"Better tuck that shirt under your a—under you," he corrected.

Wrinkling her nose at the back of his head, she did just that, not wanting the shirt tail to flap once he kicked the horse into motion.

Then she wound her arms around his waist and tried not to grip him too tightly. She didn't want this to feel familiar, didn't want him to know she wished she could wrap herself around him and press her face against his hot skin. Too many years and too many mistakes lay between them.

Colt clucked and raised his booted heels, giving a gentle nudge to the horse. They climbed the bank, both leaning forward in the saddle. She finally had to press closer and hold tighter to stay seated, but then leaned quickly away when they reached the top.

He waved his hat at his brothers, who both stood in their stirrups, too far away for her to read their expressions. But Gabe lifted a hand, and Colt pulled the reins to the side, pointing the horse toward the ranch house.

As he urged the horse into a canter, Zuri hoped she hadn't made an even bigger mistake than running from the law and David Satterly. As cold as Colt was acting, he might be tempted to turn her in without first hearing her out.

And that was something she couldn't let happen. Not with some of the cash from the robbery stuffed into the glove compartment of her car, and a flimsy story about a stalker she'd never taken the time to properly report.

Perhaps for now, she'd be better off keeping her secrets to herself. At least until she figured out whether she could trust Colt with the truth.

CHAPTER 4

ONCE HIS BATHROOM DOOR CLOSED, Colt headed to the front porch to put as much space between himself and Zuri as possible. Riding all the way back to the ranch house with her warm, damp body pressed against his back did things to him he wasn't ready to face.

He gripped the porch rail and stared out over the yard, watching Eddie Sandoval in the far corral as he walked Diego until he cooled. He wished it could be so easy to cool down his own hot blood. Seeing her again after all this time, on this particular day, when he'd been ready to move on and put the past to rest—it was too ironic. God had to be playing him.

Closing his eyes, he could still see her sweet curves as she'd stood in the water facing that bull. Still tall, still reed-thin and supple. Her breasts, crowned with small cherry-red nipples—hell, he could feel the tight little points digging into his naked back.

In the distance, the tattoo of hooves eating up the ground pulled his gaze. Gabe was riding hard for the house.

Colt wondered what the hell had kept him. Knowing his brothers, they'd already figured out who she was and had drawn straws to see who would kick her butt to town.

Gabe drew his horse to a halt in front of the house, threw a leg over the saddle horn, slid to the ground, and flipped his reins around the porch rail.

"How many times do I have to tell you that rail isn't a hitchin' post?" Colt said, keeping his voice even.

Gabe shrugged. "Don't know. Maybe it'll take a couple hundred more times for it to sink in. And don't change the subject." When he strode up the steps, he pulled a scrap of pink lace from his pocket.

Colt groaned inwardly.

"Not your color, bro," Gabe said, tossing him the pink panties. "Wasn't Old Mule's either."

"Don't start," Colt growled, not liking the way his brother's face was already wearing his bulldog expression—especially not liking the fact that he understood Gabe's animosity toward the naked woman in his shower.

"It's her, ain't it?"

"If you mean Zuri, yeah," Colt said slowly.

Gabe's cheeks were stained with ruddy color.

"Couldn't you wait to get her to the house to strip her raw?"

"That's not what happened."

"Then tell me how the girl who left you high and dry twelve years ago was ridin' naked behind you."

"She wasn't. I gave her my shirt."

Gabe's chest rose around a deep breath. "Colt..."

Colt's cheeks billowed around his own exasperated breath. "I don't know myself. I found her in the creek that way. Old Mule tromped all over her clothes."

A sneer twisted his brother's lips. "Blamin' it on a bull?"

"No, it's what happened," he said slowly, the warning to back the hell down clear in his tone.

"Did you know she was comin' back?"

"Of course not."

Gabe's expression lost some of its tension. His narrowed gaze relented, softening. "Damn, seein' her again knocked you for a loop, didn't it?"

Colt's glance slid back to the paddock. "Somethin' like that."

Gabe leaned against the porch rail, folding his arms across his chest. "Maybe you should leave her to Tommy and me to handle," he said, his tone deceptively even and soft. "I'll take her back to town."

Run her off for good was what he meant. "She wasn't stayin' in Destiny."

"She was in the cabin?"

Colt nodded and turned to Gabe, letting him see

the indecision that had to be written on his face. "With just one outfit and no shoes."

Gabe whistled silently. "Nothin' but trouble's gonna come from gettin' involved in this."

"You don't have to babysit me. I know what I'm doin'."

"Do you?" His brother snorted. "You didn't have to live with you after she dumped you the first time."

Colt grunted and straightened. "Who's watchin' over the herd?"

"Tommy and Skeeter. Almost got 'em settled in the new pasture. You think I'm bein' rough on you, wait until Tommy gets back."

"I don't suppose if I tell you both this is none of your damn business, that you might actually butt out?"

Gabe's lips curved into a rueful smile. "Not a chance."

Rubbing the back of his neck to ease the tension knotting there, Colt's gaze went back to the front door. She was probably finished with her shower and wrapping the robe—*his robe*—around her nude body. Remembering again how incredible it had felt to have her skin sliding along his, he drew a deep breath.

"Be careful, Colt. She's not the stayin' kind."

And because he knew it was true, Colt squared his shoulders, drawing on invisible armor as he walked back through the house, down the hallway to his bedroom door. With his face set in stern lines, he twisted the knob and stepped inside.

. . .

Zuri looked up, her hands pulling the belt tighter around her waist, grateful that this time she was covered neck to below mid-calf. Still, she was hyper-aware she was naked underneath it and only one knot away from making another big mistake.

"You find everything you needed?" he asked, his tone impersonal.

Oddly, she thought she might actually prefer that ragged edge of anger he'd blistered her with by the river. "Yes, thanks." She dropped the ties and smoothed her hands down her sides, nervous beneath his unblinking stare. "I don't suppose you have anything I might wear, besides this robe, that is." She flushed at how awkward this felt, how ridiculous her situation was. A closet full of clothes hung waiting for her six hundred miles away.

"You're pretty skinny. I might have some sweatpants and a T-shirt, but you'll have to cinch in the pants at the waist to keep 'em from fallin' off."

Skinny? Once he'd likened her slender frame to a filly's, and she'd taken it as the highest compliment. She lifted her chin. "That'd be fine."

She jerked when he strode for her, but he edged around the bed, headed to his dresser, and pulled out a pair of gray sweat pants and a navy tee. He tossed both on the bed, and then stood with his hands fisted on his hips.

Zuri bit back a complaint, wishing he'd quit

hovering because he was keeping her on edge. But when he didn't budge, she dragged her feet to the bed, scooped up the wash-softened cotton and turned toward the bathroom.

"Uh huh," he said, tsking softly. "My house. My clothes. *My rules.*"

She glanced over her shoulder, not knowing if she'd heard him right, but that same hard challenge he'd issued when he'd demanded the kiss was stamped all over his granite features.

She knew she ought to ignore him and lock herself into the bathroom to dress and gather her scattered wits, but the underlying tension riding the edge of his jaw excited her.

Colt had never been this dominating...except when they had sex. She'd loved it then. Her body seemed to crave it now. Heat bloomed again, winding around her core. A delicious little thrill accelerated her heartbeats.

Without a saying a word, she walked back to the bed and tossed down the clothing. Then keeping her gaze glued to his, she slowly untied the belt and let the robe fall open. With a sexy shrug, she let it slide off her shoulders and pool behind her on the floor.

Colt blinked first. His gaze trailed downward. His throat worked around a tense swallow, and Zuri couldn't help the smile that tugged at the corners of her mouth. He might think he was in charge, but she knew better. Colt liked what he saw.

His quickening breaths were the first clue. The

curving of his fists the second. When he opened his stance, just a few inches, she nearly crowed.

Reaching for the cotton pants, she wished she had something sexier to slide inside, then wondered if she'd lost her good sense to be thinking that way. She had enough problems on her plate. But how could she dress and prevent him seeing what this was doing to her? Bending and opening her legs to step into the sweatpants made her feel vulnerable, exposed in a way that just standing there naked hadn't. "I don't understand you, or why you're doin' this."

"You don't know me."

"I guess that's true. It's been a long time."

"You didn't know me then."

She pulled the pants upward, over the curve of her bottom, feeling a little less off-center now that her lower half was hidden from his view. The waist of the pants settled on her hips and she rolled the band to gather up the excess fabric. "Guess that'll have to do," she muttered.

As she dragged the T-shirt over her head, she reminded herself why she was here. Definitely not to play games with her ex-boyfriend. She needed a safe place to stay. And she needed to keep Colt clueless until she had a chance to find her car and get rid of the damning evidence before the police found it. Her story might sound a little more believable then.

When she pulled the fabric down, fully covering her body, only then did she raise her glance to Colt's again.

His brows pulled together. "Gonna tell me what's going on? Why you're here?"

"I'm a little hungry," she said, knowing her attempt to stall was completely transparent. "I don't suppose I could eat first?"

Colt dropped his fists and stepped closer, forcing her chin higher to hold his steady gaze. "If you're in trouble…"

What? He'd help? She didn't think so. Colt appeared to be the same inflexible cowboy. He'd always judged a person's actions as either black or white, right or wrong. No interesting muddying of the colors accepted. She'd forgotten that about him.

She pondered telling him part of the tale, but worried he'd use what he learned to play with her some more. He seemed to like the fact he held the reins.

Zuri licked her lips. "I need a place to stay. Just for a little while."

His gray eyes, once so warm and open, narrowed. A muscle flexed alongside his jaw.

She waited him out, knowing he wasn't satisfied with her response. The longer the moment stretched between them, the more uncomfortable she grew. Still holding his steady gaze, she shifted her bare feet, supremely conscious of the fact she wasn't wearing a stitch of underwear, and that his clothing, while freshly laundered, still carried the hint of his unique scent. She was at his mercy. Completely.

Colt inhaled deeply, and then issued a soft,

masculine grunt. He reached down, closed his hand around hers, then tugged her closer to the bed. He sat on the edge, staring at their hands before he looked up. "If you stay...you'll sleep here," he said, his voice tense and ragged.

Zuri wet her lips with her tongue because her mouth had suddenly gone dry. What he proposed sounded both wrong, yet incredibly tempting. She couldn't get words past her tightening throat. If she could have, she didn't know whether she would have told him to go to hell or given him a breathless yes. Instead, she squeezed his fingers.

So many thoughts swirled in her mind. Their past, her impossibly complicated present. It sounded so simple. She'd sleep beside him. Make love with him. Maybe she'd even find out that her memories of their being together were painted in rosy hues because she'd been younger, and he'd been her first.

Perhaps in exchange he'd give her clothes and money so that she could make a graceful exit.

Zuri crowded closer to his knees, tilting her chin.

Colt's lips curved slightly at the corners, and although his gaze remained narrow, he scooted back.

She climbed over his lap, facing him, her thighs sliding over the outside of his, not saying a word but following her instincts although they'd led her down treacherous paths before. She slipped her hand alongside his neck, felt the heavy thrum of his pulse and bent down, her mouth hovering above his. "Think you can keep this uncomplicated, cowboy?"

A deep, throaty groan seeped between his lips, and she leaned into him, settling over the ridge throbbing beneath the placket of his jeans. She could do this. She could take what she wanted from him without losing her heart again. It was just sex. Just an arrangement for shelter, for time.

She had no illusions that she'd be sought by the law, and soon. Her job would report her missing. The police would check her apartment and her background. But Detective David Satterly might want her involvement kept under wraps until he'd gotten to her, and that might work to her advantage.

As Colt's arms closed around her back, he lowered himself to the bed and brought her with him.

Sighing, she let her worries slide away. For now, she'd enjoy this little interlude. Accept the pleasure she knew he could deliver. She was older, had learned a few things about how to keep a relationship light. It was just sex.

But then he slid his hand beneath her shirt, and he scraped his callused palm upward to close around her bare breast. The sandpaper rasp of his thumb across her nipple lit a spark.

Their kiss turned instantly carnal, tongues stroking deeply, lips latching desperately together. Their bodies ground together, frustrated by the clothing separating them.

A knock sounded at the door.

"Ignore it," she whispered.

Colt sighed. "Can't. Gabe'll just barge in. Have to explain it to him first."

She sat, still straddling his hips. He slid his hand slowly from under her shirt, and she climbed off. She turned her back to the door as Colt's footsteps tapped across the bare wood.

Behind her, the brothers' voices whispered too low to make out the words, but the rapidity of their exchange, short-bulleted bursts, told her Gabe wasn't happy with her being here.

Keeping her back to them, she glanced into the dresser mirror and ran her fingers through her damp, tousled hair. Then her gaze fell on the jumbled items resting in a wooden tray. Keys, change. Silver gleamed. She stepped closer and plucked up a metal badge, *Sheriff* etched on its surface.

Zuri's hand closed around it and the sharp edges dug into her skin. The one man she'd thought she might seek refuge with was the last she could trust with her secrets.

CHAPTER 5

Dinner was an uncomfortable affair. Gabe and Tommy offered her surly glares but kept their opinions about her presence to themselves, as Colt held out her chair to seat her at the large plank table. The quiet that followed spoke volumes of the brothers' disapproval.

Zuri did her best to ignore the vibes, concentrating instead on the meal.

The wrangler named Eddie had thrown together a pot roast, potatoes, and carrots. Fluffy biscuits glazed with butter sat in a basket. Tea was served, so sweet her teeth ached at the first sip, but the men gathered at the table didn't seem to notice as they wolfed down the meal.

She didn't exactly pick at her food either. As soon as the plate was placed in front of her, her stomach remembered it had only had spoons of peanut butter she'd scrounged from the cupboard in the cabin since breakfast the previous day. She tucked into her meal, not looking up until she'd mopped the last drop of gravy, only to find all eyes resting on her plate. She'd finished her meal first.

Embarrassment warmed her cheeks, but she gave them a fierce glare, which set their gazes back to their own plates.

"Still hungry?" Colt asked, handing her the basket of rolls.

Zuri plucked one from the basket and swiftly rose, ready to leave the oppressive atmosphere. "Thanks, Eddie. Dinner was great. I was hungrier than I thought," she murmured.

Then she swept out of the kitchen, heading straight through the living room to the front porch. But not quick enough to escape the angry outburst that followed her outside.

"Seriously, bro?"

"How long's she stayin'?"

"Enough," Colt said quietly.

Zuri tried not to care that the brothers seemed to despise her. She sat on the top step and bit into the buttery biscuit, sighing with pleasure.

A soft whine behind her drew her attention to Colt's dog, He lay facing her, his gaze intent on her biscuit.

"He wants you to toss him pieces," Colt's voice came from behind her.

"Too bad for him. I'm not sharin'."

"Missed a few meals?"

"Somethin' like that."

His footsteps scuffed across the boards. He settled on the step below hers and leaned back on an elbow, staring out at the paddock and the moon rising quickly overhead. "You're in trouble."

She startled, wondering if he knew more than he was letting on. But he couldn't. Not yet. "Nothing I can't handle," she said, keeping her tone light.

"Where's your car?"

She took a deep breath. "Somewhere downriver."

His head whipped toward her, his gaze boring into hers. "Downriver from the cabin?"

"I was headin' there when I got caught in a low-water crossing." She shrugged, acting as if it hadn't been a huge deal, and that she hadn't been scared to death. "Didn't think you'd mind if I stayed in the cabin for a couple of days. I seem to remember you and your brothers only use it during huntin' season."

"That wasn't the only time I made use of it, Zuri," he said, his voice a deep rumble.

Her heart skipped a beat at the low, growling sound, but she continued nonchalantly. "Didn't figure you had to hide your women from pryin' eyes these days." Not since his parents had passed. Something she'd heard from a friend of a friend a while back.

"I don't. And you're right. We don't use it much. But the cabin's pretty rough. Can't imagine you bein' comfortable there. Why didn't you stop here?"

"I didn't want to put anyone out. And it's not like

we kept in touch."

Colt's rugged features tightened. "True. So, your car's in the river. You weren't hurt?"

"Hardly a bruise."

His brow furrowed, and his gaze lost a little of its steel. "I'll set my people lookin' for it."

Zuri nearly choked on the next bite of her biscuit. Clearing her throat, she replied as casually as she could manage, "They won't mess with it, will they? I have some personal things in the trunk and glove box."

"I'll make sure they know not to go through it when they find it. I'll have a wrecker take it to a garage, and you can deal with it."

"Thanks," she said, knowing she couldn't say more without alerting him that something was up. As it was, she was taking a huge risk.

"I'll need the make and model and approximately where it went into the river."

She nodded. "That sounded so official," she said, pretending she hadn't already figured out he was *the man*.

"I'm the sheriff, now." His gaze rested on her face, likely looking for clues that she was alarmed by that bit of news.

But forewarned was forearmed. She didn't flinch. "Congratulations. I never knew you were interested in law enforcement."

"I got my training in the Army. Seemed a waste not to make use of it."

He'd been in the Army. Travelled. How ironic. She'd wanted to see the world when she left Destiny but hadn't made it any farther than Houston.

"Is there anyone you need to call?"

She shook her head. "No one."

"Not a soul will be worried about you?"

The way he said it, slowly, considering, made her wonder if he'd read more into her admission than she'd intended. "I live alone. I don't answer to anybody." As his gaze darkened, she tossed the rest of the biscuit to Scout, her appetite gone. "Look, I know it must be a habit for you, but could you leave off with the interrogation?" Pushing off the step, she started to rise, but his hand wrapped around her ankle.

"What kind of trouble are you runnin' from, Zuri?"

"Why does it have to be trouble?"

One dark brow rose, and she blushed. She'd had a reputation for scrapes with authority when she was in high school. But that had been a long time ago. Her life since, up until the past few weeks, had been unremarkable.

He tightened his hand, and she knew he wasn't going to let go until she gave him something to chew over. She took a deep breath. "I've had some problems. With a man."

"Did he hurt you?" he asked softly.

"Not physically. But he's been watchin' me. Stalkin' me. He left pictures he'd taken when I didn't know anyone was watchin', and left me notes—first in my mail box, then under my door..." She drew a deep, shattered breath. "And on my pillow."

His eyes narrowed. "You file a report?"

She snorted. "I told my neighbor. He's a cop with the Houston PD."

"He didn't help you?"

"Said he was. He helped me fill out reports at my kitchen table."

"Why are you hesitatin'?"

Her eyes filled, and she ruthlessly blinked away the moisture. "I think he's my stalker. I think he intimidated me in order to get closer to me."

He hardened his grip. "What's his name?"

She shook her head. "I don't want trouble. I don't want you talkin' to him."

"Don't tell me. You'll handle it." He snorted. "You have a funny way of confrontin' your problems. You're runnin' again."

She pressed her lips together to still a sudden tremor. "You think everyone is brave like you? I've learned to be cautious. And I don't trust cops." She took a steadying breath, and her gaze fell away from his. "Sorry. I didn't mean you."

He grunted and looked away. "Why not? It would make us even. I don't trust you either."

Zuri stiffened. He was getting ready to show her the door. Why had she thought he might have softened over the years, maybe learned a little compassion?

"You still want to stay?"

Her head came up, her gaze clinging to his expression, which was set in firm lines that didn't give away a thing he was really thinking. "You haven't changed your mind? Your brothers didn't talk you out of it? I'm bad news, remember?"

"I don't answer to them. You willin' to stay on my terms?"

She shook her head, not understanding him—angry and unbending one moment, offering her a carrot the next. "Why are you doin' this?"

One side of his sexy mouth curved upward. "I haven't a clue."

The screen door creaked opened behind them. They both turned. Gabe gave her a hard, pointed stare, and then turned to Colt. "You have a call. It's the station."

Colt sighed and shot her a look that said he wasn't satisfied, not by a long shot. "We're not done." Then he stood and walked back into the house.

Gabe lingered on the porch, standing behind her, making her uncomfortable enough with his silent disapproval that her hackles raised.

She kept her gaze resolutely on the roofs of the outbuildings just beyond the paddock. "You have somethin' you want to get off your chest?"

"He's not a kid anymore. He won't be fooled twice."

Zuri shook her head and aimed a narrowed glare over her shoulder. "You sound like I did somethin' to him."

"Just givin' you fair warnin'."

She lifted her shoulders. "I'm not here to start anything with him. I just ran into some trouble and need a place to stay for a couple of days."

"Where you plannin' to sleep?"

She arched one brow. "Why don't you ask him?"

"I don't want him gettin' stubborn." Gabe snorted. "He never had a lick o' sense when it came to you."

She shook her head. "I don't get it, Gabe. I never did a thing to you."

"You mess with one of us, you have the whole family to answer to."

"Again, I'm drawin' blanks. I never hurt your brother. I couldn't. He didn't give a damn about me."

Gabe's lips tightened. "Your father back in jail?"

Leave it to Gabe to say the one thing sure to get her back up. "I don't know where my *stepfather* is. Haven't talked to him in twelve years." She lowered both brows, letting him see just how much he'd angered her. "You know, I never would have taken you for the prejudiced kind. I shared his roof, not his bad habits."

"So, Colt always used to say. Funny how he suddenly stopped defendin' you."

"Gabe."

Both of them froze as Colt stepped onto the porch.

He was still dressed in blue jeans, but he'd swapped his tee for a button-down shirt. His badge hung on the breast pocket, and he carried a cream-colored cowboy hat in his hand. "I have to head into town. Wade's on call and has his hands full with a wreck on Silver Tree Road. I'm headin' into the office in case anything else goes down."

Gabe nodded, and then gave Zuri a one-sided smile. "Colt keeps pretty busy. You might not see a lot of him while you're here."

"That's all right," she said, keeping her voice even. "I don't need babysittin'."

Ignoring Gabe, Colt grabbed her hand, pulled her up, and kept hold of her while they walked toward the garage at the side of the house. When they stood beside a blue and white Sheriff's vehicle, he dropped her hand. "The bed's all yours tonight. Get some sleep."

"But I thought..." She bit her lip, wishing she hadn't reacted at all. He'd think she was disappointed they weren't going to make love.

"I was just seein' how far you'd go. How desperate you really are. Makes me wonder if you've told me everything, or if you're still keepin' secrets."

Zuri closed her mouth, not wanting to dig a deeper hole for herself.

He paused as though hoping she'd tell him something more.

She sighed. "Look, I'm tired. Sleep sounds pretty good to me now."

He snaked his arm around her waist and pulled her against his chest. "I can't help you if you don't tell me everything," he said, his voice a deep, masculine growl.

"I want to," she said truthfully, fingering a shirt button. "I really do. But it's so damn complicated. And like you said, we don't really know each other."

Colt's lips firmed. His chest lifted around a deep sigh. "I'll see you in the mornin'."

His head descended, and as though it was the most natural thing in the world to do, she relaxed against the arm cinching around her and melted into his body. His kiss was surprisingly soft and over way too quick.

She must have made a sound of complaint, because he smiled, his eyelids dipping as he studied her face. "Not enough, is it?"

Zuri shook her head.

He bent his head again, but his lips hovered just above hers. He waited until she rose up on her tiptoes to press her mouth against his. Again, like a flame licking at dry tinder, sensual heat exploded between them.

Colt turned her toward the truck, crowding her against hard metal.

She slid her hands up his chest, and then snuck them around the back of his warm neck to cling to him.

The kiss deepened, their mouths circling, tongues darting inward to taste. Colt glided his hands over her, cupping one over her bottom, slipping another beneath her shirt and molding it around a bare breast.

Zuri moaned and lifted her leg, sliding it over the crest of his hip as he pushed against her, rutting gently between her legs. She broke the kiss. "This is crazy," she whispered.

"Agreed," he rasped into her ear. "Bad idea."

She raked her nails against his scalp, loving the way he groaned as though his body ached for completion as much as hers.

He slid his hand down her belly, gliding beneath the rolled waistband of the pants he'd leant her. Fingers raked downward, slipping between her moist folds.

"God, Colt," she moaned.

His mouth slammed over hers again, and he stroked her slick sex, two fingers plunging inside her.

Her body vibrated, bowed backward. Her breath hitched.

Slowly, he circled his thumb over her clitoris, the callused digit scraping and exciting her arousal to full bloom, and she cried out, the sound muffled against his mouth.

Liquid heat seeped from inside her, coating his fingers, easing his intrusion. She pulsed, dragging on his stroking fingers, forward and back, in a slow sensual ebb and flow.

He caught her lower lip with his teeth, and she opened her eyes, snared by the heat banked in his darkened eyes. "Come for me, Zuri," he whispered.

Her orgasm exploded—rich, hot, moist. She gasped, her body undulating, inviting his deepening strokes until at last the convulsions rippling deep inside her grew still, and her body quivered in the aftermath.

Colt dropped his forehead to her shoulder and pulled his hand from beneath her clothing. Then he wrapped both arms around her, rocking them together until she breathed deeply, her cheek snuggled against his.

"Gotta go," he said, his voice rough.

"Wish you weren't gonna be so long."

He pressed a kiss against her hair. "Get some sleep."

When he released her, she blinked, shaken by how fast the man had gotten to her. She hugged herself as he climbed into his vehicle.

As he eased his sheriff's SUV out of the garage, she rubbed her arms, feeling chilled and wondering if she could slip back to the bedroom without another run-in with one of the brothers.

She hadn't been lying when she'd said she was tired. Her body ached with exhaustion—from too little sleep the night before as she'd huddled naked under a blanket while her clothes dried draped over chairs, from worry that wouldn't let her go.

Colt didn't trust her. And she didn't want to be here when all his suspicions were confirmed. She'd thought she could keep this light but was quickly getting trapped by an attraction that was too hot for her resist.

CHAPTER 6

Colt pulled past the orange-and-white striped barricade, parked next to Wade Dalton's cruiser, and set his blue lights to strobe before he headed to the creek bank.

Wade had called him first, right after he'd run the plates, knowing Colt would be interested to know that an old girlfriend's car had been spotted washed up on the bank.

Colt strode toward Wade who stood at the top of the embankment. "Thanks for keepin' a lid on this for me."

Wade raised his eyebrows. "Gonna tell me why I'm not reportin' a missin' driver?"

"She's not missin'."

Wade's eyebrows rose. "She show up at your place?"

Colt nodded and glanced down into the darkened creek bed.

Moonlight glinted on the surface of the water and the top of Zuri's Corolla, which had been deposited on the bank. The rear tires were sunk in a foot of mud.

"I'd appreciate it if you'd keep this on the down low for now," Colt said quietly. "There's more goin' on here than just an accident."

"She tell you that?"

"I have a hunch." He jerked his chin toward the car. "You check it out?"

"Thought you might prefer to do the honors, boss."

Colt snorted. Wade was one of his closest friends, and not the least impressed with his higher rank. "I'll have a look. You stay up here and wait for the wrecker."

Wade pushed back the brim of his hat. "You think she's in some kind of trouble?"

"It's Zuri."

Wade grunted. "Point taken. Go satisfy your curiosity."

Colt grabbed tall bushes and exposed tree roots as he slid sideways down the bank. When he reached the bottom, his boots sank into wet sand and gravel. The closer he drew, the less he liked the look of the car. Grass clung to every metallic crevice and seam. He pulled on the front passenger-seat door handle but it didn't budge. Bracing himself, he tugged again and it opened, brackish water rushing from the interior.

Colt leaned on the door and peered inside, his belly knotting because he knew the car had been completely submerged at one point.

As unforgiving as a Texas flashflood could be, he knew Zuri had been lucky to escape with her life. And yet she'd acted as if it wasn't a big deal. He scanned the interior, noted the driver's window had been the only one opened. Anything that had been left inside the car on the seat or floors was now long gone.

Remembering her concern for the contents of her trunk and glove box, he hesitated for all of second before reaching across and popping the button to open the compartment. Water spilled out and he reached inside. His fingers wrapped around narrow bundles, and he pulled them out.

His heartbeat hammered against his chest as he gazed down at the money, still bound in soggy bank wrappers. This had to be what she'd been worried about.

He strummed his fingers across the ends and guessed he held a few thousand dollars in hundred dollar bills.

"You find something?" Wade shouted from above.

"Damn you, Zuri. Damn, damn..." Colt hung his head, breathing deeply to steady his heart. Zuri was in big trouble. No doubt she'd come up with a plausible explanation for carrying that much money stuffed inside her glove box. But she'd be lying. In his gut, he knew she'd broken the law.

He stuffed the cash into the front pockets of his jeans and turned. "Not a thing," he lied, hating himself for the deception, and angry as hell at her for putting him in this position.

Zuri had a lot of explaining to do. After he gave her a chance to come clean, he'd decide what to do next. In his heart, he wanted to protect her. If he couldn't, he'd never forgive himself. He hoped like hell he'd be left with a choice that wouldn't end his career or smear his family's name. If he hadn't already done that.

COLT LET himself into the bedroom and strode on bare feet toward the bed. He'd removed his soaked and muddy boots on the porch, not so much to keep the floors clean but so that no one would be alerted to his return.

Moonlight streamed through the windows, bathing the side of Zuri's face in soft gray. In sleep, the deep lines that had bracketed her mouth were relaxed, and she looked like she had all those years ago when they'd fallen asleep in a jumble of limbs on the mattress in the cabin.

Shoving the memories behind him, he crouched beside the bed and covered her mouth with his hand.

Her eyes slammed open, and she gave a muffled shout.

"Shhhhh," he said softly. "Not a word. Get up." He waited until she grew still then slowly pulled his hand away.

"Colt?" she whispered.

"Not a damn word." He turned to the chair beside the window, picked up his robe, and tossed it at her. "Put this on. We're goin' someplace to talk."

She sat slowly and raked back her hair, eyeing him with fear creeping across her tense features. She swung her bare legs to the side of the bed, rose swiftly and tugged down the hem of the dark T-shirt she'd worn to bed. She shrugged into the robe, belted it and followed his pointing finger toward the door. They walked silently through the house, out the front door, and then he stepped down onto the path leading toward the barn.

"I need shoes."

Fine gravel bit into the water-softened soles of his feet, but he shook his head. A little pain was deserved.

She clamped her lips closed and followed behind him, her steps crunching in the gravel. When they reached the barn, he jerked his head, telling her to get inside. Then he closed the door to lock them in together.

He walked through the darkness, found the light switch and flipped on the single bare light bulb suspended from the rafters. When he faced her, his expression was set in stern lines.

"What's wrong? What's happened?" she whispered. Then her gaze trailed down his body to his water-soaked pants and the mud staining the bottom of his blue jeans. Her gaze widened and shot back up to lock with his.

"I'm gonna give you a chance," he bit out. "One chance to tell me the truth. If you do, I promise I'll do everything I can to help you. But for once in your life, you have to play straight with me."

Her mouth opened to speak, but her words died. Her chest rose and fell swiftly. "Why should I trust you?"

"Zuri, I'm all you've got. You don't have a choice."

"I didn't do anything wrong."

"I'll be the judge."

She shook her head. "I don't want to drag you into this."

"I'm already there." He reached into his pockets and pulled out the cash.

Her eyes closed; her head bowed. "I know it looks bad."

"Baby, you have no idea."

Zuri's face crumpled, tears streaming from her eyes. "Colt, I swear I didn't do it."

He tightened his jaw and waited her out.

Her shoulders dropped. "There was a robbery yesterday...at the bank where I work. One armed man. He had a gun. Killed my boss." She paused on a soft sob.

Colt kept silent but slapped the bills across his

palm, no sign of compassion anywhere in the set of his steel-edged jaw. He was never going to believe her, had likely already decided she was guilty.

Still, she lifted her chin. "I'm being framed."

Colt lay facing the window, unable to sleep. After the story he'd heard, he didn't know what to think or believe. It was far-fetched, like a really bad made-for-TV movie. But unless Zuri had grown into one helluva an actress, it just might be true.

The sorry fact was he *wanted* it to be true. Then he'd know exactly what to do. He'd call in a friend from the FBI to give her protection until everything was sorted out.

If it wasn't true, if she'd been stringing him along for a chance to lay low and make good her escape, he wasn't sure he could turn her in. The thought of Zuri, *his Zuri*, spending the rest of her life in jail made him sick.

Which meant, for now, he couldn't say anything to anyone outside his family.

He heard a sniff from the far side of the bed, but closed his eyes. Touching her now would be the wrong thing to do. He was angry, twisted up inside, confused about how he felt. The revenge he'd originally planned had been tossed out the door with the possibility she really was innocent. He'd be using her when she was her most vulnerable.

At her next sniff, he swung his legs over the side of the bed, determined to leave so he wouldn't be tortured by the sounds of her crying.

"Thought we had a deal," she said, her voice thick. "Your bed. Your rules."

"Things have changed," he said gruffly, even though his cock perked up at just the thought of what she suggested.

"Don't see how. You knew I was trouble soon as you saw me."

"What do you think fuckin's gonna get you, Zuri?" he asked, then winced at how crass it sounded, even to him.

Her breath caught. "I thought *maybe* we could both blow off some steam. I sure as hell can't sleep. Doesn't appear you can either." She turned, the sheet twisting around her body to mold to her slender curves.

Damn. He wished she hadn't been so blunt. That what she said didn't appeal so much. Things were complicated enough. Colt's body tightened. "What are you suggestin'?"

Zuri sat up. "I know I've put you in a bad spot. That I've compromised you. I'm sayin' that what happens between us isn't about any bargain. No one has to know."

"I'd know. My brothers would know. What the hell am I supposed to say when the FBI comes callin', because, honey, they will. If they think you're involved, they'll come to Destiny. They'll seek me out since I'm the law in these parts. When they learn about our connection..."

Zuri's jaw firmed. "When they come, I'll hie off to that cabin and swear on a stack of bibles you didn't know I was hidin' there. Do your silent-cowboy thing. I think your brothers wouldn't mind one bit backin' you up. But until they do come, can't we take a little pleasure for ourselves?"

Colt's chest expanded around a deep, indrawn breath. He wanted to fight with her, argue until they both lost their tempers, because then he'd have an excuse for letting lose. He curved his fingers, sinking them into the bedding because what he really wanted to do was drag her across the mattress and expend the tension gripping his groin.

When the law came, he'd have to tell the truth. One thing he wasn't was a liar. But right this moment, he didn't care what he'd have to admit. Anyone looking at her now, seeing her tangled hair and large frightened eyes would get why he'd thrown his principles to the winds. "Lord help you if you're playin' me," he whispered.

"I'm not, Colt," she said, her voice breaking. "I'd never have come if I'd known you were the sheriff. I don't mean to ruin anything for you. But I'm scared. And I'm just askin' you to give me what you promised."

"Why, Zuri?" Was she only trying to get under

his skin to make sure he'd protect her? Did she hope he'd help her make a run for it when the time came? More than anything, he hoped she felt the same way he did. Helpless against this attraction.

Her breath came in a ragged gust. "Because it was good between us once. And that spark's still there. Let's just forget our problems for a little while. Please, Colt."

He hesitated. No doubt she saw the effect she had on him, his boxers tented by the strength of his desire.

Slowly, her glittering gaze locked with his. She drew off the T-shirt he'd given her, baring her breasts then shoving down the sheet to remind him she'd already gotten rid of the pants. Lying back, a hand resting on the pillow beside her head, she stretched the other across to his side of the bed.

An invitation he couldn't refuse.

Whatever the consequences, he had to have her. Tomorrow, he'd figure out what he *should* do, at the very least, reading his brothers into the situation. The coming fight with them would be a trial all in itself.

Colt cupped himself through the thin cotton, then rose and pushed the garment down, letting it drop to the floor. He stood still, enjoying the fresh air wafting around him and the slowing of her breaths. Zuri had always had a fascination with his cock, every bit as much as he'd enjoyed her feminine bits. Once they'd passed the barrier of her innocence, they'd drowned in their lust, spending endless hours touching each other, finding new ways to give the other pleasure.

Her gaze slid down, halting on his erection. She licked her lips and crawled across the mattress, reached her hands out to cup his hips and draw him closer. Then she slid to the floor between him and the bed, raised her face and glided her cheek against his sex. Up one side, then down the other. She opened her mouth and licked along the same path.

His groin tightened painfully hard, balls drawing up, as she worked her magic. Cupping her head, he dug his fingers into her hair and speared his cock into her mouth.

Her gentle suction wasn't nearly enough, was a blatant tease because she chuckled.

Colt growled deep in his throat and pulled her hair.

Her lips latched around him, sucking him deeper into her mouth, pulling harder.

He would have loved to come like that, spurting in her throat, but it had been so long since he'd had a woman, and far too long since he'd slid inside Zuri's hot, tight pussy. No way was he going to spend himself in her mouth. Not this time.

He pulled her off him, urged her up to bend over the bed. Her arms reached wide, hands digging into the sheets for purchase.

The small of her back was curved, pushing up

her ass. Whatever he wanted, she'd give him. And what he craved was the slick heat he remembered.

He cupped both cheeks, squeezing them apart, then pushing up until she rose on her toes. Her pussy glinted wetly in the moonlight, and he slapped her with his cock—once, twice—watching the way her lips clasped, eager to hold him. Another slap and her moisture glazed his cockhead. Waiting was killing them both.

Swirling his hips, he screwed into her in slow, shallow circles that had him gritting his teeth because she was so hot, so wet, he wanted nothing more than to slam his entire length into her. But he wanted this to last. Instead, he pulled free and went down on his knees behind her.

Parting her folds, he found her clit at the bottom and nuzzled into her, lips latching onto the hard little knot while he began to play with her cunt, thrusting a finger inside.

Sweet God, she was still small and tight. Everything he'd remembered but more now, because she needed him. The fact she was here, at his mercy, offered a lush temptation. Dominating her had always been one of his favorite fantasies.

Even if it was only for the night. Even if tomorrow meant he'd have to pay a huge price for this momentary weakness, he would enjoy this time.

"God, Colt that feels so good," she groaned.

He added a finger, pointed the tips down and slowly slid into her, feeling for the spongy spot of nerves he'd learned to manipulate with other partners.

Her breath hissed and her legs and buttocks trembled.

He swirled on her sweet spot then added another finger, filling her completely with three fingers to fuck in and out of her pussy.

His cock oozed pre-come, bubbling over. His balls drew high and tight to his groin. Pulling free, he crawled onto the bed, sat with his back to the headboard, and held up his dick. "Come here, Zuri," he said, keeping his voice firm.

She edged onto the mattress on shaking knees and crawled toward him. He turned her. Surprise was evident in her widening eyes when he moved her with firm hands until she faced away and straddled his lap, her juicy cunt poised over his tip.

"Ride me, baby. Make it good."

"I was never much of a rider," she said, her voice husky.

"Need a little incentive to get movin'?" he growled.

Her body tingled in all the right places as she realized he was taking control, something they'd learned in their last few months together ratcheted up the sweet tension. She glanced over her shoulder and pouted. "Hardly seems fair. You're the one getting most of the pleasure."

The corners of his lips climbed. "There's plenty you'll enjoy, but for now, be a good girl. I want your hands where I can see 'em."

So she couldn't touch herself? Her eyes narrowed, but she did as he said, putting her hands on the tops of her thighs, for now, while noting her body was getting way ahead of her in excitement. Her pussy clenched; the muscles of her sheath pulsed. Holding over her, her thighs burned, as she waited to see what he'd insist on next.

"Slide on down, cowgirl."

Instinctively, she reached between her legs with one hand to guide his cock into her body, but a tap on her bottom had her quickly replacing it on her thigh again.

Oh, she'd give him a ride he'd never forget. Zuri eyed him over her shoulder, drew her bottom lip between her teeth and slowly eased down the rigid pole.

His hands were hard metal bands on her hips, guiding her progress, making sure she took it slowly. There was a feral gleam in his eyes, and that added to the predatory edge of his jaw and flaring nose that turned her on like never before.

She faced forward, holding that image in her mind and gave a sexy whirl of her hips as she slowly came down his shaft again.

He tightened his hand again, digging his thumbs into her ass, and he pushed her up, which she allowed, but she bounced several times coming down, squeezing her inner muscles to constrict around him.

His breath caught, held. He gave a sharp, bitter laugh. "Damn, Zuri. Don't even want to know how you learned to do that."

She laughed and arched her back, giving him a show as she raised her arms above her head and began a sultry dance as she came up and down, again and again. She teased herself into near orgasm then halted, breathing deeply because she didn't want it to be over this quickly.

However, she hadn't really taken control at all. He roamed his callused hands up her back, down her sides, then pulled her back until she had to brace her hands on his belly while he reached around to palm her breasts. He leaned toward her and nipped the back of her shoulder, her neck, then settled to the bed again, because she was moving, unable to stop the sensual movements, forward and back, slightly up and down, circling because his thick cock touched every part of her walls and deep shivers were sliding up and down inside her.

"Colt," she moaned.

"Tell me, baby. Tell me what you need."

"Can't move. I need to touch myself. So damn hard."

"What's hard?"

"You, Colt." Her pussy convulsed, rippling all around him. "So damn hard. I have to come, baby, please."

He pushed her up and off his cock. Then he turned her roughly so she sprawled across the bed, feet toward the head board, and crawled atop her, his wet cock sliding up one thigh then nestling against her swollen lips.

He circled his hips, screwed in a couple of shallow inches, then came down over her, his chest against hers, his arms sliding under her to cradle her close.

Lord, it was too much. There was tenderness in the way he held her. And all that masculine strength, his weight pressing down, the rigid wall of muscle surrounding her. She whimpered.

Then he began to move, pumping his hips, stroking into her, so deep, but she wanted more. "More, Colt," she whispered nearly out of her mind for want of him.

"Climb those sleek legs up," he said, bringing first one arm then the other out from under her as she did.

She clung to his hips, but he pushed on the backs of her thighs until they rose again. Not until he had her body curled beneath him, her legs collapsed against her body so tightly she could barely breathe, did he seem satisfied.

He used his large hands to place her ankles behind his neck. He was so deep now, she nearly wept. "Move, move, move," she chanted and reached around to dig her fingernails into his ass.

Colt's face was hard, his eyes glittering in the

deep shadows beneath his heavy brows. The tension was frightening, exhilarating.

She dug her head into the mattress and gritted her teeth as he began to stroke. Sharp, targeted digs built friction in her already scalding walls. Her labia swelled, constricting around her opening. Her pussy was on fire. She said so in a rushed, thready whisper.

"Feels so damn good, Zuri. Fuck, it's good."

And although the backs of her thighs burned with the stretch, she thrashed her head side-to-side while he rocked against her hips, shoving into her in powerful surges until at last, her entire body stiffened.

Zuri keened, the sound coming from her constricted lungs, choked and shrill. "Yes, yes, yes," she shouted.

Colt pushed her legs from his shoulders, shoved his hands under her ass and curved his own body to slam her harder, his movements scooting them both down the bed.

His powerful plunging hips shredded every ounce of pride and self-preservation, and she wrapped her arms around him, sobbing, coming apart.

Scalding spurts erupted, filling her. And still he didn't stop, his breaths coming in jagged gusts, then slowing, as his hips lost rhythm and he unloaded inside her.

He came to rest against her, his skin sliding against hers, slick with sweat. She molded his buttocks, the heavy ropes of muscle cording his back, then thrust her finger into his hair and turned her face to meet a last, ravenous kiss.

He pulled back and rested his forehead against hers. He pushed her legs from where they were wedged between them until he fell against her breasts. "Dammit, Zuri. Why'd you go?"

CHAPTER 7

Colt knew he'd made a mistake the moment he blurted the words. He pulled out of her heat and rolled to the side of the bed, coming to a stand even though his legs were shaking in the aftermath of the most explosive orgasm he could ever remember.

"What did you say?" she gasped.

"Never mind," he growled, wanting nothing more than to escape and shore up his ravaged emotions.

She swung her legs to the side and sat on the edge of the mattress before pulling the sheet to cover her nude body.

"Little late for that," he muttered.

"I'm not used to havin' conversations when I'm naked."

He turned his back to her, hands on his hips as he stared down at his cock, still semi-erect and coated with his come and her juices. Damn. "Well, don't worry about it. We aren't. Havin' a conversation, that is."

"You can't just say something like that and expect me not to respond."

"It's water under the bridge."

"Not the best analogy right this freakin' moment," she said, anger sharpening her voice. "What did you mean, why did I go?"

Colt didn't suffer the same modesty she did. He turned fully toward her, not caring his cock was still mostly hard. "All right then. Why'd you leave me? I gotta ask. It's not like you left me for something better than you coulda had here."

She lowered her eyebrows were in a fierce scowl, twisted her lips in a snarl. "You didn't want me," she said, her voice huskier now, laced with tears.

"Didn't want you?" Something inside him snapped. "I had a goddamn wedding ring in my pocket when you dropped your bomb," he shouted. "'My car's packed,' you said."

She shoved off the bed, letting the sheet slide away as she stalked toward him. When she was in front of him, she stabbed his chest with a finger. "It was packed because Jed kicked me out. Said he was done the day I graduated. I woke up that mornin' and he had all my belongings sittin' in the trunk and back seat of my car. I had no place else to go."

Her body vibrated with anger, shaking so hard he was tempted to catch her to steady her, but then everything she'd said struck him like a blade. "You could have come here," he said hoarsely.

"Well, you didn't ask me to stay."

"You should have known I wanted that. I told you I loved you."

"So did every high school boy who wanted in his girl's pants."

Colt swallowed hard, cold chasing the heat from his body. He dragged in a deep breath. "Would you have stayed if I'd asked?"

Her eyes closed. Her head hung, but not before he saw a tear trickle down her cheek.

"Guess it doesn't matter," he said, feeling as hollow as he sounded. "You didn't trust me."

"I still don't trust anyone," she said, her shoulders shaking. "It's not like I had anyone to teach me how."

Colt raked a hand through his hair. "Well, fuck." He returned to the bed and sat. "All this time, I thought you left because you didn't care."

"I cared." She turned slowly. "You're the only man who ever mattered to me."

The tears came freely now, and he felt at a loss. He patted the bed beside him. "Sit."

She crossed her arms over her middle, ambled slowly forward then sat beside him, inches separating their thighs.

He slipped an arm around her shoulders and pulled her against his side.

Zuri turned and snuggled against him, her hand

cupped over his heart. "I'd have stayed. All you had to do was tell me not to go."

For years, he'd carried around his resentment and confusion, afraid to trust his heart again, and for what? She hadn't trusted him, but he sure as hell hadn't given her his trust. He'd assumed she didn't care a lick when she'd walked toward her car and driven away. "We're a pair, Zuri," he whispered, then kissed her cheek. *Both fools. What a damn waste.* "You should get some rest."

She sniffed and raised her head. "What about you?"

"I have to read Gabe and Tommy into the situation. They have a right to know."

She nodded. "If they have a problem with me stayin', I'll leave."

"And go where?"

She lifted her shoulders. "Do you want me to turn myself in?" Her head came up. Her lashes were starred with her tears.

"Not until we can figure out how to keep you safe. He's had all the time in the world to set you up."

"You believe me?"

Colt sighed. "I want to," he said truthfully.

She gave a little nod, slid deeper onto the mattress and lay on her side. "Guess I am pretty tired."

He hesitated for a moment, then bent toward her, gave her cheek a kiss and pulled the bedding from the floor to cover her. "For tonight, don't worry. I'm in your corner."

She sniffed again and looked away. "I would have stayed," she said, her voice so ragged his chest hurt.

He gave her another kiss. This time on the lips. Damn, if he didn't believe her.

"And you believe her?" Tommy asked, eyebrows high.

Gabe snorted. "Course he does. He's all soft on account he just fucked her."

Colt bit back a curse. "I'm not an idiot." He'd woken both his brothers from a deep sleep, and now they sat alone in the kitchen, mugs of instant coffee on the table in front of them. Colt took a sip of his and made a face.

"You're an idiot when it comes to her," Gabe said, his eyes narrowed. "No offense, bro."

Colt bristled. "I told you, she and I both made mistakes."

Tommy sat, arms crossed over his bare chest. He tilted back on the kitchen chair, his expression pensive as he stared back. "So, what do you want to do?"

He eyed his youngest brother, surprised at his even tone. Tommy had always been just as adamantly anti-Zuri as Gabe. "Not gonna tell me I should turn her in?"

Tommy's lips firmed into a narrow line. "Not if you think there's a chance her story's true."

Colt felt relief spill down his spine. He leaned forward, both elbows on the table as he stared into his cup. "If she's tellin' the truth, this cop's gonna be lookin' for. He'll come here. She thought she saw him just before she went into the river, so he could already be close."

Gabe rubbed his jaw then sat forward as well. His gaze swung between his brothers, and he took a deep breath. "Can't say I'm happy havin' her under our roof. I still remember how it was after she left. She changed you, man. Whether this is her fault or not, she's trouble. But if this is what you want to do, I'm in. I'll talk to the men. Make sure none of them says a word to anyone about her bein' here."

"Better we all stick close to the ranch," Colt said, nodding.

"I'll make sure no one goes out unarmed," Gabe said, "and we should probably set up a patrol."

Colt nodded. "I have to talk to Wade. He knows she's here. If he sees anything come in about her, he'll have to know how to handle it."

"You expect him to keep quiet?" Tommy said.

"I'll tell him everything and give him the choice of what he wants to do. Only fair. His ass would be in a sling too, if shit goes sideways."

"You're takin' a big risk," Gabe said, shaking his head. "With your job. Hell, you could wind up in jail for harborin' a fugitive. You sure this is how you want to do this?"

Colt's jaw tightened. "What I want is a little time to sort out her story."

"And if she's not tellin' the truth?" Gabe arched a dark brow.

Colt grunted. "That patrol works both ways. No one comes in—and she doesn't take a step off this ranch."

"I'll tell the guys." Tommy pushed up. "I'll hit the bunkhouse now. It's gonna be a long day."

When Tommy left the room, Gabe's gave him a hard stare.

Colt stiffened. "Go ahead and spit it out. It's not like you've ever held a thing back."

The hard edge of Gabe's jaw eased a fraction and his gaze reflected worry. "I know she's pretty."

Colt snorted and picked up his cup to take a sip.

"Okay, she's beautiful. I get why any man would want her. But you've been down that road before. It didn't work twelve years ago. It sure as hell can't work now. All I'm gonna say is be careful."

"I'm not a kid anymore. And you're my younger brother. I could tell you to mind your own business, but I know better." Colt set his cup on the table and raised his gaze to meet Gabe's. "I love her. Always have. Always will. She's under my skin. As long as we've been apart, I never forgot her smell, her taste. When she looks at me like I'm a dream come to life, somethin' happens." Colt paused, realizing this was the longest personal conversation they'd ever shared.

Gabe shifted in his chair, then scraped it closer so he hunched beside Colt. "I won't pretend I understand, because I don't. For all the reasons I've said 'til I'm blue in the face. But I can see she's dug deep. If you're set on helpin' her, I'm in. Not for her, but because you're my brother. This is about family. Ours. We'll stand together." He rose and clapped a hand on Colt's shoulder. "I'll take a walk around the yard."

Colt sat for a long moment, swallowing past the burning lump at the back of this throat. He'd brought trouble into the house. He hoped like hell he could keep everyone safe.

When he returned to his room, he quietly opened the door, then stripped off his jeans and climbed into bed beside Zuri.

By her deep, even breathing, she slept.

In his head, he replayed their conversation, heard the heartbreak in her voice when she'd demanded to know what he'd meant. He believed that much was real—that she'd thought he'd been happy to see her go when they'd parted after graduation.

And he'd held tight to his resentment. Harbored it. Let if fester until it had colored every relationship he'd ever had.

Zuri would have stayed. Would have been his wife. He'd fucked up big time, and now she needed his help. Whether she lied about the rest... Well, he'd deal with that as it came. In the meantime, he'd keep her safe and find her a damn good lawyer.

Moonlight silvered her hair and skin. Gabe had called her beautiful. Looking at her now caused that lump to burn his throat again. He snuck an arm over her waist and pulled her closer, doing his best to ignore the heat stirring in his loins as he nestled his nose into her hair and breathed deeply, taking in her fresh, sweet scent. Colt realized in that moment how much he'd missed this, having her here beside him. He'd never stopped loving her because she'd been imprinted on his mind and body. There wasn't another woman on the planet who'd ever made him feel anything so intensely.

Lord, how would he ever let her go?

COLT DIDN'T SLEEP A WINK. When dawn broke, just before light peeked through the curtains, he called Wade, who went from groggy and annoyed to instantly alert as Colt described Zuri's predicament.

His friend agreed to keep quiet and urged Colt to stay home to watch over her. Colt's stomach churned, wondering how the hell he could help her and keep his brothers and friend out of trouble too.

Zuri stirred, rolling to her side and snuggling her cheek against his chest. "This is nice," she whispered. "You sleep good?"

"Yeah," he lied, smiling as her eyelids fluttered open.

Her soft brown gaze roamed his face, touched on his lips, and he knew what she wanted because she lingered there.

He came closer, but she pulled back, wrinkling her nose. "I need to brush my teeth."

"Don't worry about me," he murmured and kissed her although she kept her mouth firmly closed. His lips smiled against hers. He nudged her hip with his cock.

Her eyes widened. "Been like that long?" she asked, her voice husky.

"A pretty woman lying right beside me, what do you think?"

She brushed her hair from her face with her hand. "I must look a sight."

Colt caught her fingers and threaded them with his before placing both their hands on the pillow beside her head. "Have any better plans?"

CHAPTER 8

Zuri breathed, taking in his crisp male scent. No man had ever smelled like that. Of horse and sage and his own male musk. Wearing his clothes had cloaked her in it, even freshly laundered. When she was surrounded with that smell, she couldn't help but remember all the times they'd been like this, waking in the dawn, weak morning sun casting rays to chase away the shadows that made their loving something private and secretive. Something she could handle because he couldn't see every expression flitting across her face.

Mornings revealed, inspiring fresh passion as well as fear. She worried over how she looked. Could he see the wrinkles beside her eyes? Would he think she'd grown old? Did he compare her to other women, more generously endowed women?

But mostly, she feared the honesty light revealed. With him, now, she couldn't put on a careless face.

He'd see how much every little caress meant, how wild he made her.

He came up on an elbow. Morning was more than kind to the man. Dark stubble on his jaw and chin added a dash of danger to his appearance. His large hand cupped her small breast and his callused thumb rasped the tip.

She bit her lip against a moan. Lazy heat burned between her legs. She angled toward him, unable to resist the challenge in his gleaming eyes. Reaching beneath the covers, she cupped his erection in her palm. "Have to say, Sheriff Triplehorn, you do know how to get a lady's attention."

His cock surged against her hand, and she wrapped her fingers around his shaft, loving the steamy heat and the soft satin feel of the skin surrounding his steely hardness. She gave him a gentle stroke, strumming her fingers over his length.

A deep growl rumbled through his chest, and he slipped the hand on her breast around her hip to cup a buttock. "Don't tease if you don't mean to do something about it. I'm in a world of hurt here, Zuri."

"And it's my fault? All I was doin' was sleepin'."

"You breathed, baby. That's all it takes."

This time when he leaned in to kiss her, she didn't demur. Her mouth opened, her tongue slipped out to lick his bottom lip, then slid inside. The moist warmth she found fanned the flames building in her core. "Colt?" she whispered against his mouth.

"Anything, baby. Say it."

"Fuck me. Jesus, fuck me hard."

Abruptly, he rolled, covering her chest to toes, his hard cock trapped against her belly. She would have opened her legs, welcomed him inside, but his knees settled at either side of her and kept her closed.

"That's not how this works," she said, angling her head to trace the edge of his strong, square jaw with her tongue.

His stormy-gray eyes glinted before he scooted down her body, moving quickly but not missing a spot as he licked and nipped his way down to her breasts.

And as she had learned long ago, her breasts might be small, but they contained all the necessary nerve endings. Already engorged, the hard points tingled as his tongue flicked, shooting sparks south to warm her core and release a wash of arousal that dampened her sex.

She wound her fingers tightly in his hair and pulled and scratched while shivers shuddered through her. Her head thrashed, her pelvis bucked.

When he bit her nipple, she screamed, creaming in an instant. "Colt, Colt..."

But Colt wasn't ready to end her agony. He moved farther down, pressing kisses against the hollow of her belly, tonguing her belly button then her mound.

When he nudged apart her legs and settled between them, she nearly wept. She opened for him, sliding her heels up the mattress and letting her thighs fall to the side.

She let go of his hair and slid a hand between her legs, two fingers parting her folds and pulling up to expose her clit, begging silently for him to pay attention to her need.

Maybe he was in a generous mood because he didn't make her wait. Hard lips surrounded the swollen nub and he began to suction.

Her body vibrated, her torso curling up. "So good. So good."

Fingers thrust into her pussy. She widened her sprawled thighs again and began to pump shallowly, up and down, while she hummed with pleasure.

Colt twisted and swirled his fingers, fluttered the tip of his tongue against her sensitive knot. She was close. Nearly there…

And he pulled away.

Sweating, she fell back, breathing like she'd run a race. "Not nice," she gasped.

"Not finished," he bit out. "Get up."

Hard hands rolled her, gripped her hips and backed her up as she got her trembling arms beneath her. Before she even had a chance to brace herself, he was at her again. His head behind her, his teeth nibbling at her swollen cunt.

Breaths breaking apart like sobs, she lowered her back to tilt her ass higher, coming down on her elbows, sinking her head between her shoulders as he took all the power from her shaking frame.

Rough thumbs parted her folds and his tongue rimmed her entrance before dipping inside.

She tossed her head, hair feathering and sticking to her sweaty cheeks. "Yes!"

He withdrew, placed his large hands on her ass and spread her cheeks. His weight on the mattress shifted. The blunt, fat head of his cock butted against her entrance then pushed inside.

Zuri clutched her hair with one hand and pulled hard. Anything to distract her from the overwhelming pleasure.

Colt stroked inward, short measured thrusts that juiced her up.

She wriggled her bottom. "More, Colt. God, fuck me hard."

He readjusted his hands and split apart her buttocks. Warm liquid dropped between her cheeks and fingers smoothed it down her crack to her tiny hole.

She shot up on her arms and aimed a startled glance behind her. "Colt?"

"My bed. My rules," he said.

His gruff, hard tone added an edge of dangerous delight. Not ready to concede, she pushed back, trying to take his cock deeper into her body, and succeeding once, twice, before his fingers shocked her again.

A thick thumb rubbed her asshole, pressed and dipped inside.

A thick, garbled moan slipped from her throat.

"Like that, sweetheart? Want some more?"

She shook her head, but backed up again, dropping on her arms until her breasts touched the cotton sheet. Then his strokes pushed her forward and back, abrading her turgid nipples, filling her rippling channel. His thumb pulled free and two fingers slipped inside her, pumping in time with his deepening thrusts.

Beyond protesting now, she whimpered and shook, rocked by the strength of his motions and the wicked swirling of his fingers.

"I'll take this ass. Someday soon."

Relief made her sob. Not today. God, she didn't think she could take it today. On sensory overload already, she melted to the bed, bottom suspended high by his strong hands and powerful thrusts. When he quickened his movements, she cinched around him, knowing he was close and wanting to feel his ecstasy explode with hers.

Fingers pulled from her ass, gripped the corners of her hips, then he slammed against her, the sound loud and wet, jolting her and making the bed thump against the wall.

Pleasure burst and Zuri screamed hoarsely, body stiffening, back arching, her arms burning as she thrust backward to meet his jarring thrusts.

Colt shouted, body going rigid behind her, and searing jets of come bathed her inner walls. He jerked against her, losing rhythm but still tunneling deep. He bent over her, hands sliding beneath to cup her breasts, and he pulled her up to sit against his lap, their bodies still joined as the last sweet convulsions ebbed away.

Sitting with his arms wrapped around her, hands fondling breasts, belly, lips grazing her neck and shoulder, Zuri floated in a sensual haze…happy, free… Something she hadn't felt in a long, long time. "I love you," she whispered.

He cupped her chin with his palm and turned her face. He slid his mouth over hers, gentle suction locking them together.

When their breaths slowed, their kiss turned softer. A blending of lips that rubbed and pushed, so sweet tears pricked her eyes.

Colt saw the shimmer in her eyes. He gripped her hair and kissed her temple. Then he brought them to the bed, his softening cock slipping from her slick channel.

She sighed, seemingly happy to be in his arms.

"Feel like ridin' this mornin'?" he rumbled behind her.

"Thought we just did."

He smiled into her hair. "Ride horses, sweetheart. Get some fresh air."

Her head turned, eyes brightening with excitement. "I'd love to. But don't you have to work?"

"Wade's handlin' things. Said he'd call if he hears anything."

"You told him?" she asked, worry digging a line between her dark brows.

"Had to, Zuri. I have a supposed fugitive in my custody."

"Did you tell him about the money?"

"No, and you're not to worry about that. I have it locked away."

Zuri drew back. "I should shower."

He raised his eyebrows. "Nothin' stoppin' you."

"Well, it's broad daylight and…"

"Not shy, are you? I know every curve of your body."

"We were…busy. In the moment." She wrinkled her nose. "This feels a little…premeditated."

"I think I'm good."

She crossed her eyes then scooted toward the edge of the bed, trying to drag the sheet with her, but he bunched it in his fist and held tight.

"Never knew you were a perv," she huffed.

"Sure, you did. It's just one of my more endearing qualities."

Zuri let go of the sheet and studied his expression. "You're different today. You're not as growly."

He fingered the faint blue tracings of veins at her wrist. "I had a lot to take in yesterday."

"You believe me?"

Her soft, hushed tone did things to him. Made his insides melt. "I'm trying."

She lifted her chin. "Guess that's more than fair. My story sounds like a tall tale, even to me. Can't imagine how it sounds to you as a lawman. You must hear stories like mine all the time."

"Not really," he said with a wry smile. "This is Destiny. The most exciting things that happen around here are barroom brawls and cattle on the highway. You've certainly livened things up." He pointed his chin toward the bathroom door. "Any time you're ready."

With a twist of her lips, she slipped from beneath the sheet and darted to the bathroom door, white cheeks jiggling.

Colt grinned until she closed the door. Reaching down, he adjusted his cock. If she'd bumped against it, she'd have known just how close she'd been to being under him again.

He flipped back the sheet and strode toward the bathroom door. The shower was running. The chuff of a toothbrush sounded. She must have found his spare in the drawer. When he heard the soft snick of the shower door, he tried the bathroom door handle.

She hadn't locked it after herself. Maybe she wanted company. And even though they'd just made love, it wasn't enough.

He slid inside, opened the shower door and stepped in behind her.

She glanced over her shoulder and grinned. "Wondered if you'd be able to resist. I saw you starting to tent the sheet again."

He smoothed his hands around her waist and

came up against her, letting his cock ride the crack of her ass. "My shower..."

"Your rules? Huh." She handed him the shampoo and shook back her hair.

"And my rules say I get to wash every inch of your skin."

"I would expect no other punishment."

Not something they'd ever shared. A skinny dip in the river, yes, but never the luxury of soap in his hands, fingers deep in her dark hair. He kneaded her scalp, loving her soft sighs as ropes of lather slid down her pale skin. "Time to rinse," he murmured.

"You're good at this," she said, groaning.

He felt a pang in his chest. If he didn't get things figured out soon, they might not have a lot of time to figure out what else was good between them. "Sorry, no conditioner."

"I'll make do."

"I'll put together a list of things for Tommy or Gabe to pick up in town. I'll add that."

She glanced back. "Is it wise? If they see you buyin' things for a woman, someone might get suspicious."

"You forget. We have some pull in this town. If we ask folks to look the other way... Don't worry about it. But I will need sizes." He pushed her head beneath the stream of water and coaxed the soap from her hair. "All the shampoo's gone. Want to hand me the soap?"

Zuri groaned. "It'd be so much quicker if you let me do this myself."

"My shower..."

"Yeah, yeah." She handed him the soap.

When he nudged the inside of her feet, she sighed, but braced them apart.

"Hands on the tiles."

Her back straightened, but she did as he commanded, placing them flat against the slate tiles.

"Higher. No moving 'til I'm done."

When he moved his soaped-up palms around to cup her breasts, she leaned her forehead against the tile. "Best pat-down *ever*."

Zuri wasn't lying. His callused palms did a number on her skin, roughing up her nipples as he massaged them in lazy, circular motions. Standing with her back to him, she couldn't help jumping every time his cock touched her buttocks.

She was too aware of every movement, of the hot water sluicing down her skin, the warm breaths gusting in her ear. But especially the way his fingers were moving, kneading the sensitive globes, moving them around and around until her hips followed the same slow motions.

"You're killin' me, Colt." Teeth nipped her ear and she shivered, curling up her shoulder but tilting her head the other way to let him slide his warm lips across her slick skin. "You're gonna get a mouthful of suds."

"Oh, I'm gonna get a mouthful."

He moved his hands down, scrubbing over her ribs, her soft belly. A finger rimmed her belly button then trailed lower, sinking into the tops of her folds.

Her pussy contracted, her ass tilted. She rubbed her buttocks against him until he gripped her hips and centered her for him to ride the split.

Then Colt went back to work, lathering her pussy, washing the creases between her labia and thighs, parting her folds to wash between. When the soap was gone and everything squeaky clean, he turned her.

Somehow, facing him, her breasts and pussy exposed, even though he'd had his fingers everywhere, she felt naked in a very fundamental way.

When she reached for his shoulders, he bent, kneading her back and buttocks as he mouthed her breasts.

Each sweet biting caress sent electricity darting toward her core. He knelt lower, rubbing the bristles on his cheek against her belly, making her tremble and moan. When he knelt lower still, she trained her eyes on the etched glass door and surrendered as he dove between her legs. He urged one thigh over his shoulder and rubbed his cheeks against her inner thighs before nuzzling upwards. Because she was expecting it, her body shuddered the moment before he actually touched her there, her pussy clenching.

His tongue pushed between her folds, slid into her entrance, and her calf tightened as it hugged his back. He petted her mound with his fingers then spread her folds and scraped a callused thumb across her swollen clit.

"Colt. Oh!"

His tongue withdrew, then feathered upward, tapping the hard little knot before swirling wetly over and over it. He slid his fingers inside her, pumping in and out of her hot channel.

Her hips moved forward and back, pushing her mound against his nose, urging him to stroke deeper. "Please, please," she whispered.

Colt shrugged off her thigh and rose. His hands gripped her ass and slid her up the slippery tiles. She wrapped her legs around his waist, waited impatiently while he fit the thick head at the opening of her vagina.

Only then did he press into her, pushing upward, sliding her down then up the wall with the strength of his hard thrusts.

Water streamed like heavy rain atop their heads, beat their shoulders, dripped off their noses.

His eyelashes were starred with liquid, but he kept his eyes open, as did she. They locked glances, and she marveled that a man who looked so hard, his face tight and sharp-edged, could still hold onto his control to deliver the long, precise strokes she needed.

He broke apart her breaths, not with sharp thrusts, but with endless rolls of his hips, firm up-and-down lunges of his hands on her bottom to control the surging tension.

Up and down the slippery tiles, up and down his thickening cock. The friction inside her burned. The juicy sounds they made coming together and apart were louder than their straining breaths.

"Let go of my waist," he growled.

She began to lower her legs, but he pressed closer, released her buttocks and hooked his arms beneath her thighs. Then the sensual movements quickened, sharpened.

Already so near, she let her head bump back against the tile and surrendered, letting him control everything, her limbs lax, her pussy convulsing, strong ripples traveling down to caress every sweet inch of the cock shoving up inside her.

"Colt..." Her mouth opened and her eyelids fluttered closed.

His knees dipped, and he came up harder, pulling her thighs to bounce her on his shaft. There was violence in his movements, a gentle rage that ripped away every last sense of self.

Zuri arched her back and screamed, rocking her legs within his hold, rubbing her breasts against his chest, needing to be closer, needing him deeper.

The moment and her body locked and held although Colt continued to plunge inside her. Her pussy clamped down, milking him with strong contractions she felt all along her channel to her gripping entrance. The scalding spurt of liquid flooding her now was him and her, a wave of their excitement so hot and pure that she wrapped her arms around him and held on with all her might, because she didn't want to let it end. Didn't want to leave his embrace.

But he was shaking, leaning into the tiles, his head sinking to her shoulder as he dragged in deep, shuddering breaths.

Zuri, eyes still closed, mouth still slack, rubbed his cheek as she fought to breathe enough air into her lungs so she wouldn't pass out. "Best…pat-down…ever."

Colt grunted, not letting her go, just rocking ever so slightly against her as the pulsing of his cock slowed. He kissed her neck, lifted his head and skimmed his mouth along her jaw. Then he angled his face to press his lips against hers.

When at last they both drew back, Zuri slowly opened her eyes. His blazed back with a look she'd never seen. One of feral possession. A look that filled an empty place inside her, because she'd always wanted to belong to this fierce, strong man. "I love you, Colt."

His jaw tightened. He didn't give her back the words, but he held her safe inside his embrace.

CHAPTER 9

Colt glanced over at Zuri who sat her horse rather gingerly. He suppressed a self-satisfied grin, surprised at just how much the tenderness she felt pleased him in a very primal way.

Colt cast a trained eye around the rolling hills, looking for anything out of place. He'd wanted to treat her to an outing, but wasn't taking any chances. To the south, he saw a rider, Eddie Sandoval, his horse halted on a rise.

Eddie raised a hand to let him know he'd keep watch. All the men were party to keeping Zuri safe now. Whatever Tommy had said had galvanized them. When he and Zuri had stepped out onto the porch after they'd showered, they'd been greeted by a pair of cowboys flanking both ends of the porch. At the barn, another armed man had stepped from the shadows to tip his hat.

Zuri had given him a glance filled with alarm, but

he'd explained they were only there for protection, so that she could feel safe moving around. After that, they'd both firmly ignored their security detail.

At her next wince, Colt took pity on her. "Would you like to rest a bit before we head back?"

She glanced over, her eyebrows lowering into a scowl like she'd guessed he knew exactly what was bothering her, and she warned him not to say a word.

He pretended not to notice and tipped his chin to the live oak at the top of the next hill. "How about we stretch our legs and let the horses graze. There's shade under the tree."

She nudged her horse and led the way, her legs stiff from trying to hold herself off the saddle, which only meant each impact was sharp rather than a gentle roll.

He chuckled quietly, pleased with himself. Happy in way he hadn't felt in a long time.

All because he'd had the most explosive sex of his life and expended all the pent-up anger and resentment he'd kept inside him all these years. He hadn't known he'd been carrying it around for so long, not until it slid right off his shoulders. Zuri was back. He'd move heaven and earth to keep her now. Even proving to her she'd never find a more attentive lover.

They dismounted, and he took the saddlebags he'd filled with their lunch. They'd both been too late for breakfast, and his stomach was growling. She had to be starving too.

He spread a blanket on the buffalo grass under

the tree, opened two chilled bottles of sparkling water and handed her one. Then he sat and patted the blanket beside him.

"I think I'll stand for minute," she muttered.

"Been a while since you rode?" he drawled, keeping his expression innocent.

Zuri turned away, but her shoulders shook. When she glanced back, a crooked grin stretched across her face. "You know darn well what my problem is. It's all your fault."

"You complainin'?"

"About the fact my lover wore me out?" She sighed and knelt in the blanket, before sitting gingerly on her bottom. "Not complainin'," she said a wry note in her voice. "Just wonderin' how I'm gonna get back up on that horse. Is it too far to walk home?"

He patted the rounded saddlebag. "I brought lunch. We can take our time. You can even take a nap if you need it."

"It's not fair. You should be just as raw."

"I am," he said quietly, a small smile tugging at his lips.

She huffed. "Think anyone else knows?"

"Anyone in a hundred yards of the house heard you scream."

She groaned and hid her face. "Your brothers?"

"Congratulated me."

"*No.*" She laughed and dropped her hands. Her cheeks were a fiery red. "I can't believe they weren't ready to dump me at the edge of town."

"I told them everything. They're the ones who set up the patrols. We'll all keep you safe."

"They believe me?"

"They're...open to it," he said, giving her a steady gaze.

Her cheeks billowed around a quick puffed breath. "So, the guard works both ways."

Colt nodded. "No one out. No one in."

"You can't do this for long. The FBI probably already suspects me of collusion because I disappeared."

"They probably do. Let's not worry about it. Not right now. Let me feed you."

Zuri sat across from him, her eyes bright and wide, her mouth still red from his kisses. He wondered if she knew that her cheeks were raw from whisker burn, but he kept that to himself.

From the pack, he pulled out thick roast-beef sandwiches and two apples.

She took hers, unwrapped the plastic and then opened her sandwich, reset the lettuce, sliced tomato and onion before being satisfied.

"Don't trust I know how you like it?"

"No, I always look. It's just habit."

They ate in silence. When he stowed away the plastic wrap and emptied bottles, they sat side-by-side, staring out over the green pastures and the highway in the distance.

"Think you can sit a saddle?"

"It's a long way back. Too long to walk, huh?"

The whine in her voice had him grinning again. "I have an idea."

He brought her horse beside his, tied a rope to its halter and the other end to his saddle horn. "He can follow us." Then he mounted, scooted back as far as he could, then reached down and pulled her up in one fluid movement to sit sideways in front of him. He cradled her back in one arm. "Better?"

Her lips pouted. "They'll laugh at me when we ride in like this."

"They wouldn't dare."

"It's kind of nice," she said, settling against his body as he nudged his horse into motion.

They kept a slow, steady pace, Zuri asking him questions about the ranch and the cattle they passed until they neared the last hill before coming to the house.

A sharp report echoed in the distance. His horse halted, gave a heavy, snuffling snort, then began buckling beneath him.

Colt realized in an instant what had happened, kicked his boots free of the stirrups and dove for the ground, pulling Zuri with him as the horse fell the other way.

Zuri's mare whinnied wildly, rearing on her hind legs and bucking against the rope.

Colt slipped the knot, turning her free to run, then pushed Zuri down to lie beside his horse, whose legs still twitched. He cautiously slipped his rifle from its scabbard and scanned the horizon around them.

"What was that?" Zuri asked, her voice hushed and small.

"A rifle."

"Someone shot at your horse?"

"Someone shot at us."

Her eyes grew round, all color leaching from her face.

Blood bubbled from Diego's nostrils, but Colt couldn't think about it. Not right now. He dug a hand into his shirt pocket, pulled out his satellite phone and hit the speed dial.

As soon as it connected, he barked, "Gabe, someone's on the range just to the west of the house. He shot my horse."

"Stay there. We're comin'." But already, he heard hooves pounding from the far hills.

Zuri was crying, her hands petting Diego's nose trying to comfort the horse, but he was already gone, his breath shuddering out one last time.

Colt pressed his hand against the top of her head to keep her down and positioned himself to the outside, kneeling with his weapon as he continued to scan for whomever had done this.

"I'm so sorry," she sobbed behind him.

"Not your fault," he bit out, his body tense, kicking himself for putting them both at risk.

"He followed me. You know that's what this is."

"Yeah. Figured that out."

"You believe me now?"

"I do, sweetheart. No good lawman would have taken that shot. Not and risk hurtin' me, too."

The growl of engines sounded in distance. A truck and three motorized mules coming at a fast clip topped the hill and fanned out around them.

Gabe jumped out the passenger door of the truck before it stopped, then waved it and the other vehicles to move on. He hunkered down beside them. "They'll check to see if anyone's still out there."

"He's probably long gone. Plenty of places to hide," Colt said, thinking of the miles of arroyos and brush.

"That was pretty damn bold," Gabe said, gazing at Colt then Zuri whose tears were making muddy tracks down her cheeks. "Guess this means any more field trips are out. And it means you weren't lyin'."

Zuri's tears came faster. "I'm so sorry about Diego."

So was Colt. He'd had the horse since he was a teenager. "I am too. I just didn't think Satterly would come onto the property. Not like this."

"Sure he's workin' alone?" Gabe asked.

Zuri lifted her shoulder. "Only one man held up the bank."

"He's a cop," Colt said. "I can't see him trustin' anyone else with his dirty business."

The vehicles returned. Colt helped Zuri into the truck cab then stood on the side rail while Gabe leaped into the bed. Then all three vehicles took off across the pasture.

Back at the house, he hustled Zuri inside and called Wade.

"Someone took a potshot at you?" Wade asked, his voice sharpening.

"Killed my horse," he bit out.

"Do you want me to pull a couple of officers in to provide security?"

"We've got it handled at the house, but we're gonna have to keep her inside."

"What are you gonna do now? Looks like your girl's in deep."

"I have a friend at the bureau. I'll give him a heads up. Looks like we've got a dirty cop. Zuri doesn't think he knows she's onto him. So, he may still be pretty comfortable operating' in the open. Be sure to let Roy Givens at the garage know he's to call me if anyone comes sniffing' around about that car. I'm coming' in. Much as I hate not being here, I can't do anything from here."

"Might not want to ride in alone. Make sure someone watches your back."

Colt hit disconnect then glanced up to find Zuri hovering in the doorway. She'd changed her shirt and wore one of his sweaters although it was pretty warm inside the room. Her slender frame was lost in the bulky fabric.

He opened his arms. She walked quickly toward him and sank against his chest.

Hugging her tight, he bent to her ear. "I'm not gonna let anyone hurt you, Zuri-girl."

"I don't want anyone hurt because of me. I'm nothing but trouble, Colt."

He tucked a finger under her chin to lift her face. "You sit tight until I get back?"

She nodded.

"Turn the blinds in any room you enter. Stay away from the windows."

"You're callin' the FBI?"

"I have to. Now we know he's desperate, we have a chance to get him to make a move. We have to do this right. Make sure you're left in the clear."

"What if they arrest me?"

"They might take you into custody, for your protection, but is that such a bad idea?"

She snuggled closer. "Guess not."

"I won't let you go alone."

Tears welled in her eyes. She blinked them away and gave a little laugh, like she was embarrassed. "I'm not used to anyone takin' care of me."

"You're not alone in this. I'll keep you safe. Every man on this ranch is lookin' out for you." He gave her another hug and she gasped. Holding her away, he asked, "Are you okay? I took you down pretty hard when Diego got shot."

"We're lucky all we got were a few bruises." She reached behind her and rubbed her bottom. "I'll be sitting funny for a while."

Colt chuckled and pulled her gently against his

chest. He pressed a kiss into her hair. "Maybe you should take a long, hot soak. Might help what else hurts."

Zuri gave a soft, feminine snort. "I think I'll make it. But what about you? Are you gonna be safe? He might try to get to you while you're out."

"I won't ride in alone. And once I'm in town, I'll be sure to keep a deputy close. I'm no John Wayne. I'll be home tonight. I should have news to share then. 'Til then, don't budge from this house."

She nodded and he set her away from him, gave her mouth a quick hard kiss, then strode out of the room.

Zuri watched him go then stood beside the window with the blinds turned, but lifting one slat to watch him stride confidently across the front porch, sliding his cowboy hat atop his head while he barked orders to the hands who were gathered in the yard.

When he walked out of sight toward the driveway, Gabe followed him. She let out deep breath.

"Maybe you should stay away from the windows."

She turned to find Tommy watching her. Not sure how much blame he was ready to place at her feet, she eyed him warily. She stepped back from the window. "I can't just sit here."

He cocked a brow. "Can you cook?"

She nodded slowly.

"The men are takin' shifts. Some seein' to the stock and horses. The others on patrol. It'd be a help if you could cook something for everyone to eat in shifts. Stew or chili."

"I can handle that."

Tommy gave her an approving nod. He started to leave, but hesitated. "Colt told us everything, even about why you left. Said some of the blame was his, for not askin' you to stay."

"We should have talked. I should have trusted him more."

"I understand why you didn't, but Zuri, you hurt him again…"

She lifted her chin to meet him square in the eye. "The last thing I want to do is hurt him. He doesn't deserve that. Not any of this."

"Your old man…"

She stiffened. "Isn't part of my life. Never was. Not after I left. Don't know where he is or what he's doin'. And I don't care."

"He was bad news. Guess I couldn't look any farther than that."

"You thought I was just a white-trash girl lookin' for a piece of your ranch. That's not what I was after."

Tommy frowned. "I wouldn't have put it quite that bluntly."

"But it's what you and Gabe always thought. That I was out to get me a Triplehorn. Well, all I ever wanted was Colt. If he hadn't had a nickel, I still would have wanted him."

He gave her a nod. "Well, that was awkward."

Her lips twisted into a small smile. "Let's not repeat it."

He grimaced. "It'd be nice if you didn't mention it to Colt. He'd kick my ass."

"Never happened," she drawled.

When he left, she felt raw. As though her skin had been peeled back and everything inside her exposed. Well, it wasn't like she hadn't known all along what Colt's brothers had thought about her. And if she'd been on the outside looking in, she might have had the same suspicions.

Her stepfather was an ex-con who'd served time for drug possession and burglary. Her mother had married him, even knowing that, then up and died, leaving Zuri to be raised by a man who resented the imposition.

He'd provided her food and a place to live, but anything else she'd needed—clothing, spending money and extra expenses for school— she'd had to earn for herself starting at a young age.

She'd come up hard and had a chip on her shoulder before she'd met Colt. He'd been the golden boy. The high-school quarterback, a good student. What the hell he'd ever seen in her, she'd never figured out.

At first, she thought all he wanted was to get into her pants. Like any boy who'd ever paid her any attention. But when she'd refused that first time, he hadn't dropped her for an easier mark. He'd stayed the course. Dared to be seen with her in daylight. Had faced his parent's disapproval and the strange looks he'd gotten from his friends.

Not that she'd wanted to go anywhere to be seen. She'd much preferred quiet picnics. Like the one they'd had today. Or fishing in the creek. Then at last, when both of them hadn't been able to resist each other's young bodies any longer, meeting at the cabin for their trysts. She'd fallen so hard for him, but had always had the thought in the back of her mind that she was undeserving of anyone as fine and good as Colt Triplehorn.

Which was why she'd walked away from him without looking back. She'd expected it all along. That she'd go on with her life alone.

Zuri headed to the kitchen, thinking about the past, worrying about what was coming, but determined that at least she'd prove she could do one thing that would contribute to the ranch. She'd make them the best damn chili they'd ever tasted.

CHAPTER 10

It was nearly dinner time before Colt was finished with his calls. His friend at the bureau had barked in his ear when he'd first mentioned he had Zuri at the ranch house.

"Are you out of your mind? Do you know we're inches from issuin' a warrant for her arrest?"

Colt had gone on to explain the special circumstances, including the shooting that day.

Billy Slater had listened, not saying a word until the end. "There's no proof anyone was shootin' at you, Zuri or your horse, much less some dirty cop. Could have been a hunter poppin' off a random shot."

"I know. But I don't believe in coincidence."

"How much you trust this girl?"

"We have a history. She's scared, Billy."

"You a hundred percent sure about her?"

Colt let out a breath and went with his gut.

"She's tellin' the truth. She's mixed up in this, but I believe she's been set up. Still, I have men watchin' her and watchin' out for this guy. She's safe and stayin' put for now."

"Let me find out where the field team is with the investigation. I'll get hold of the agent in charge. I have no doubts he'll want to head straight for Destiny to pick her up."

"I want to go with her. She won't feel safe if I'm not there."

"I'll let him know, but he won't take any interference from you."

"I understand. I won't give him any so long as he keeps her safe and at least gives her the benefit of the doubt." He rung off and sat back in his desk chair.

Wade stuck his head in the office. "Sheriff."

Colt raised his eyebrows at Wade's use of his title.

"Someone's pokin' around Zuri's car."

Colt pushed up, took his weapon from his desk drawer and headed to truck.

At Roy Given's garage where he'd asked the vehicle be stored, he bypassed the office and went straight to the bay. A man was leaning through a window of the Corolla, peering inside

"That vehicle is in police impound. Did you not see the yellow tape on the doors?"

The man pulled out and turned. He was nearly six feet and lean with sandy blond hair and blue eyes. Pulling a badge from his sports jacket, he held it up for Colt to see. "I'm Detective David Satterly out of

Houston. We're looking for the woman who owns that car."

"That car was pulled from a river," Colt said, not offering anything more.

Satterly closed his eyes and looked away. "I hope like hell she made it out. No one's seen her? She's from these parts. Name's Zuri Prescott."

Colt held still, not answering.

Satterly appeared to collect himself then glanced back. "Look, I know this is a small town and everyone knows everyone else's business, but the young lady is in some serious trouble. I'm trying to do her a favor."

Colt's skin crawled at the thought that Zuri had been forced to turn to this sleazebag for help. He held himself still and forced a neutral expression on his face when all he wanted to do was put his hands around the other man's neck and squeeze. Colt set his hands on his hips. "How do you know her?"

"I'm a neighbor. Same apartment building. There was a robbery at the bank where she worked. A man was shot, and Zuri's the only witness. I know she has to be spooked, but she really shouldn't have run. It looks bad."

Colt studied his expression. The man was either really worried about her or a very good actor. Either way, Colt didn't want Satterly anywhere near Zuri.

"She's in big trouble. I don't know if the reports have crossed your desk here yet or not, but she was tied up, blindfolded. From her statement to the officers who responded, she was pretty sure the robber intended to kill her, but the bank manager distracted him."

Satterly leaned against the car. His gaze locked with Colt's. "Even before the robbery, she was having some trouble with a stalker. I don't know if the two things are related or not, but if she made it out of that river, she's not safe."

Colt narrowed his gaze. "If she shows up, we'll take care of her. It's what we do in small towns."

The other man's lips thinned. He reached into a pocket, flipped open a small case and handed Colt a card. "You see her, if she needs help, ask her to call me. I've got more than a few gray hairs worrying about her. She's a pretty thing. Independent and stubborn as hell. She might not want help."

"Why do you care? It seems a long way for a detective out of Houston to come for a neighbor."

Satterly gave a small crimped smile. "Well, I guess you have me figured out. I like her. I wouldn't be operating on my own all the way out here if I didn't." He glanced back at the car, his expression turning grim. "Good day to you, Sherriff."

Colt watched him walk away, every bit as sure as Zuri that he was looking at the robber. In the morning, he'd give Satterly's boss a call and see what more he could learn about the man.

When he returned to the ranch, Wade flipped his truck's siren in farewell and turned at the gate to head back into town.

Colt pulled into the driveway, nodded to a hand

sitting on the porch with a rifle lying across his lap. "Might want to find a shady spot. A sniper could pick you off right where you sit."

Skeeter tipped his hat and moved to a far corner of the porch. "Boss, your woman's a fine cook."

My woman...? Colt squinted at the man but didn't respond, following his nose to the kitchen where his brothers and a couple of the hands sat at the large table along with Zuri.

She was sitting with a cup of coffee between her hands, but when she spotted him, she jumped to her feet and headed to the stove. "Have a seat, and I'll get your supper. It's something simple, since everyone's eatin' in shifts."

Colt arched an eyebrow at Tommy who shrugged and smiled.

"Zuri, you didn't have to do this."

"I liked having something to do. If you like it hotter, there are jalapenos on the table. And I made cornbread muffins."

His stomach growled loudly, and Tommy and Gabe laughed.

Gabe pushed up from the table. "Guess we'll head on out and see what needs to be done before everyone beds down for the night."

Chairs ground on the Saltillo tiles and booted heels tapped as they fled the kitchen, leaving Colt alone with Zuri.

She set a bowl on the table and a basket with

muffins beside it. "You sure know how to clear a room."

Colt grunted. The men had thought he'd want her to himself, and he did.

Hanging his cowboy hat on the coat tree next to the door, he took a seat at the table and tucked into the meal. The first bite had him groaning. "Where'd you learn to cook like this?"

"Always had to make my own meals and Jed's, after Mama died. You just never knew because we didn't have a kitchen at our disposal."

We'd only cared about a bed. But he kept that to himself.

"You like it?" she asked, her hands twisting together.

"Mmmm," he groaned around another bite.

Her cheeks glowed with pleasure.

"Never would have taken you for the domestic type."

Her brown gaze narrowed. "Just because I don't like fast food or TV dinners, doesn't make me a domestic goddess."

"Just tryin' to make conversation, baby."

"You don't have to," she said, a little snip to her honeyed tones. "I'm fine when you're quiet."

He finished the bowl, broke a muffin and used it to clean the bottom of his bowl. When he glanced up she was smiling softly. "Didn't want to waste it."

"I can see that," she drawled.

He pushed back the bowl, but when she reached

for it, he grabbed her hand and pulled her down to the chair beside him. "We need to talk."

Her chest rose around a deep breath. "You find out anything today?"

He nodded. "I called my buddy at the bureau. He's gettin' hold of the team in Houston."

Her throat worked around a swallow, but she nodded, her gaze not shying from his own.

"And we had a visitor to town. Detective David Satterly."

All color drained from her face.

"He gave me his card. Said he was real worried about you. That if I see you, I should tell you to call him."

Her head angled away. "Are you tellin' me to call him?"

"Hell, no. I don't trust him, Zuri."

Her forehead wrinkled when she frowned. "I can't be sure it's him. The cologne. The fact he knew my routine. Maybe it's not him at all, and he's just tryin' to be a friend."

"Don't believe it. No one comes that far for a friend who's gone the wrong side of the law. Not unless he's in love with you. And he's not. My gut says he's mixed up in this. First thing in the morning, I'll call his department and see if they have any idea he's up here, and whether there's been anything funny with him before."

"Did he mention anything about me bein' here?"

"I didn't tell him you were at the ranch. Figured

if he's not the one who took that potshot at us, he doesn't need to know anyway."

Suddenly, Zuri leaned toward him, cupped his cheek and kissed his mouth.

Colt blinked then slowly smiled. "What was that for?"

"Not dismissing me. Even if you have reservations that I'm tellin' the truth, you protected me today."

Colt held the back of her hand and pressed a kiss to her palm. "I won't let anything happen to you. We have dishes to do?"

She shook her head. "Everyone pitched in. Let me put your bowl into the dishwasher and we're done."

"Hurry it up."

She gave him a blinding smile and bustled around the kitchen to cover the pot warming on the stove and toss the muffins into the oven.

When she came back to him, he took her hand and pulled her behind him, straight down the hallway to his bedroom.

She dug her heels in and pulled on his arm. "Don't you have to talk to your brothers?"

"Later. The guys are on alert after what happened today. They know the terrain. If anyone comes sneakin' in, they don't stand a chance."

He pulled her straight into his bedroom, closed the door then shoved her gently against the solid oak.

His kiss was swift and hard, but she didn't seem

to mind. She wound her arms around his neck and stood on her toes to deepen it. The tips of her small breasts hardened, and he felt them dig against his chest as she scraped upward.

She tasted like apples and cinnamon. "You make pie?" he murmured.

Her mouth stretched. "I did. Want to go back for a piece?"

"Hell, no." Again, he kissed her, tasting her until she sucked on his tongue and his cock hardened in sympathy to the steady pulling pleasure.

Hands smoothed over his back, fingers pinching as she grabbed for his shirt and shoved it up. Then she was gliding on his naked skin, and he wanted the same as fast as he could manage it. He thrust his fingers under her shirt, shaped her slender middle then moved up to mold her small, firm breasts.

"Kinda like that you don't have any bras," he growled.

"All of the guys kinda like that too," she said, her eyes nailing him.

He cleared his throat. "I'll be sure to fix that tomorrow."

"Do that. Only man I want ogling me is you."

He leaned back and dragged her shirt over her head, his gaze falling to the soft cherry cones topping her pretty breasts.

"Oh no. Not so fast," she whispered when he started to move down her body. She raised his shirt and pulled it off once he lifted his arms. Then before he had a chance to go to work on the rest of her clothes, her fingers got busy opening his belt, sliding down his zipper then reaching into his pants.

The feel of her warm hand around his shaft was pure heaven. Already hard, it swelled inside her fist as she gently pumped up then down, staring down between them.

"Just gonna look?"

Zuri flashed him a devilish grin and pushed on his shoulder to make him back up a step. She went to her knees, and he found he had to reach out an arm to lean against the wall to keep from falling because her soft, warm mouth went straight to his cock, swallowing him down.

"Baby..."

"Better keep quiet. We're right by the door. Everyone will hear."

He didn't give a damn if they did. He thrust his fingers into her hair and dragged on her scalp to hold her right where she was. His toes curled inside his boots as she gripped his shaft and swirled his cockhead around and around inside her mouth while her tongue lavished him with licks that made his balls harden like river stones.

She came off him then licked him up one side and down the other, wetting him. Her hands surrounded him and began to pump. Her head tilted back and her lashes fanned downward. "Used to think cocks were ugly, 'til I met yours. Those first times at the cabin, when you felt me up under my clothes, it gave me the courage to explore. When we finally did it, I had this wonderful new play toy." She stuck out her tongue and swabbed the soft cap. "I liked playin' with it, watchin' it fill. I mapped every vein with my fingers, then my mouth." She pointed her tongue and licked beneath the ridge surrounding the cap, flicking then laving it.

When she pulled him inside her mouth and suctioned, he cussed under his breath because he knew he wasn't going to last long, not the way she was warming him up with her firm grip sliding on his shaft. "Baby, come up. Let me get the rest of your clothes off. Get you on the bed."

She palmed his balls, wrapping her fingers right around them, and gave him a gentle tug. "Want to spoil my fun?"

"I want to make sure you're there with me when I come."

Only Zuri wasn't paying him any mind at all. She sank on him, taking him all the way to the back of her throat.

He reached down and ringed the base of his cock, squeezing to stop him from shooting into her mouth. "Uh huh. Not like this. Get those clothes off now."

He backed away from her, pulling from her mouth although it nearly killed him. She shoved down the sweatpants she wore and walked toward the bed, glancing behind her as she crawled atop the mattress, her soft white ass wagging in an invitation he couldn't refuse.

Following, he palmed both cheeks and bent to give her lush backside nips that had her gasping and giggling. He pushed her face down, leaving her legs dangling over the side.

Then he stripped quickly and came behind her, touching her between her legs and finding her so wet he couldn't resist the urge to kneel beside the bed and take her with his mouth.

He slid his tongue between her folds. His fingers traced the length of her slit, tucked into the crease between her thigh and thickening labia, teasing her before he dove in for a taste of her salty cream.

When he suckled at the bottom of her folds and found her little clit, he latched on and thrust his three fingers inside her pussy, filling her.

Her bottom lifted and held, and he smiled and sucked harder, enjoying the way her body shivered and her thighs and ass grew tight.

When he stroked his thumb over her tiny asshole, she grew rigid. "Colt! What are you doin'"

"Playin'."

"Play somewhere else."

Only he was just getting started. Because he wanted her pliable again, he returned his attention to her clit and vagina. The lush wet heat he sank inside had his dick pulsing, but he didn't stop, adding a finger and cupping them together as he thrust inside her tight sheath.

She mewled like a kitten, her hands fisting in the sheets, her back sinking and her ass rising higher.

At last satisfied she was ready, he rose behind her, urged her to her knees at the edge of the mattress, spreading them wide until she was at just the right height. Then he pressed into her, gliding straight inside until his groin met her sweet cunt.

When he was as deep as he could go, he placed a hand beneath her and circled on her clit, licked the fingers of his other hand and slid them between her cheeks.

This time, air hissed between her teeth, but she didn't complain. Instead, she held still as he swirled over her tiny hole. When he pushed and sank a fingertip inside, her head dropped to the mattress and her breaths came faster.

His cock was swollen, getting impossibly harder because her pussy was clamping down on him, moisture spilling from deep inside. Slick, wet heat surrounded him, and then her inner muscles began to convulse.

He sank his finger deeper then began to move it and his dick, forging in then pulling out, slick heat surrounding him. The lush sounds adding to his ragged gasps and her shaky moans.

Zuri came up on her arms and began to push back every time he plunged forward. They found a rhythm that pleased them both and rocked together and apart while sweat coated their skin and the smell of sex wafted in the air.

"Colt," she gasped.

"Baby?"

"God, please, please. Can't hold up."

He withdrew, flipped her over then climbed onto the mattress and shoved her up until they both lay in the center.

Then he climbed over her, found her center again and pushed inside.

She drew her legs up, bent her knees and gripped them to hold them high and out of the way as he braced on his arms and began to power into her.

Her face was red, her features tight. When she bared her teeth, he felt just as savage, plowing into her, over and over, until she tossed back her head, digging it into the mattress, and gave a keening cry.

Colt leaned back, kneeling between her legs and cradled her buttocks. He gave her shorter, sharper strokes, faster and faster, while her channel heated all around him. He came, giving a roar, not caring how far the sound carried, because his body exploded, balls emptying their tension in successive surges of come.

When he slowed, which he had to because he was gasping for breath, he opened his eyes to find Zuri staring, a lop-sided smile quirking up one corner.

He pushed deep then came down on top of her, not wanting to give up the connection or the feel of her hands smoothing over his back. With his breaths evening, he got his elbows beneath him and lifted his chest slightly. "Breathe now?"

"I was breathin' just fine," she said, her smile wider now.

"Happy?"

She sighed, her fingers playing with the curve of his ear. "Incredibly so."

He bent and kissed her smiling lips until they softened and suctioned against his, sealing them together.

CHAPTER 11

Zuri woke slowly. Something tickled her nose and a bad, bad feeling snaked down her spine.

A shout sounded from the yard in front of the house, Scout's excited barks punctuated the air. Her eyes fluttered open. Even though it was the dead of night, light chased across the walls of Colt's bedroom. Bright red light that flickered and waved. The smell of smoke filled her with dread.

"Fire!" came more shouts. Boots thudded on the porch.

Instantly alert, Zuri pushed up from the bed, heart racing. She swung her legs over the side of the bed and ran to Colt's chest of drawers, found another tee and too-large pants and dressed. She put on socks to protect her feet, then ran out the bedroom and down the hallway toward the front door.

Just as she reached for the doorknob, she felt a presence behind her. A moment later, a large hand closed around her mouth. Something hard nudged her ribs, and she knew.

She smelled his cologne, felt the gust of his hot breath against her cheek. She went still as her blood chilled

"Have to stop meeting like this," he whispered in her ear. His hand slid away from her mouth.

Torn between screaming and fighting, she quivered against him. Outside was chaos. Even if she had the courage to shout, they'd never hear her above the roar of the fire, the shrill whinnies of frightened horses and the shouts from the men as they scurried to put out the fire.

Tamping down her fear, she lifted her chin. "What did you do?"

"Set a fire in the barn," he said, his tone weirdly gleeful. "It'll give us a little time."

She thought fast. Had all the hands left to take care of the fire? Even the ones watching the house? Stillness surrounded them. He'd done something. She just knew it.

"No one's coming. Your guard's gonna have a helluva headache when he comes to."

A shiver racked her frame, but she stiffened her back. "I don't know who you are," she said, lying, because this time she recognized his voice. "You've already got me in the FBI's crosshairs. You should have just let them find me. What more damage can you do?"

"I can make sure they stop looking. Point all eyes your way."

"Bastard."

A finger toyed with the hair beside her ear. "Too bad your sheriff didn't show better judgment. If he'd locked you up, we wouldn't be having this conversation."

"Leave him out of this."

"Can't. It's too late now. He already harbored a *person of interest*. You disappear on his watch, they're gonna think he let you escape. That maybe he knew all about the money, and you cut him in so he'd look the other way."

"He'll be cleared. No one will believe he's involved.

"But it will take some time. Long enough for me to get far, far away." He shifted behind her. "Open wide." His hand appeared in front of her face, holding a wad of fabric

She didn't want to open, but she didn't really have a choice. He had a gun to her side, and she didn't want anyone else hurt. She opened her mouth and waited while he stuffed the fabric inside. Panic welled because it was too large to push out with her tongue, and he wasn't done. The gun fell away and tape covered her mouth, holding the wadding in place.

Then he dragged her toward the kitchen and the door leading to the driveway, away from all the commotion in front of the house. Opening the door, he pulled her out sideways, past the prone body of one of the hands.

She sobbed, the sound muffled. The urge to vomit rose up, but she tamped it down because she'd choke.

"Like I said, he'll wake up. They'll think you started the fire. That you hit him over the head making your escape."

She dragged her feet, anything to slow him down, hoping like hell someone would see, but there was no one. The quiet enveloped them as he forced her quickly through a pasture toward the vehicle parked on the highway.

He didn't pause at the fence. The barbed wire was cut. Another nudge on her ribs and he forced her into the passenger seat of the sedan and quickly restrained one hand with metal cuffs dangling from the oh-shit handle above the passenger-side window.

As he pulled away from the shoulder of the road, sirens sounded in the distance from the opposite direction. Fire trucks heading to the ranch.

Zuri watched as the Triplehorn Ranch faded in the distance.

She laid her head against the headrest and closed her eyes, praying for intervention, because she knew the farther down the road they got, the less her chances of ever being found were. She couldn't imagine what Colt would go through when he discovered her gone. He loved her, had told her so, but would he hold onto that last nugget of uncertainty and believe she'd left willingly?

At least she'd had a chance to set things right. They'd had two days. Two perfect days. She could almost die happy. Almost. Except it would mean that David had won, and that thought made her mad as hell.

COLT JAMMED the truck into park in the middle of the road and yanked open his door. Two more county trucks pulled in, spitting gravel from beneath their tires, forming a barrier at the highway intersection. He'd used graveled ranch roads and a cutoff to get here quickly. He'd planned for just such an eventuality, coordinating with the sheriff from the next town over.

Wade stepped down from his truck. "If he makes it through this road block there's another forming on down the road."

The radio squawked. "Colt? Colt?"

Colt cussed under his breath. Gabe had never got the hang of the police radio.

"Got his taillights in front of me now. We're about a quarter mile from you. Get ready."

Colt clamped his hat on head, pulled out his rifle and opened his truck door to rest the barrel against the bottom of the window frame. In the distance, he saw the glint of metal in the early morning sunlight.

Wade clapped his shoulder. "We've got him

boxed-in tight. No place he can go. We knew it was a diversion the second the barn went up."

"Didn't count on the fact he was already inside the damn house," Colt ground out. "We were watchin' the pastures, the roads."

Gabe had seen him and Zuri slip across the pasture, but the bastard had a gun on her, and his brother had to hold back so Satterly wouldn't spook and kill her on the spot. "Gabe's been followin' with lights off so he wouldn't know he was bein' trailed while I called in support. Should've arrested his ass the moment he nosed around the Roy's garage."

"Didn't have cause," Wade said from where he stood, rifle braced in the window on the other side of his truck.

Colt gave him a glance across the cab. "Wouldn't have mattered. Zuri'd be safe. I should've been there. Should've stuck to her like glue."

"You're the law. It was your duty to alert the feds. When Satterly moved out of his hotel room, the deputies scrambled me. Had to call you, boss. It's what you've been waitin' for."

Colt narrowed his gaze on the car approaching at a fast clip. The glint was Satterly's sedan. He reached into the dash and flipped the switch to set the blue lights strobing. The other trucks followed suit.

The sedan slowed. Colt bent his head and stared through his rifle sight. It was Satterly behind the wheel all right. Beside him sat Zuri, her hand hanging from a set of cuffs. His gut tightened. She looked scared.

The car weaved then swerved, running off the road as the wheels turned and Satterly began to make a U-turn but discovered his way was blocked by another set of vehicles coming from the direction of the ranch.

Gabe slowed and flashed his headlights. Behind him were three more trucks, all from the ranch, ranch hands crammed in the cabs and tail beds, all armed.

"Hope they know not to let off a shot while she's inside," Colt growled.

"Your brother Tommy might think he's so good with that rifle of his that he could take him out where he sits."

"I'd have his ass if he tried."

Satterly's car halted, half in the ditch, then lurched back onto the road and headed slowly toward Colt and his deputies' cars.

"Come on, buddy, do the smart thing."

The car kept coming, the engine building. No sign from the driver he was going to stop.

Colt shook his head, pulled his rifle from the window, and slammed his door closed. With his rifle held against his thigh, he strode down the center of the highway toward the car.

WAS HE CRAZY? Zuri froze, watching Colt saunter like a gunfighter of old right down the center line. He was dressed for the role in his crisp blue shirt, a badge hanging from his pocket. His cream-colored cowboy hat sat square on his head. His expression was hard, his body held like an unmovable mountain. Only she knew he was flesh and blood, vulnerable in the open.

"Sonofabitch," David said, sweat beginning to drip down the side of his face. "Who does he think he is? Rambo?"

More like John Wayne. Zuri made a noise behind her gag and rattled her cuffs.

"Shut the hell up." David reached sideways and slapped her with the back of his hand.

Her eyes watered, but she blinked the moisture away. Through the windshield, she realized Colt must have seen the blow, because he flipped up his rifle and jammed the butt against his shoulder. Still walking down the center line, he took aim.

"Don't guess he cares a damn about you, sweetie." David jerked his steering wheel to the left, drove down into the ditch and up the other side, the car tilting sideways at a dangerous angle until he rode the edge of the fence line. It looked like he intended get around the vehicles parked nose-to-tail blocking the road.

A shot fired, pinging off the tarmac.

Her scared glance shot toward Colt, but he was pointing in front of them. The shot was just a warning.

David punched the gas pedal, and the car shot forward, dragging the steel cuff on her wrist, which was already swelling. She moaned and braced her feet on the floor, trying to take some of the abuse off her wrist.

Another shot rang out. And above the noise the squeaking shocks made, she heard a hiss.

David cursed. "Shot my damn tire."

He ran down the ditch and back into the middle of the road, but he fought the steering as he aimed the car straight at Colt.

Colt stood firm.

Zuri couldn't believe the two of them. Both stubborn as hell. David had to know there wasn't any escape, but he wasn't giving up. Colt was an even bigger idiot, standing right in the car's path. His expression was hard as stone. His eyes narrowed with deadly intent.

No way was she leaving her fate in either of their hands. Zuri brought up her legs and jabbed her feet toward David.

He took one hand off the steering wheel and reached for her. The car careened right into the opposite ditch and came to a rest against a fence post.

Her airbag exploded, plastic and chemicals slapping her in the face, dazing her.

David's never deployed. His hands scrabbled for a hold of her legs, but as the bag deflated, she roused, wriggling and kicking, catching him with the edge of her heel against his jaw.

His head whipped back and hit the window glass.

Zuri kept kicking even though he lay still. She

grunted with exertion, tears streaming down her face.

The door beside her jerked opened. Arms reached inside. The cuff was released, and she fell sideways out the door, but someone caught her. She kicked out again, bucking her body to free herself, still half-crazed.

Colt dragged her out the door and into his arms to hold her against his shaking body. "I've got you, baby. It's okay, Zuri. It's over."

Her breaths came in jagged sobs. He ripped away the tape across her mouth and removed the wad of material. She dragged in a deep breath and screamed.

Colt pressed his cheek against hers and squeezed her tight. "Shhh...shhh, baby. Take a deep breath."

She did, hiccupping, then jerked inside his embrace until he loosened his grip and she could turn toward him. She slammed her mouth against his and kissed him, awkwardly, crying at the same time.

Colt cupped her head, digging his fingers in her scalp and kissed her back.

When they came up for air, she leaned away, lifted her arm and slapped him as hard as she could across his face.

He didn't move a muscle, although his expression shuttered.

She reached back again, but his hand shot out and caught her forearm in a firm grip. "Sure you want to do that?"

Everything she'd held inside erupted in a blistering scream. "You asshole! Think you're Superman? That his car would bounce right off you? You scared the shit out of me!"

When she stopped, she realized that all the noise around them had, too.

Her glance slid to the side to find Gabe fighting a smirk. One of the deputies, who looked awfully familiar, cleared his throat. Officers began moving around them again.

"Guess I shouldn't have popped the sheriff in the mouth," she grumbled, not ready to apologize.

"Got it all out?" he said, his voice even.

"No." Her gaze dropped away from his steady glare, and she pouted her lips. "Never saw anything that damn dumb."

His grunt made her look up again. Dark humor gleamed in his eyes and quirked up one corner of his mouth. "You all right? Did he hurt you?"

She shook her head. "No, but I was s-scared."

"I know. I was too." And then he gave her a wide smile. One she returned.

"I'm not gonna hit you again," she said, shaking her arm.

But he didn't ease his hold.

Not that she cared. Not with all the noise surrounding them, more sirens blaring, more feet running. She leaned toward him, pressed her face into the corner of his neck, and breathed in his scent. "I didn't want to go. He forced me."

A kiss touched her forehead. "He was in the house."

She nodded. "He surprised me. Pushed a gun into my ribs and gagged me. I didn't fight because I didn't want anyone else being hurt. The man at the back door?"

"Will be fine. Don't you worry."

"Good. Didn't want anyone hurt on account of me." She stirred, becoming aware that she sat sprawled across Colt's lap as he sat in the dirt on the side of the highway.

Scrubbing a hand across her face, she wiped away her tears.

"Better?"

She nodded and offered him a smile, although now with the adrenaline leaving her system, she felt every ache and was weary to the bone.

"Let me get you up." Colt gently slid from under her then stood and picked her up from the ground.

She grabbed for his shoulders. "I can walk."

His gray eyes met her gaze. A dark brow lifted. "Do you want to?"

She ducked her head and blushed. "Not really."

"Then let me take care of you."

She liked the sound of that, however foreign the sentiment in her life. She'd never had anyone say that to her before. Still, pride made her blurt, "I'm not hurt. Not really. Just a little bruised."

He didn't answer as he strode away from David's car. The detective lay prone on the ground, an EMT kneeling beside him. His mouth was bloodied, his gaze on her, hatred radiating from his cold blue eyes.

She shivered and snuggled closer to Colt's chest. "Don't you worry about him."

"Hey, Colt." A man dressed in a dark suit approached, his features flinty until his gaze fell on her. He gave her a nod. "She okay? She need medical attention?"

"She's fine, Billy."

"Taking her to the station?"

Colt's arms became rigid bands around her. "Yeah, heading there now."

But she knew he hadn't been thinking that, not by his tone. He'd forgotten for a moment that she was still in deep trouble.

Billy's hard gaze didn't blink. "I'll follow you."

"Great." Colt approached one of the deputy's trucks, which was when Zuri realized why he was so familiar. Wade Dalton had been one of Colt's running buddies in high school.

Wade, looking older and more handsome than the last time she'd seen him, held open the door to the back seat. "Zuri," he said, nodding to her. Then to Colt he said, "Want me to drive you two?"

Colt leaned down and set her on the seat. "Scoot."

Surprised he intended to ride with her in the back, she moved quickly, her gaze never leaving his as he ducked inside and sat. His hand reached for hers, and he held it between both of his as Wade put the car in gear and pulled onto the highway.

CHAPTER 12

After pulling down the yellow crime-scene tape from the door, Zuri unlocked her apartment with the spare key the super gave her and stepped inside. She closed the door behind her then leaned her back against it, glancing around.

The air was musty. Dust lay on the surface of the bureau sitting near the door. She glanced around and her heart fell to her toes. Her apartment was trashed. Couch cushions were tossed, drawers emptied on the ground. Nothing was as she'd left it. Whoever had searched her apartment, Houston PD or the FBI, maybe both, had left no stone or pillow unturned.

"What a mess."

After days in custody, she'd finally been released on her own recognizance, even though David Satterly still swore up and down she'd been a part of the robbery, that *she'd* recruited him. The prosecutor hadn't bought his story and, instead, had offered her immunity from prosecution for her testimony. A bad cop was more newsworthy than a greedy bank teller.

Colt was sure she'd be cleared in the end. Once all the facts were sorted out.

Colt. She sighed. He'd been a rock—hiring the best attorney money could buy, hovering every time she was led away for questioning. She was sure his stolid presence had worked in her favor, swaying the investigators. How could a stalwart man like Colt Triplehorn get involved with someone unsavory? In the end, she was sure he'd tipped the scales in her favor. That and the fact that despite a thorough search of her home and financial records, they hadn't found any proof she'd been in league with the detective.

With just his word against hers, they'd jockeyed for a deal. One she'd been too exhausted to protest. Like Colt had said, the truth would come out in the end, and she'd be cleared.

In the meantime, she was out of job. And likely wouldn't find another with the investigation hanging over her head.

Colt didn't see the problem. Which was why, without telling anyone where she was going, she'd taken a cab from the FBI building straight home.

She needed time to think, which she could do while she cleaned up her apartment. Pushing away from the door, she rolled up the sleeves of the blouse Colt had bought her. After he'd seen her dressed in the jail's white jumpsuit, he'd sent Tommy on a mission to buy her clothes.

Zuri shook her head. The man had so much money all he had to do was snap his fingers and things happened. She wished she could snap her fingers and make this mess go away, but she wasn't a Triplehorn. If she didn't shake the stain of her arrest, she never would be.

Dragging her feet, she headed straight into the living room area and picked up pillows from the floor. When she bent to replace the chair's cushion, she noted a long gash cut into the bottom, stuffing pushing out. Her hands shook as she reached down to push it back inside. But it was ruined. Everything was ruined. She dropped it to the carpet, leaned her head against the sofa, and cried.

Colt heard her sobs as soon as he pushed through the front door. Moving quietly, he entered, noted the mess and guessed the cause of her sorrow. He'd have spared her this, but she'd given him the slip. Tommy had followed her to the apartment and called him to let him know where to find her.

For whatever cockeyed reason, Zuri had begun to withdraw from him. Pulling away the moment she realized her problems were going to linger for a while. He suspected that she worried about hurting his reputation, that she'd be a burden, but they hadn't had the privacy to talk about what was weighing on her mind.

Coming up behind her, he knelt and reached for her upper arms. He pulled her back against his chest then wrapped his arms around her. "It's going to be okay, Zuri."

She didn't fight him, but also didn't cling. She lay limply against his chest, her body shaking with her deep sobs. "You can't know that. You're a sheriff; you can't want this."

You can't want me was what he heard. He tightened his fingers on her upper arms and gave her a gentle shake. "Don't tell me what I want." It came out more harshly than he intended, but it seemed to do the trick.

Zuri stiffened. Her sobs subsided. When she reached up to pry his fingers from her arm, he let her go. She crawled forward on her knees then turned to face him.

Her expression nearly killed him.

Her soft brown eyes were large in her face, her lashes wet and spiked. Her chin wobbled. Gone was any hint of stubborn pride.

At a loss for what to say next, he took off his cowboy hat and raked a hand through his hair. "Billy says I can take you home."

"This is my home," she said, her voice thick and raw.

He shook his head. "You're not stayin' here."

"I have work to do. A mess to clean up."

"I'll hire a cleaning team. You don't have to do this."

"It's my own damn mess." Her chin firmed, lifted.

Now *there* was the hint of starch he'd hoped to find. "Then we've got ourselves a problem."

"What's that?"

"I have a job. One that requires I be in Destiny County to perform."

"There's nothin' stoppin' you here."

"Sure, there is," he said softly. "You see, Billy says you're my responsibility."

"They released me."

"With promises from me to make sure you met your court dates. And he expects to contact you in the meantime at my home."

Her chin lifted. "You'll just have to tell him my plans changed."

He almost smiled. Her eyes gleamed, not with tears, but with anger. Something he could work with.

Slipping his cuffs from his back pocket, he dangled them from a finger. "Now, we can do this the easy way…or…"

Her eyes narrowed to slits. "You wouldn't."

"I will if I have to." He held out his other hand. "Gonna come peaceably?"

He read relief in the lowering of her shoulders but not defeat.

Her glance cut to the side. "I'll need to pack."

"There's not a thing you need. I have a suitcase in

the truck. All those pretty things Tommy bought you."

"I'm not some charity case."

"Never wanted you to feel that way," he said honestly. "Didn't mean to ride roughshod over you these past few days, but I wanted this over. For us to be able to move on. Fact is, I need you, Zuri."

"I'm not right for you. Not—"

"Don't say you aren't good enough."

Her eyes filled. "You know what I came from, what I've been accused of. Folks can't be that forgiving, not in Destiny."

"Folks will learn to judge you by the company you keep, by the good things you do."

A tear escaped her eye and trailed down her cheek. "I don't want to hurt you, Colt. I couldn't stand that."

Colt reached out a finger and wiped the tear away. Then he cupped her face between his hands, locking her gaze with his. "The only way you'll hurt me, Zuri-girl, is if you let me walk out that door alone."

She drew in a breath, opened her mouth to speak, but then came up on her knees and flung her arms around his shoulders. "I'm so glad you said that. I wanted to give you an out, but it would have killed me to say goodbye. Guess I'm selfish."

Colt held her close, smiling into her hair. "Guess I'm selfish too, because I wasn't jokin' about those cuffs."

"We're a pair, aren't we?"

Tugging on the back of her hair, he forced her head back. "If you come home with me, you're gonna live under my roof. My rules."

Her lips curved. "Didn't mind your rules so much the last time."

"Glad you're so eager," he drawled. "But I've got this ring that's been burnin' a hole in my pocket for twelve long years."

Her breath caught. "You kept it?"

"Belonged to my grandmother. I wasn't gonna throw it away. It's been waitin' for the right girl to come home."

"Your rules?" she said, arching a brow.

"You have to come home as my wife."

She wrinkled her nose. "Think we can leave out the whole I'm-in-your-custody bit when we tell our kids about this?"

"Don't you want to be the coolest mom ever?"

She laughed and sprang against him, kissing his mouth.

He caught her against his chest…felt her heart thudding against him, his own heart racing to catch up.

When she pulled back, she held up her hand and fluttered her fingers. "I want to see it."

He grinned. "You haven't said yes."

Dropping her hand to her thigh, her lips twisted. "I'd have said yes twelve years ago, but you still haven't asked."

Colt couldn't help it. He laughed.

Zuri giggled.

A door opened and closed. "Holy shit," came Tommy's voice. His footsteps drew near. "Zuri, you better say yes quick. No way is *Mrs.* Triplehorn gonna have to clean up this mess."

Colt laughed harder.

Zuri leaned into him, her body shaking with laughter.

When he got his mirth under control, he shifted onto one knee and reached into his pocket. He pulled out a small jeweler's box and opened the lid, glancing at the sparkling diamond inside before turning it toward her. "Zuri Prescott, will be my wife?"

Her glance fell to the ring with a soft gasp. "It's beautiful," she said, her voice soft and uncharacteristically high.

"She still hasn't said yes," Tommy whispered.

"I'm thinkin'," she murmured, her gaze still glued to the ring.

"What's there to think about, sugar? He's crazy about you."

"His rules..."

Colt chuckled. "I promise they won't be anything you can't live with."

Her gaze narrowed then darted up to his face. "I'd still like to hear them."

Since he didn't really have a list, he cleared his throat. "We have an audience..."

His brother's breath gusted on a laugh. "Your audience ain't leavin' now."

Zuri's eyebrows waggled. "We're all waitin' to hear."

Colt aimed a glare at Tommy's grinning face then turned back to Zuri. "My rules. No other man but me for the rest of our lives."

She appeared to consider that one for a long moment then nodded. "Agreed."

"No clothes between us when we lay together."

"*Wherever* we lay together?"

He didn't know how that made a difference, but he nodded.

"Agreed."

Tommy snorted. "Man, you've got no imagination."

Colt snorted. "No panties when I take you out on a date."

Zuri's eyes widened. "Colt, you said that in front of Tommy. Now, he'll know!"

"Yes, I will," Tommy said, laughter in his voice. "And won't that be fun."

Zuri aimed a blistering glare at Tommy, but gave Colt a curt nod.

Colt ignored his brother's chuckles until he fell silent again, and Zuri's blush receded. "And no secrets, Zuri. If I leave anything unsaid, you tell me."

He knew she was thinking about graduation day. He was too. They'd wasted years on hurt feelings, all because neither of them had had the courage to say what was on their mind.

"Agreed." She held up her hand again.

He plucked the ring from the box and held it poised at the end of her finger. "Still haven't said yes, sweetheart."

Zuri rolled her eyes. "Yes, Colt. Yes to your rules. Yes to gettin' married."

He slid the ring on. Both their faces stretched with wide, happy smiles.

"Well, halleluiah," Tommy muttered.

They married in the living room at the ranch house the very next day in front of a preacher and with all the hands present. Wade stood beside Colt as his best man. Tommy and Gabe led her into the room, one at each elbow.

Zuri could scarcely believe everything had happened so quickly. Apparently, Gabe had been left to make all the arrangements, even before her release was assured.

She wore a beautiful white gown that Tommy had purchased along with her get-out-of-jail wardrobe. Of course, it was strapless, which had made her nervous given her meager measurements, but the laces up the back assured nothing gaped. The pretty handmade lace train swished on the wood floor as she approached.

Colt's gaze when it found her made all her efforts

at primping worthwhile. She'd realized as she'd prepared that he hadn't seen her in makeup and with her hair styled. Even she was aware of the transformation. A delicate blush stained her cheeks and lips. Small pink roses and baby's breath were pinned strategically to her upswept hair to resemble a crown. She felt like a princess as she took those final steps.

When he closed his hand around hers and drew her close to his side, she sighed. She was where she belonged. Where she'd always belonged.

∿

IN TOO DEEP

THE TRIPLEHORN BRAND, BOOK 2

New York Times and *USA Today* Bestselling Author
Delilah Devlin

IN TOO DEEP

TRIPLEHORN BRAND

NEW YORK TIMES BESTSELLING AUTHOR

DELILAH DEVLIN

ABOUT THE BOOK

Some things never change. And some things change everything...

Gabe Triplehorn can think of no better getaway from his heavy responsibilities at the ranch than to go back to a time and place where he didn't have a care in the world. When there was just a campground, a river, and a girl. When he gets to Red Hawk Landing, the campground and the river are still there. He just never expected the girl would still be there, too. Only now she runs the place.

Lena Twohig can think of no better place to raise her young son than the family-owned campground that holds so many memories. Especially, the romance with Gabe that lit up one long-ago summer like a wild electrical storm. Now he's back with a ranch-hardened body she knows she shouldn't want so badly.

No amount of lies, or the years that have passed, can tame this tidal wave of passion.

CHAPTER 1

With the window of his Ford F-150 rolled down and a breeze whipping his face, Gabe Triplehorn didn't mind the sultry, mid-summer heat. For the first time in years, he felt completely free.

Free of responsibility.

Free of Colt telling him what he ought to do with his life.

Free of Tommy giving him disgusted glances, because the last thing Gabe wanted to do lately was ride behind a herd of cattle kicking up dust in his face.

But he was especially free of the evidence of domestic bliss stinking up the air in the Triplehorn ranch house.

Gabe wasn't usually this grumpy, but he'd lost sleep for weeks due to the lusty goings-on inside the Triplehorn ranch house. Unaccustomed to sleepless nights when he was home and lying in his own bed, and irritated at having to keep himself decently dressed every time he stepped foot outside his bedroom door, he'd become as nasty as a growling bear to be around.

And who could blame him? Sounds echoed down the bedroom hallway into the early morning hours. Sexy sounds—soft moans, warm chuckles. Sharp, urgent cries. Sounds that put erotic images into a horny man's head. Stuffing a pillow over his face didn't muffle them enough to cut through the pictures flooding his mind, especially after he'd gotten an up-close eyeful of one particularly hot-'n'-heavy petting session in the kitchen. Thankfully, neither one of the newly married couple had noticed as he'd hastily backed away from the door. But after that, he couldn't look at melted chocolate or Zuri's small breasts in quite the same light.

Not that he wasn't happy for his brother, Colt. The eldest of the brothers deserved every bit of the happiness he'd found with his new wife. He just wished the two of them had kept their newfound wedded bliss a little more private. Having a beautiful woman under the same roof, one whose lusty spirit apparently matched his brother's stroke for stroke, played hell with Gabe's own desire. The fact he hadn't had time to court a new playmate to handle his excess frustration only added to his ill humor.

At least, Gabe had at last gotten over the major case of indigestion that adding Zuri Prescott to the family had caused. She'd turned out to be all right.

Far from the heartless heartbreaker he and Tommy had pegged her for.

Still, it was hard to shrug off over a decade of animosity and resentment in just a couple of months. Harder still to listen to the sounds of his brother's hard-won satisfaction night after night.

When Colt had suggested that Gabe take a vacation, sew some wild oats—anything to get his head back on straight—Gabe had been a little angry at first, wondering if Colt was trying to push him out of the nest because he was cramping the couple's style.

But Zuri had pulled him aside, surprising him after he'd been so rough on her when she'd first arrived. He hadn't believed her story of being framed for a bank robbery or that the true robber had been a cop. Given who her father was, and what Gabe had thought she'd done to his brother, he'd suspected the worst.

Just that morning, after Colt had baldly told him he needed to get out of his system whatever was making him cranky, she'd stopped him on the front porch.

"Gabe," she'd called after him.

He thought about ignoring her, had his hat in his hand as he stomped down the steps heading to the barn to saddle his horse.

"Gabe."

He paused, sucked in a deep breath, and pasted on a smile before he faced her. "What do want, Zuri?"

"For you to be happy."

"Who says I'm not?"

She arched a dark brow while she silently studied him.

Gabe had to admit he could see his brother's attraction to the woman standing before him. Her curves were subtle, but the length of smooth leg exposed beneath the hem of her short skirt could make any man stop and take notice. Add the healthy shine to her straight, chin-length dark hair and the wide, puppy-dog eyes, and he knew why his brother had risked his life and his career as sheriff to protect her.

"Zuri, I have chores to do," he said, his voice gruff.

"He's not trying to ease you out of the house, Gabe. There's plenty of room here still. And we have plans to build another house to make room for any kids we might be lucky enough to have."

Luck isn't gonna have a thing to do with it, honey. He kicked at the dirt beneath his boots. "Colt's the oldest. The house is his."

Zuri shook her head. "Fact is, I think he wants Tommy to have this place. He loves it the most. Works the hardest. Colt's got his sheriff's job, but Tommy eats, breaths, and sleeps with the cattle. You're the one he worries about."

"Sounds like you've both been doin' a lot of talking behind my back."

"He just wants me to understand you."

A flush of guilt heated his cheeks. "I said I was sorry for how I treated you," he muttered, dropping his head to watch himself scuff his boots together.

"And I've forgiven you," she said, her musical voice filled with earnest intent. "You had your reasons for distrusting me. And I can't blame you for holding a grudge."

Although he knew she was only acting out of concern, Gabe didn't like the feeling that crept over him, like Zuri and Colt considered him a problem they had to fix. He was a grown man. He could take care of his own damn problems.

"What's your point?" he asked, then cringed inside at his terse tone.

Zuri sighed. "Why don't you do as he suggested. Get away for a bit. Find whatever's missing in your life or figure out how to go about finding it. We'll be fine. Our honeymoon's over. Colt's ready to dig back in and take up any slack your absence might leave. No one will look sideways if you want to get away for a while on your own."

Gabe released a deep breath, and then raised his head. "Where the hell would I go?"

Zuri pursed her lips. "Isn't there some place or person you're missing?" she asked softly. "Go there."

The moment she mentioned it, a place did enter his mind.

Tall elms flanking a riverbank, clear water burbling over rocky shelves, and a slow current that invited a man to plant a fishing pole in the mud while he lay on his back, chewing on a blade of grass.

Then another picture seeped into his thoughts. A woman with laughing blue eyes and silky blonde hair that always looked in need of a comb. Curves that would overspill a large palm.

"Gabe?"

He'd drifted a moment on that slow-moving creek.

"You thought of a place?"

He shook his head. Last thing he wanted was to share even a shred of that treasured memory.

She arched a brow. "Then why'd you smile?"

Gabe flashed her a quick grin. "Because you're every bit as stubborn as your husband."

"I sure like that word," she said, a smile stretching her pretty mouth.

Boot steps echoed from inside the house. Colt swept open the door, wearing a pale-blue shirt and dark trousers. His silver badge was clipped to his shirt pocket. "You think about what I said?"

Ten minutes ago, Gabe would have bitten his head off and told him to mind his own business, but Zuri's expression, so earnest and hopeful, made him stop. "I have," he said nodding. "I think I'm goin' campin'."

Colt's eyes narrowed. "To the Red Hawk?"

"Yeah, haven't been there in years." Gabe stared back, daring him to say anything more.

"Think she's still there?"

Gabe shook his head. "If she's there, she's long married and has a passel of kids. I'm just gonna do some fishin'."

Colt grinned then leaned down and kissed Zuri's cheek. "Don't know what you said to him, but thanks."

Zuri laughed. "I swear it didn't take much persuasion on my part."

Later that morning, he'd stuffed a few changes of clothes into a backpack and left rubber as he'd peeled out of the drive, he was so eager to let loose. Suddenly hopeful that something extraordinary might lie at the end of his journey.

A deer darted into the road. Gabe swerved slightly and tapped the brakes. A doe stood in the center of the road, her flanks quivering, but Gabe understood why she didn't move when a fawn on spindly legs trotted past her.

When they both leaped into the bushes on the opposite side, he pressed on the gas. He'd better pay attention to the road and stop daydreaming or he'd wind up in a ditch. And he was impatient to see Red Hawk Landing—the small campground with a pier that stretched to the center of the river, the ramshackle collection of wooden cabins that sat in a horseshoe to the side of the small lodge. Not anyone's idea of a luxury vacation spot, but it was a place a man could hear his own thoughts.

He'd found the campground by accident when he was a teenager and driving, blowing off steam after yet another argument with his father over his grades and late-night partying. He'd been seventeen, and Colt had joined the Army and wasn't there any longer to help deflect attention from his bad habits. Not that Dad hadn't had a point. Something Gabe had thought about long and hard after he left a note on the table for his mother to find, telling her he'd be back in a week.

But one week had turned into two when he'd found the campground. Old man Twohig had hired him, needing someone handy to help with repairs and blowing up inner tubes for guests to float the river. What Gabe hadn't known at the time was that Mr. Twohig had called his dad the first day he'd arrived, and the two men had made an arrangement to help Gabe blow off some steam and have time away from all the expectations of being a Triplehorn.

Gabe had spent the two weeks in cutoff jeans and barefoot. And he'd taken a shine to the old man's granddaughter, Lena.

She'd come to spend the summer away from the city. She made breakfast every morning for the guests, and then leant a hand with the chores, working side by side with Gabe.

Even though she was a couple of years older than he was, she'd been shy at first. Maybe she'd felt those two years placed him in the do-not-flirt-with zone, but he'd been persistent. Then one late afternoon, a couple of days before his dad and Colt had shown up to take him home, he and Lena Twohig had shed their clothes for a dip in the stream. For one sparkling afternoon, he hadn't just been romanticizing about being in love. He'd sunk his toes in the mud and pebbles and fallen hard for a woman who'd taught him what real passion meant.

So, what the hell was he doing now, heading back there? It was doubtful the old man was still alive. Even more so that the woman would still be there. She'd had plans for college, another life to begin in Dallas. But still, when he'd spoken to Zuri, his first instinct had been to go back there.

Now, the light, expectant glow that had sustained him for most of the trip began to fade.

At a bend in the road, he saw the sign nearly hidden by bushes because it tilted at an angle. *Red Hawk Landing. Open Memorial Day to Labor Day.*

The crackled, worn paint on the leaning sign didn't bode well, but he took the turn anyway, his truck bumping along an uneven gravel trail that worked its way down a steep decline, heading toward the river's edge.

When he made the clearing, he heaved a sigh of relief. The place was still in operation. Kids in cutoffs and swimming suits took running dives from the pier. Cars and pickups were parked in front of roughhewn wooden cabins.

He hoped like hell there was still one vacancy left for him and pulled up in front of the small lodge house. The place was clean but showing its age. Looked like the owner needed another handy man to help with a broken spoke or two in the wraparound porch rails and a window frame that appeared to be rotting away.

He put his truck in park and pushed down on the handle to open the door, but halted the moment she stepped onto the porch.

Lena Twohig. *Sweet Jesus.*

His breath caught, nostalgia blurring her appearance in a golden light that masked the years etched lightly into her features.

Sure, her figure was a tad fuller, her roots darker, but the feeling he got just looking at her as she lifted a hand to guard her eyes against the brilliant sunshine was exactly the same one he'd had all those years ago.

A slow throbbing built in his groin. His body stiffened, going on alert. His gaze swept her womanly frame again, snagging on the generous swell of her bosom, the long, well-toned legs displayed beneath the hem of her shorts. Ten years had been kind indeed.

Then something glinted on the fingers cupping her eyes. A flash of white metal.

He remembered a slender band he'd given her. His last gift. A promise he'd never fulfilled. However much he might wish it wasn't so, the ring she wore now killed his pleasant dream of rekindling their romance. The desire he'd allowed to build while he'd ogled her began to slowly unwind. Lead settled in his stomach.

Lena was strictly on the look-but-don't-touch list. *What a cryin' damn shame.*

And how awkward. He considered backing out of the lot and heading to the coast to Corpus Christi or Galveston, but he couldn't work up the interest.

Would she even remember him? He wasn't the same tall, lanky kid with shaggy hair, all elbows and knees and horny burning need.

His hair was darker, cut short. His face was tanned and toughened by the sun, the blades of his cheeks more pronounced, the corners of his jaw sharper. His body was filled out by years of physical labor.

His hand let go of the keys, and he felt a smile tug at his lips. So, maybe he couldn't hope for a lusty trip down memory lane, but how much fun would it be to pretend he'd never met her, never been here before? While never touching, he could tease and flirt using his intimate knowledge of her, and she'd never realize he knew exactly what he was doing.

And the mister? Well, he'd keep the games well away from him. He didn't want to stir up trouble. Just wanted to have a little fun—a challenge that didn't have a thing to do with cattle or balancing the ranch's books.

He reached for the cowboy hat on the seat beside him, pushed open the door to his truck and stepped down to the ground. Once there, he put on his hat and strode toward the porch steps.

Her gaze swung his way and swept him briefly

head to toe. She pasted on a smile of welcome, although he noted caution dug a line between her brows.

"Howdy, ma'am," he said, touching the brim of his hat.

"Can I help you?" she asked.

Her voice was huskier than he remembered but still had a lilting quality that caressed his nerve endings. Damn shame she was taken. He'd like nothing better than to hear that voice greeting him in the morning from the pillow next to his.

The throbbing that had begun at his first glimpse of her tall, statuesque figure intensified. Inconveniently, because he couldn't think past the urgency in his loins. He cleared his throat. "I was hoping you had a vacancy. One of the cabins."

"I'm sorry. We're booked up." She gave him a polite smile. "All I have are a couple of rooms in the lodge."

She's hoping I'll pass. He returned her smile with a grin that stretched slowly across his face. "That'll be fine then."

"We aren't fancy," she said, eyeing his Lucchese boots. "I do provide meals in the dining room, but we don't have a lot of amenities. Most folks come on weekends to float the river. The cabins have added features, their own barbeque pits and small fridges, but you'd have to take your meals in the dining room, and you'd have to share a bathroom."

Gabe gave her an easy smile. "I just came to fish. Do you have poles to rent?"

She raised her brows a little bit. "Of course. And we can provide bait—worms and crickets. The gift shop has some fancy lures."

"I'm hopin' I don't actually catch much." He gave her a brief smile. "Fishin's man-code for bein' lazy."

"Oh." Her cheeks flushed.

Had it been his smile?

"Well, you can register inside," she said, pointing toward the door behind her. "Kayla's at the desk. She'll get you settled." She cleared her throat. "How long do you plan to stay?"

"A couple of weeks, ma'am." He looked around the clearing and then swept her body with a quick glance. "That ought to be long enough."

He could see the questions in her eyes. And a hint of anxiety.

He hadn't meant to make her worry and wondered at its cause—unless she was feeling the same lazy heat that was burning through him.

Damn inconvenient she was married, because he'd have loved to entice her into his bed. Gabe wasn't the least shy about going after what he wanted, and he wanted her. At least to see whether she was still as hot-blooded and adventurous as she'd been all those years ago when he'd been a boy not yet sure of himself, and she'd been a girl ready to take on the role of sexual tutor.

Again, he touched the brim of his hat and walked

toward the door. He fought the urge to glance back and see if she was still watching him.

Best not take this little game too far. The last thing he wanted was to walk into the end of a shotgun held by a jealous husband. That had already happened to him once, and he'd been damn sure ever since that any woman he pursued was completely free.

He stepped through the lodge's door and pulled the scents of Pine-Sol and lemon oil into his nose. Neither could quite mask the lingering floral scent of her perfume. He shook his head, wondering why he'd insisted on staying. There was nothing for him here. He'd have been better off heading straight back to the ranch, but then he suspected he'd just be surlier than ever since his expectations hadn't been met.

Still, for a moment when he'd first seen her, he'd felt something inside him relax. At the very least, if he stayed he could satisfy his curiosity about her life. And maybe he could finally let go.

CHAPTER 2

As soon as the cowboy strode inside the lodge, Lena gripped the porch rail with both hands and blew out a deep breath. The man was one tall order of temptation, a long buffet of delight for a starving woman.

Dressed in a neatly ironed work shirt that stretched across sturdy shoulders and Wranglers that lovingly molded his powerful legs and rusty-brown hand-tooled boots, the man made her mouth water. His face, though shaded by the brim of his pale hat, was a study in masculine lines—as sharp-edged as his gaze. She'd felt an instant attraction that nearly buckled her knees.

Good Lord, and he wanted to stay for two weeks?

She pressed a hand against her pounding heart and fought the urge to fan her suddenly hot face. The things she wanted to do to him would have her arrested in most Southern states. When was the last time she'd let loose and gotten a little wild? Just one look at the cowboy's rugged good looks, and her insides had given a rebel yell.

When the door closed behind her, she shot a glance over her shoulder to watch him through the window. Yes, he looked as good going as he had coming. The sight played havoc with her hormones.

Lena shook her head at the direction of her thoughts. Lord, she must be desperate to think about jumping some stranger's bones. Anyone who knew her would be surprised. Except for one glaring lapse in her youth, she was the model of propriety. A private woman who kept the running of the family business second from the top of her list of priorities.

The season so far had been filled with families and college kids. Busy enough to keep her from feeling lonely. And too tired at night to even dream about some mystery lover. But now, here was this cowboy who didn't fit in with her usual brand of guests—single, handsome, and with money. And by the glint in his eyes—interested in her.

Lena reached up and undid the clip that held up her hair. She ran her fingers through the messy curls and then twisted it all into bun and clipped it again. Why was she primping? He hadn't been wearing a ring, but so many married men never did. Someone that yummy had to have a woman waiting at home.

Through the window, she watched as Kayla laughed and twirled a lock of dark hair while she gazed up at the man standing on the other side of the counter. Lena gave her a glare, which the younger woman blithely ignored. It really shouldn't have taken that long to check him in.

The cowboy glanced back through the window and caught her looking. Lena whirled around and stepped off the porch. Her toe caught in the lattice next to the step, and she fell hard, bumping down two steps. She landed on one hip, gravel digging into a palm.

Tears pricked her eyes, and she winced at the pain. Worse, the door behind her slammed and heavy booted footsteps stomped down the steps.

When the handsome cowboy came down on a knee beside her, Lena wished the ground would open up and swallow her whole.

"Are you all right?" he asked.

The deep timbre of his voice did a number on her nerves. She shivered.

Something he must have taken for shock, because before she knew it, his hands were under her thighs and behind her back, and he lifted her high against his chest.

"Put me down!"

"I will. Soon as I get you inside."

"I'm too heavy for you to carry."

"Darlin', there's some meat on your bones but not anything I can't handle."

Lena's face burned with embarrassment. Had he meant it *that* way?

Kayla met them at the door, opened it, and then stood to the side as the cowboy swept inside. As they passed, Kayla gave Lena a wink and a thumbs-up. "Her bedroom's just down the hall to the left," she called after them. "Across the hall from yours, cowboy."

"Thanks, Kayla. I'll settle up with you in a few."

"Take your time," her helper sang.

Lena wiggled her legs. "I swear, you can put me down. I'm fine."

He didn't look down, but Lena watched one corner of his firm mouth twitch. "There's gravel embedded in your thigh. Your hands are scraped. Why not let me help? I'm willin'."

They reached her bedroom door, and he drew to a halt. His gaze dropped. "You're gonna have to turn the knob."

Every word that came out of his mouth felt as though it was charged with sexual current. Her body tightened against the thrill of it all. Lena reached to the side and twisted the knob, excitement buzzing inside at the thought of him entering her bedroom.

He turned sideways and stepped into the room, giving it a quick glance before he strode to the bed. He set her down on the coverlet, and Lena instantly swung her legs over the edge.

The cowboy stepped so close one of his thighs brushed the naked inside of one of hers. She glanced up to find him towering over her, his hands on his hips.

"Are you gonna stay put?"

Lena drew in a quick breath. The man had nerve. "I don't take orders well."

"Like givin' 'em, do ya?"

Jesus, his voice was smooth as dark silk. Her throat went dry. She nodded.

His gaze narrowed as he studied her. "Just to be straight. Is there a mister?" His gaze went to the slender silver ring on her finger.

She considered lying or at least dancing around the point, but the thrill of him even asking the question had her insides tingling. "I'm not married. It's a promise ring."

His forehead wrinkled, and he reached for her hand. He curved her fingers over his and lifted it to take a closer look. When he swept his glance back to hers, she almost drew back. So much heat was banked in that one predatory glance.

She cleared her throat. "You think if I was married I would have let you carry me here?"

"What's your name?" he asked.

"Lena."

"Last name.

"Twohig."

His head shook. "A woman like you never married?"

Lena straightened her shoulders. Why did everyone think it was an attractive woman's duty to marry? "It's none of your business why I decided to remain single."

He swallowed. A dark gleam in his eyes and the

stubborn set of his jaw kept her from saying anything more.

"I'm...Tommy," he said softly.

"Last name?"

"Just Tommy, for now."

He didn't look much like a Tommy. She'd have named him something rugged and harsh. Something as severe as the cut of his square jaw.

Was the fact he'd only given her one name some kind of clue? Like he wanted to keep a little mystery going? Was he hoping she'd be into it as well? Lena took a breath and decided to stop pretending she didn't want him in her room. Needing to take back a little control, she pointed toward the bathroom. "You'll find washcloths in the cupboard beside the shower."

"Antiseptic?"

"Under the sink."

When he turned on his heel, she waited until he was out of sight before she mouthed the words, *Oh my God!*

A seriously sexy man was in her bathroom and looking through her cupboards. Her cheeks burned at the thought of the intimacy. She'd never been one to bring men home. A once-in-a-blue-moon rendezvous at a motel was the most she'd allowed herself over the years. She wasn't a prude, but with grandpa and Jake to consider, she lived a pretty circumspect life.

She'd never had an opportunity like this one land in her lap. Summers were usually spent with both of her guys constantly underfoot, but grandpa's accident had put the burden of running the campsite squarely on her shoulders.

Why shouldn't she take advantage and see where this might lead? She was a free agent. Tommy seemed interested. Now, if she could just let him know she was too, without looking too desperate for her own pride's sake, why not have some fun?

While he was gone, she kicked off her flip-flops and struck a pose, one knee raised, the other stretched. Did it look natural? She slid her knee back down and glanced sideways, because he was standing beside her wearing a one-sided smile.

"Nice scrape," he murmured, nodding his chin toward her right knee. "Better raise it again."

Mute with embarrassment, she slid it up.

He sat on the edge of the bed, one leg folded under him as he bent toward her knee and began to gently wash it with a wash cloth.

"All this fuss," she murmured, "and it's just a little dirt."

The skin was angry looking when he'd finished. He picked up the antiseptic spray, coated the abrasions, and then blew on her skin to dry it.

Her gaze snagged on his pursed lips, staring a little too long, because a grin stretched there, bringing her gaze to his eyes, which were wrinkled with amusement. Gray eyes. Nearly a slate-blue.

She'd once known a boy with eyes just like that. Framed by long dark lashes and set in a pretty-boy face. They'd both been young. She'd been a couple years older and had known better, but he'd been so eager to learn everything she wanted to teach him.

This grown man, sitting so close she could smell the scent of his musk and a hint of something sagey, didn't look as though he needed instruction. No, he exuded a sexual confidence she found impossible to ignore.

"Any place else need some attention?" he asked softly.

Her breath released in a slow whoosh. She could think of more than one. Her nipples ached. Moisture seeped to wet the crotch of her underwear. How had he managed to arouse her so thoroughly? So quickly?

She turned her hands and held them up, side by side, to show him her palms.

He washed both, sprayed both, then clasped her wrists in one hand as he bent to blow. "Better off without a bandage," he drawled as he leaned back to meet her gaze.

With her cheeks on fire, she gave him a quick, nervous nod.

"Kayla said my room's across the hallway."

"Yes."

His gaze narrowed on her mouth. "Will we be sharin' a bath?"

He did it again. Made her think of naked skin and sinning with one innocently phrased sentence.

She shook her head. Then blurted before she had

time to talk herself out of it, "I have my own. But if the one at the end of the hall is in use..."

A sparkle of devilment shone in his eyes. "You won't mind? I promise to knock first."

Knock away. She might pretend she didn't hear. Let him surprise her in her bath...

The images that bombarded her mind while he sat on her bed, his large frame so close she felt the heat coming off him, set her heartbeat thundering inside her chest. She shook her head. "You're welcome to use it any time."

"I'll get settled in. Then maybe you could show me the best spot to set my pole."

Her jaw sagged.

A wily grin parted his lips.

He knew damn well which pole her dirty mind had conjured. She gave a short laugh and shook her head. "You're trouble, cowboy. Knew it soon as you stepped out of your truck."

He gave her a wink but scooted off the bed and strode away.

Lena dragged in a deep breath and whistled between her teeth.

The moment his footsteps clomped down the hallway, Kayla skimmed into her room. "Was he not the yummiest thing you've ever seen? I thought I'd die when he walked inside carryin' you. It's so romantic!" She squealed the last.

Lena fanned her face. "He needs a fishing pole. No, two. And a carton of worms."

Her brown eyes widened. "You takin' him fishin'?"

"He said he wanted me to show him where the best place to go was." The last thing she'd acknowledge was he'd asked where to plant his pole, although that's exactly what she'd be thinking about for the rest of the afternoon. She closed her eyes and groaned. "I'm a slut. A horny, desperate slut."

Kayla giggled. "You should take him up past the falls. No one goes that far. I'll steer anyone who asks *down* the creek."

Lena leaned her head to the side and aimed a narrow-eyed glance at her helper. "You tryin' to match make?"

Kayla wrinkled her nose. "Someone needs to get a little some-some out of that man. If it's not me, you at least have to share all the sordid details."

Lena laughed and shook her head. No way would she share any sexy details with the twenty-year-old. Any sordidness would be hers alone to savor. She swung her legs off the bed. "Get those poles ready. I need to freshen up a bit. Don't let him leave without me."

Kayla grinned. "A little lipstick. Something soft and pink, and he won't be thinkin' about any grubby ole worms."

Lena shut the bathroom door and stared at her reflection in the mirror. Her hair was a wild mess. Dirt stained the sides of her shorts. She stripped and put her clothes in the hamper.

A quick shower, and she'd be ready to face him again. Maybe by then the excited blush scorching her cheeks would fade.

THE NEXT TIME she saw him, she took a step back. He wore knee-length swim shorts and a pair of boat shoes. His broad chest was completely bare, a wide expanse of warm caramel with a light dusting of dark brown hair.

Indecently masculine. Or maybe it was the way he made her feel so indecently feminine, because lust rose up so strongly that, once again, her knees grew weak.

His gaze swept over her frame. When he reached her face, that dark glint was back in his gray eyes. She'd donned a tankini top and cutoffs. Her bikini bottoms were underneath, just in case they succumbed to the lure of the cool water.

Kayla gave her a broad grin. A carton of worms and a small picnic basket sat on the counter. "In case you two get hungry," she said, winking discretely.

Tommy held the poles and picked up the worms.

She took the basket. "Follow me?"

"For now."

Every word out of his mouth was a tease—unless she was reading more into his words than he meant.

The fact she'd only just met him, but was already thinking about sex, should have rung alarm bells, but something about him made her want to jump his bones—to hell with propriety. Folks were busy with their own adventures. Other than nosy Kayla, who else would care if she acted a little fast and loose?

At least she'd had the good sense to stuff a line of condoms into her pocket. Just in case he was every bit as eager as she was.

The moment she stepped out onto the porch, the midday heat hammered the top of her head. "Let's follow the river bank," she said over her shoulder. "There'll be more shade."

"I'm right behind you."

Right behind her. That made her ass tense. Made her gait a little stilted. Sweet Jesus, they'd better do it soon, or she'd be gibbering mess.

They left the clearing, walking down a path that paralleled the pier, but then led left, following the edge of the creek upstream.

In the shade, with leaves fanning the air, the temperature was a good ten degrees cooler. The path was a narrow dirt trail with thick brush to the left and a steep bank to the right. They trudged forward, and she worried he might think they were travelling too far, but the place she wanted to bring him was magical. Worth the extra effort.

When she edged around a boulder and climbed down to spot where the bank was flatter and the water fell over a series of large stepped rocks, she glanced back.

His appreciative gaze was on the falls. "It's nice," he said, smiling back at her. "And private."

The steps and the curve of the river made this short bend a favorite necking spot for guests. A fact she'd taken advantage of when she was younger. This was her skinny-dipping hole. The place she'd brought a boy a couple of years younger than herself and had her wicked way with him.

She walked to one rock that jutted over the edge of the water. "See this groove? You can set your pole in here," she said, adding a sultry texture to her voice, because it was now or never.

He laid the poles on the bank and toed off his shoes. "Wanna cool off first?"

Lena noted the hint of challenge that gleamed in his eyes. She swallowed, stalling a second while she worked up the nerve. But she was done with him being the only one issuing oblique teases. "Nothing would please me more."

"Nothing?"

Her gaze slid down to his shorts, and then slowly made its way back up to his face. She cocked an eyebrow, wondering how far he'd take the dare.

"Lady, don't look at me that way if you're not ready to play with fire."

She lifted her chin, waiting to see how he'd answer her challenge. Her heart skittered to a halt when he pushed down his shorts and strode nude into the water.

Her jaw loosened as she stared. His cock was only beginning to stir, lifting from a shaved groin. As he strode past, she remembered how to breathe and glanced at his retreating figure. His ass was hard, round, two deep dimples above it. Her mouth watered at the thought of dipping her tongue into those grooves.

He stepped off the underwater ledge and began to swim away, not trying to influence her with any sexy cajoling or burning glances. He'd left the decision in her hands. The invitation hers to accept or not.

Well, this was what she'd wanted—no, *needed*. She glanced around the clearing to make sure they were still completely alone, and then quickly started stripping away her clothes. Not nearly with as much confidence as he had, but then she carried a few extra pounds, and her belly was soft.

Taking a calming breath, she strode into the river.

CHAPTER 3

Gabe listened to the rustle of clothing being shed and her quick, excited breaths. When water splashed behind him, only then did he turn in the water to acknowledge her presence. He didn't betray any emotion over the fact she'd dumped propriety on its ass to join him—deliciously nude.

Only her breasts were visible, floating just beneath the surface of the water. The cream-colored globes were naturally full. The tips were tightened little buds. The areolas were a little larger than he remembered but still cotton-candy pink.

His cock hardened, pulsing as he imagined gently chewing on a stiff bud while her legs writhed around him.

She swam closer, but not so near he could sweep out a hand to bring her against him. She was ready to flirt but still held onto a little caution.

Gabe struck out for the first rocky ledge, and

pulled himself up to sit, while clear river water sluiced around his body. His cock was prominent despite the blurring water. No way could she pretend not to be looking where she was.

Her gaze was caught, her pupils growing large as she stared at his erection.

He patted the rock beside him. "Why not join me?"

Her eyes widened, but she firmed her mouth and swam nearer.

He held out a hand, which she accepted after giving him a long, searching look. He pulled her up beside him to rest on the ledge. With her knees pulled up against her chest and her body curled, she hid most of her interesting bits. Her shyness amused and enchanted him.

That same combination of boldness and reticence had excited him as a youth. He'd wanted to make her blush with embarrassment one moment and with searing passion the next. In the end, she'd given him both.

"Tell me something," he said softly. "Something about you." He hoped she'd answer the questions abounding in his mind. Like why was she still here? Had she finished college? Or given up? Why was she still wearing that cheap promise ring he'd given her all those years ago?

She gave him a sideways glance. Her body still folded tightly, she wrapped her arms around her knees to hide herself.

Not that she looked anything but completely sexy. The long expanse of her back was golden and smooth. The sides of her breasts a creamy white.

She slicked back her wet hair then set her cheek against her knee as she stared back at him. "There's not much to tell. I run this place in the summers for my grandfather."

"And during the rest of the year?"

She lifted her shoulders. "I teach art in middle school."

She'd wanted to study graphic design and work in a marketing firm. What the hell had happened to that dream?

"What about you?" she asked.

"I'm in cattle."

Her eyelids dipped, and she glanced away. The tiny catch in her breath made him wonder if she was remembering a boy who'd been a rancher's son.

"I have to ask you, because, well, it'd a little embarrassing if you knew him..."

He let a smile curve his mouth. "Who?"

"His name was Gabriel Triplehorn. He was here years and years ago. Lived on a ranch, too. Just wondered if you knew him. Your eyes kinda remind me of him."

Gabe gave her an easy smile although inside his chest warmed. She hadn't forgotten him. "Was he someone special?"

Her smile seemed a little brittle. "Like I said, it was years ago. We barely knew each other."

"How well did you know each other?"

Her glance flashed, a hint of annoyance digging a line between her brows. "That's hardly any of your business."

"If I knew this Gabe, maybe it would be."

She huffed a breath. "It's not like you'd be stepping on any toes. It was a long time ago. Forget I even mentioned him."

Gabe kept quiet, studying her face for a hint of what she was really thinking. Something about his appearance had sparked her memory, but by the tightness of her shoulders and the crimp of her soft lips, not every memory she had of him was rosy.

All his memories of her were fond ones. Had he done something, said something there at the end of that summer that had left a bitter taste in her mouth?

For the first time since he'd arrived, he wondered if he was doing the right thing. Playing this game. Perhaps he shouldn't have given in to the temptation to extend the game after he'd discovered she wasn't married. He didn't understand what had inspired him to lie. Part of him had wanted to know whether the spark would still be there, without her memories of their previous entanglement swaying her. Part of him had wanted to protect himself. The moment he realized she wore his ring, something inside him had frozen for just a moment. He didn't know how he felt about that. Likely, the ring held no meaning for her. But once, it had meant everything to him. He'd known when he left he'd likely never see her again, but he'd left his heart behind. No woman had ever moved him as much, and even though time had passed and dulled the emotions he'd felt back then, there was still a twinge of nostalgia plucking at him that scared him.

More than her beauty, more than her, he was afraid that he was ready to be in love again, and if she wasn't the right person, he didn't want to make a mistake.

Though why he was thinking this way left him confused. Perhaps seeing Colt so happy had changed him. Truth was, he hadn't been in the mood to join his younger brother in their usual carousing ever since the wedding. Maybe his churlishness stemmed from the fact he was envious of what Colt and Zuri had found.

Something of his thoughts must have played on his face, because Lena's expression changed. The light of arousal began to fade. "Look, if you've changed your mind..." she said, bit her bottom lip and looked away.

Did she think he didn't find her attractive now she was naked?

Gabe swore silently and pushed aside his concerns. Yes, he was worried that maybe he shouldn't have gone into this based on a lie, but he did think this attraction was worth exploring. And his body hadn't cooled down one bit.

Gabe leaned back to rest on one elbow and closed his eyes as the water poured over his body, rushing over his stomach and the jut of his thick cock.

He snuck a peek to watch her gaze running greedily over his male flesh and made up his mind in an instant that all teasing was done. He swung his head toward hers, catching her hungry gaze. "I won't mind if you touch. But I left condoms on the bank."

Her gaze searched his for a long moment, and a little smile played on her lips. She lifted her hand to uncurl her fingers. A plastic packet lay in the center of her palm.

"Are you nervous we're moving too quickly?" he asked, giving her one last chance before he was too far gone to be a gentleman.

Her breath gusted. "I'm holdin' on by a thread, cowboy. I think if we don't get past this, I won't ever remember how to breathe." She lifted her chin to point at his cock. "Raise it above the water. I'll put it on."

That voice. A soft but firm command. She'd been like that back then, and he'd been eager to obey. For now, he'd let her lead since she seemed to need to be in charge.

Holding her gaze, he lay back on both elbows and raised his hips above the water.

Lena tore the packet open, stuffed the wrapper into a crevice in the rock and turned to face him, giving him a full view of her luscious body. Her fleshy frame was thicker but more beautiful than ever. She was full and rounded, her waist narrowing above generous hips. Every curve in lush proportion.

His breaths shortened as he raised his glance to meet hers. He read doubt in her eyes and gave her a smile. "Lena Twohig, you're one beautiful woman."

Her cheeks flooded with color. "Thanks."

He could see the fortifying breath she took before she firmed her pretty mouth and bent over him to roll the condom down his shaft.

The sensation of her strong hand gliding down his length had him groaning, something he didn't hold back because he didn't want her worrying again about his attraction. When the latex clothed him, she gave him firm up and down pumps with her fist as though testing his hardness.

"What now?" he asked.

She wrinkled her nose. "Seems a little rude me climbing right on, seein' as we've never even kissed."

He liked the lazy ease of her comment and the husky texture of her voice. The sensual note was like a caress, stroking his balls. "I agree. Think we might manage to do both at the same time?"

Her mouth curved. "I didn't want to seem too greedy."

"I don't mind greedy. I'm lettin' you lead. Whatever pleases you, sugar."

Lena came up on her knees and slowly straddled him, trapping his cock between their bellies. "Truth is..." she said, rubbing lightly against him, "I can't think straight...because all I want...is you...inside me."

She settled her hands on his shoulders and she bent, pressing her breasts against his chest. "Lord, I love the way this feels," she moaned, the hard tips of her nipples scraping his skin.

With his elbows beneath him supporting them both, Gabe couldn't do anything more than lie there as she took her pleasure. Every part of his body was tense. His balls ached as he held back. "Lena, give me one of those," he whispered, staring at her full breasts.

"No pretty please?" she said, with another sexy glide.

"Please, baby. In my mouth."

Her hands clenching his shoulders, she shifted her knees beside his hips and rose, aiming on large breast at his face. Gabe opened wide and lapped her nipple with his tongue, then latched his mouth around as much of the soft flesh as he could and drew hard.

Damn, he loved the way she shivered against him. She released his shoulders and dug her fingers into his scalp, massaging him as he burrowed. He wagged his head, sucking harder, trying to fit more flesh inside his mouth. Who was greedy now?

He couldn't remember ever being this hungry, this aroused. Her sun-warmed skin was delightfully salty. The tiny pebbled tip teased his tongue as he laved it inside his mouth, stroking it over and over, roughing it with the flat of tongue then tapping it until it extended even more. His mouth worked her flesh, suctioning so hard he wondered if he'd leave marks.

He pulled off and paused to nibble the tip. He kissed the upper crest of her breast, her collarbone, and moved to the other nipple.

Lena's entire breast hardened, and she inserted a hand between their bodies to reach down and stroke his cock, wrapping her fingers tightly around him as she pumped.

Gabe groaned and nuzzled, his body tensing more, his balls drawing up against his groin. His cock expanded, painfully hardening. He pulled away. "No more, sweetheart. I'll blow."

Lena leaned away, her gaze catching his. When she pushed up on her knees, he nearly howled he hurt so bad.

Both their gazes shot downward.

Fascinated by the sight of her plump lips and the light thatch of dark blonde hair, he held his breath.

She took him in her hands, guided him between her folds, and centered him at her entrance.

With just the cap snug against her pussy, Gabe's breaths gusted hard.

"I like it when a man begs," she whispered, her voice tight.

His gaze flicked to her face. "Do you like it dirty?" he asked, but he already knew.

She nodded, her expression eager and strained.

Gabe cleared his throat and willed himself not to smile. "Put my dick in your pussy."

She dipped her eyelids, but her mouth pursed. "Um, nice start."

He narrowed his gaze. She wasn't satisfied. She wanted it raw. Something that didn't take any effort on his part. "Wiggle that ass, baby," he rasped. "Screw that pussy down my dick."

She gave a soft snort. "You're not beggin'. You're tellin'."

Gabe's chest shook with a bark of laughter. "Sweetheart, baby...*please*. I need that sweet, hot cunt fucking me. Please, sugar."

She grinned. "Your mama ever wash your mouth out with soap?"

Gabe gave her back a brazen smile. "Nope, but I'll let you do it, if you'll just put me out of my misery. Fuck me, Lena. Please."

She shook her head. "Why do I get the feeling the last thing you're used to is beggin' for it?"

"Because I never beg. And just you wait. First chance I get you under me..."

She flipped back her hair. "Think I'm gonna want this again? With you?"

Gabe held still, his gaze raking her chest then lowering to where she still sat poised above his cock. "Really think we can fight this?" he asked, more to himself than expecting a response from her.

When his gaze locked with hers, they both fell silent for a long moment.

"Any way you want it," he said, lowering his voice. "Fast or slow. But if you don't move, I will."

. . .

Lena sat on the precipice of an excitement she hadn't felt in forever. Her entire body shook with it. Her pussy clasped the head of his dick, making the decision for her. She pressed against his chest and slowly screwed, swirling down his length, dragging her hips in shallow circles as she worked her way down his substantial cock.

"Feels so good," she said, closing her eyes. "So fucking big."

"Glad you're enjoyin' it," he murmured. "I like it dirty, too. Tell me more."

She opened her eyes to find a crooked smile stretching his mouth. She circled her hips again and ground downward, her mouth sagging against the overwhelming sensations. "I could see how big you were, but I wasn't expectin' to feel this stretched." And she really hadn't. Motherhood had robbed her of that little joy with the other men she'd had. "You're a blessed man, Tommy."

He gave a little wince at the name. "Maybe a little less talkin'?"

With her hand flat against his chest, she raised her hips and powered down his cock. When their groins met, she held and rubbed forward and back. "I could get off just like this," she said, hissing between her teeth. "My clit against your pubic bone."

"That's just plain cruel, talkin' about your clit."

His eyelids dipped halfway and his nostrils flared. "I'd love nothin' better than to suck it 'til you come."

"Next time, maybe." She gasped as she gave him another deep rub. But then she was past thinking, because the tension building in her body demanded she move.

She pushed off his chest and clasped her breasts, rolling them in her hands, squeezing them, knowing he was watching as she began to rise and fall in short little thrusts that warmed her inner walls and churned the water around their hips.

"Baby, it's burnin' hot in there," he growled. "Pinch your nipples. Tug 'em. Let me watch. Least you can do."

Lena laughed and shook her head. "I like you. You're a real sweet-talker."

His laughter shook his body. "And you're a tease. Come on," he moaned, "gimme something."

While she rose a little higher and dove deeper, she lifted her mounds, raising them enough she could lick the tops of her breasts. Each fluttering lap made his cock jerk inside her. She toyed with the tips, flicking them with her thumb while she continued to stretch. When she lapped at her own areola, his hard, muscled belly quivered.

The groan that followed was deeply satisfying. So, she ringed her nipples and squeezed them, letting the tips peek between her fingers. Then she gave him what he'd asked for, pulling the tips hard enough her pussy cinched around his cock with the sweet sting.

"Sweet Jesus. If I had you under me..."

"What would you do?" she asked, giving her breasts a shake that made him suck in a deep breath. The man liked tits.

His gaze remained glued to her jiggling mounds. "I'd force you to your knees and back you onto my dick. Then I'd hold that sweet ass still and hammer you into the ground."

Her breaths shortened until she was gasping. The tension wound so tight inside her, she couldn't move with any grace or rhythm. She pumped wildly on his cock, her breasts bouncing. When she started panting, she stopped and came off him.

He pushed up to rest on his hands. "Want me to take over?"

She nodded, unable to speak.

He sat up and slipped off the ledge. Then he turned and opened his arms. She slid forward, encircling her legs around his hips to ride them as he strode toward the bank, cradling her back with his hands.

Lena felt shell-shocked, trembling all over. When he lay her torso down on the sandy bank, her hips still surrounded by cool water, she didn't protest. She reached out, welcoming his weight on top of her.

His broad shoulders filled her sight. His face was tight, his jaw sharp-edged with hunger—a feral look that thrilled her to her curled toes.

Her cowboy slid his hands beneath her and cupped her bottom. "No mercy," he whispered.

"Don't want any," she said, surprised by how small and crimped her voice sounded.

He dipped down, hovering his mouth over hers. "Never did get that kiss."

The moment his mouth touched hers, something inside her unlocked. A groan clawed its way up her throat. She wrapped her arms around him and dug her fingernails into his muscled back. Raising her legs, she encircled his hips, pulling them into hers.

He rooted once at her opening, then thrust hard inside, forcing a gasp from her that spilled into his mouth. He thrust his tongue boldly, and she sucked on it as he began to move, driving deep, cramming his thick cock through hot, engorged walls.

Shock made her rigid as she came apart in a blinding instant. Her back bowed. She dug her head into grass and sand. Her eyes squeezed shut and light exploded in her head, pinpricks stinging the backs of her eyes. Lena gave a muffled shout.

Her cowboy disengaged with her mouth, rising on his arms as he continued to pound inside her, drawing out her pleasure until she keened and moaned and then at last lay limp beneath him.

His body sagged against hers.

She huffed a laugh, amazed she'd been so consumed with her own orgasm she'd missed the moment of his.

When a kiss landed on her cheek, she opened her eyes to find him grinning down.

"Not disappointed?" he asked, his voice a soothing rumble.

Lena shook her head, too weak to form words. A moment later, her pleasure faded as she realized she'd heard those exact same words from another younger cowboy years ago. She stared for a long moment as her body grew chilled.

Icy fury spilling over her, Lena dug her nails into his shoulders and shoved. "You bastard!"

CHAPTER 4

When Lena began slapping his chest, Gabe grabbed both hands and forced them to the ground beside her head. "What the hell?"

Her mouth twisted in a snarl. "Get off me."

Gabe glared down, wondering why the sudden change. One moment she'd melted beneath him. The next she was a writhing wildcat. And the fact he was still eight inches deep inside her only made him more confused. "What's wrong, Lena?"

"Liar," she roared, the sound so raw his heart stuttered.

All fight left her. Her body relaxed beneath his, but her expression worried him even more. Tears welled in her eyes. The corners of her mouth turned down.

"Did I hurt you?"

She shook her head, sniffing as moisture filled her

eyes. "What kind of game are you playin', Gabriel Triplehorn?"

His stomach lurched. He bowed his head, breathing deeply for a moment before forcing his gaze to meet her accusing one. "What gave me away?"

"I'm a fool," she rasped. "You're all grown up. Nearly unrecognizable. But I knew those eyes."

Gabe released one of her hands and cupped her cheek. "I'm sorry I lied about my name. I'm not sure why I did. I guess I just wanted to be some guy you'd never met." At her continued glare, he sighed. "I didn't mean any harm. I just wanted the chance to get to know you again, without you thinking about that clumsy boy."

"You weren't clumsy," she muttered. "You were sweet. Energetic, but you were utterly perfect."

"And that makes you sad?"

She blew out a gust of air. "It makes me an idiot. The one man I should never have anything to do with..." She closed her eyes. Another tear leaked from her eye.

Gabe still didn't get it. So, she'd figured out who he was. Why was she so damn against him? "Why not have anything to do with me?"

She snorted. "Not enough time or tears to explain."

Gabe frowned. "Lena, I'm not movin' until you tell me what's wrong."

Her chin jutted. "Isn't the fact you got me here under false pretenses enough?"

"This was fun. You enjoyed it. If it's not something you wanted, all you had to do was tell me to go to hell."

"I didn't get the chance to say that to Mr. Triplehorn, did I?" she said, her voice getting a little louder.

"All because I'm not some stranger?"

"Don't look at me like that. You don't know me."

"But I want to," he ground out in frustration.

"It's a little too late. Now, please. Get off me."

Gabe dreaded doing that. So long as he was locked inside her body, she had to keep talking to him. He sensed once he let her go, she'd withdraw, and he'd never understand what went so wrong. "Sweetheart—"

"Don't call me that."

Gabe dropped his glance. "Lena..." He swallowed, and then lifted his gaze again. Triplehorns weren't cowards. "I'm afraid if I let you go, you'll run."

Her hard stare would have had his brother Colt backing away, but Gabe held firm. "I know I was dead wrong not tellin' you up front. But that doesn't mean there's not something here between us. Tell me the truth. You feel it, too."

Her mouth formed a tight line, and he almost relented.

But then her eyes filled with tears. "This is all wrong."

"Doesn't have to be," he said, adopting a more soothing tone. "Lust always took the lead with us, but that doesn't mean we can't make this about so much more."

"It's too fucking late. Years late to make this into anything but a really bad dream."

"I don't understand. Was it something I said back then? Something I did?"

"It's what you left," she said, bitterness roughening her voice. "Let me up."

"We're not done."

As though taunting them both, his cock twitched inside her, surging again inside her steamy heat. He chose to ignore it.

But a moan seeped from inside her. Her bottom lip trembled, and her pussy gave away her state of arousal. It clenched, cinching around him to keep him deeply embedded.

Gabe narrowed his eyes as he studied her expression. He noted the deepening of her breaths, the tension quivering through her frame. Slowly, he lowered his head, giving her one last chance to say no.

But she never did.

Their lips touched, softly at first. He rubbed her mouth, gently circling, and then suctioned to pull at her lips.

She dug her fingers into his skin, raked his chest and then dragged her hands around his sides to his back.

He'd have the marks there for anyone to see but

didn't care. He ended the kiss and jerked his hips to dig inside her, tunneling hard.

Her eyelid fluttered then closed. Her mouth gaped as her head tilted back. The sweat on her cheeks gleamed in the bright sunlight.

Gabe straightened, pushing up on his arms, pulling away from her tight embrace. Without breaking their connection, he went to his knees, stuck his arms beneath the crooks of each of her knees and raised her bottom. With his arms controlling her movements, he continued thrusting, jerking her against him in opposition. He dropped his gaze down to where their bodies joined and watched his reddened cock glide between her swollen vaginal lips.

"Let me see your clit," he ground out.

Without hesitation, her hands smoothed down her soft belly and pulled up on the top of her folds, exposing her engorged nubbin. Slick and bright red, he wished he could dip his head between her legs.

"Tonight," he said, with another glide into her silky hot depths, "I'll come to your room. Don't lock your door. I'll suck on that pretty little button until you come. Then I'll spank your pussy until it's wet and your legs are shaking. I'll make you come again like that."

"Shut up. Just shut up," she groaned, but her hips fought his hold, her bottom bounced.

He raised his curled arms tighter and spread

them to open her as he pounded deep and hard, each thrust thudding against her body.

Lena cupped a breast with her free hand and pinched her nipple. Then her belly undulated in uneven motions as her cunt squeezed around him. "Jesus, Gabe. Fuck me. Fuck me harder!" She stuck two fingers into the top of her folds and rubbed hard. "Jesus, oh fuck."

Gabe was so deep, so fucking hard, his teeth hurt. His balls drew up, hard as rocks, banging against her ass. He gave everything he had in a violent flurry of motion. Not relenting even after a long wail erupted from her.

Gabe banged her with more force, wanting to mark her, make sure she never forgot what it was like to be truly taken by a man who wouldn't accept anything but complete surrender. He wouldn't let her refuse him again, wouldn't ever let her go.

At that thought, something inside him snapped into place. Joy exploded at the same time his cock erupted, spewing inside the condom. Whatever grievance she had against him couldn't withstand his sheer determination. He'd make it up to her, make her see that no other man would ever be as good, ever want her as much.

He gritted his teeth as the last surge of come spurted. Lowering her thighs, he came down on top of her, his heaving chest resting against her soft breasts. "This was good, Lena. We're good together. That's not changed."

She covered her face with an arm and turned her head to the side. "This was never the problem. It's even better now."

"Forgive me for lying?"

"It's not for me to forgive."

She eased her arm away and gave him a look filled with so much emotion it nearly killed him. "You're gonna hate me."

He didn't believe her. With her warm, pliant body cushioning his own, he held still. "Tell me."

Tears filled her eyes and tracked down the sides of her face into her hair. She held his gaze as if silently begging for understanding before she whispered, "We have a son."

Gabe blinked. He shook his head, sure he'd heard wrong. "What?"

"We have a boy. He's nine."

He'd been so hot a moment ago, but now the sweat dripping from his hair felt cold as ice against his skin. He pulled free, scrambling away to kneel beside her. "A boy? My son?" He heard the hoarseness in his voice. Felt his throat close up, unable to utter another sound.

Lena moved, also coming to her knees.

She reached out a hand toward him, but he jerked back. "You were just a kid. Still in high school."

"You think I wouldn't have wanted to know?" he whispered harshly. "It was my right."

"I was afraid. Alone. Except for grandpa. My

mother and father were furious. Cut me off. When I went back to school, I had to do it on my own."

His lips curled up in a snarl. "You didn't *have* to do anything on your own. One damn call would have fixed it." Gabe pushed up to his feet and quickly rolled the condom off his cock. He dropped it to the ground.

"Um, we have to pick up our trash," she said, vaguely waving at the condom.

He gave her a glare, shaking his head as he backed away. "You do it. I have calls to make."

"Wait," she called after him.

But he was already moving to the clothes they'd flung away.

"Gabe."

He gave a sharp shake of his head but didn't look back. Moments later, dressed, he crashed through the brush, heading down the sunlit trail, his chest tight, his mind completely blown.

He didn't want to be anywhere near her. Didn't want to talk. Beyond shocked, fury shook his whole body. He had a kid. One he'd never met. Didn't even know his name. He wanted to curse her but couldn't make himself stoop that low.

She'd had her reasons. He'd been a teenager. But he didn't buy that one. His parents had married young and look how many years they'd had together.

No, he could think of only one really good reason she hadn't told him. She'd been scared of his family, no doubt. Thought maybe she couldn't fight him and keep custody of her child.

But she was dead wrong. He wouldn't have stripped the boy from her. He'd have been there for her. *Married her*. Damn her to hell. He'd been in love with her, missed her—for fucking years—until he'd built a shell around his heart and learned to be with women without giving a damn about their emotional needs.

He'd played and caroused. Shared women with his brother, Tommy. He'd become a goddamn whore, fucking anything with tits because he hadn't found that same feeling of connection, of completeness, with anyone else.

He'd half-convinced himself he'd been operating on teenage lust, that he couldn't have really been in love with her. That love was a myth dredged up by too many hormones.

Until he'd seen his brother with Zuri. Watched Colt's anger and disappointment melt beneath an all-consuming hunger. And he'd remembered what that felt like. Knew exactly why Colt hadn't been able to give up on Zuri. Not for a minute. Not even when he thought she'd robbed a bank.

He stomped into the clearing and ran up the steps, passed Kayla at the desk, but ignored her greeting. When he got to his room he went straight for his cell phone.

"That you, bro?" Colt asked on the first ring.

"Colt." Gabe's throat closed again, but he cleared it.

"Anything wrong?"

Gabe sat on the edge of the bed, dropping his elbows on his knees as he dragged in deep breaths to calm his racing heart. "I have a kid. A boy."

After a long pause, Colt asked, "Lena Twohig the mom?"

"Yeah."

"That boy's a Triplehorn," Colt said, his voice dead even. "Bring him home."

"I can't... Jesus, I've probably already blown it," he said, remembering her face, the crushing disappointment that had clouded her eyes when he'd jerked away from her.

"No, Gabe," Colt said, his tone firm. "I don't care what you have to do. You bring that boy home."

"He has a mother. One who didn't want anything to do with me. Never bothered to tell me even though she knew where to find me."

"Doesn't matter. You know now. You have to make it right."

Gabe shook his head. He was sick to his stomach, his head still reeling and unable to think. "She can't just pick up and leave. She's got a campground to run."

"Leave that to me and Tommy. You talk to her. She's family now—whether she's married you or not. He's our kin."

Gabe nodded, relief spilling through him. He

groaned. "She's probably mad as hell at me right now. Soon as she told me, I got up and ran. Had to get away. I wasn't sure I wouldn't shake her."

"Get a grip. You talk to her."

After he ended the call, Gabe sat in his room thinking about his life. About what could have been. Regret piled on top of regret. He took a shower and dressed. All the while running through everything he might say to a woman who couldn't have had it easy raising a boy on her own. Who might resent him if he waded in and tried to take over.

He listed in his mind all his arguments. He was the boy's dad, and a child needed a father. He was wealthy, from a stable, respected family. Lena's child would never want for a thing and stood to inherit a lot. She'd be a fool to deny him his place at the Triplehorn.

And then there was their relationship. Sure, they'd made missteps along the way. She'd withheld something so important most men would find it hard to forgive, but he was willing to overlook her sin of omission. He'd lied to her in order to seduce her, but only because he'd been in denial over the fact that he'd always yearned for her.

Fact was, he'd held other women up against her and never felt the spark. Not until he'd been intimate with her again and held her so close there was no hiding the truth, not even from himself, had he realized. She was his one and only. Same way Colt had never been able to love another woman. Neither had he.

Sure, they'd been kids. But for two weeks in one golden summer, he'd become a man. She'd left an indelible stamp upon his soul. He'd left behind living proof that their brief affair was meant to be so much more.

Feeling surer of himself, more determined not to let her push him away or deny everything he offered, he set out to convince Lena Twohig to become his wife.

CHAPTER 5

Lena served dinner with a brittle smile and one eye on the entrance of the dining room, dreading the moment Gabe joined them. She'd had time to think about how he'd reacted, time to pile regrets on her shoulders for the fact she'd succumbed to temptation, and then spilled her guts in a stupid moment of weakness.

"Just plain stupid, that's what I am," she whispered to herself. What had she expected? That he'd sweep her into his arms and tell her everything would be okay? That he'd forgive her for never seeking him out?

Now, she worried about what he might do. The Triplehorns weren't unknown in these parts. They owned a major spread in the big state of Texas. They could buy better lawyers, come after her and Jake with all guns blazing. And just maybe, they'd win.

"Dessert's on the buffet table," Kayla said, coming to her side. "Gonna eat?"

Lena wiped her sweaty hands on her apron, glanced around the tables filled with families eating meatloaf, mashed potatoes, green beans, and biscuits straight from her oven. "I couldn't swallow a bite."

"He sure had me fooled. I thought he'd be a gentleman," Kayla said softly.

Lena stiffened. "We had an argument. Wasn't any of his fault. Don't you worry about me." She reached behind her to untie her apron and draped it over a chair.

"Um, don't look now, but you-know-who just walked in. Want to slip out the kitchen door?"

Lena shook her head. "How about you sit him at a table. I'll start emptying the dishwasher."

Kayla nodded, pasted on a smile, and swept toward Gabe, whose laser gaze locked on Lena.

Lena's stomach did a somersault, and she turned on her heel to push through the kitchen door and hide.

Only, of course, that didn't work. The door swung open with a whoosh behind her, but she didn't glance back. Instead, she opened the dishwasher and began unloading glasses into the cupboard.

"We have to talk."

She stiffened, but then grabbed another glass to put away. "Nothin' more to say. I got your message loud and clear."

Hands landed on her hips and firmly turned her.

He was standing too close. She didn't dare lift her head. Instead, she stared at the collar of his shirt.

"I didn't handle that well, back at the river."

"I'm not grading you on your ability to handle upsetting news."

"Teacher, if you were, I'd have earned a big fat F. I was dead wrong for the way I behaved."

He tucked a finger under her chin, and she resisted for a moment but didn't want to seem cowardly. Now was the time to show some strength. Let him know she wasn't cowed—not by his rudeness, not by the power he might wield if he had a mind to fight her for Jake.

She slowly let him raise her head and met his stormy gaze. For a moment, she softened inside. Felt that familiar spark and nearly swayed toward him. But she caught herself just in time because she couldn't read his expression.

"Come walk with me," he said softly.

"I have work to do here."

"I'll help you with it, later."

"It's not your place. You're a paying guest."

He drew in a deep breath, and then let it sift slowly out. "I don't want to start this conversation with an argument. I'm calm now. I apologize for my reaction earlier. I have no excuse for leaving you like that."

The backs of her eyes began to burn, but she blinked. No way was she going to cry. She was made of sterner stuff than that. Lena Twohig didn't disintegrate into tears just because a man made a pretty apology. Not even if the way he'd exploded, rushing from the river, had been the worst, most harsh rejection she'd ever received.

She gave him a nod. "All right. We'll walk." When he didn't move away, she arched a brow. "You first."

Gabe cleared his throat and backed up a step.

She slipped to the side and walked as sedately as she could manage to the door leading out onto the back porch. But she didn't want to talk with the possibility of anyone overhearing, so she continued striding toward the river, hoping the sound of the water gently trickling by would soothe her nerves.

At river's edge, she sought a picnic bench and sat.

Gabe removed his hat and lowered beside her. They both stared out over the water.

He cleared his throat. "I'm sorry as hell for what happened. I didn't act like a man. It's embarrassing to admit. But your...news...was unexpected. I felt sucker punched."

"I shouldn't have said anything. Should have let things go on as they have for ten years, but I was surprised as well." She shot him a sideways glance. "I never would have taken up with you if I'd realized it was you, Gabe."

"Did you ever intend to tell me about the boy?"

She shook her head. "I'd have told Jake when he was older and let him make up his mind whether he wanted to seek you out. He'd have had my support."

He raked a hand through his hair. "Why didn't you want to tell me? I thought we had...a thing. I cared about you."

She swung toward him. "You were seventeen years old. I was nineteen. When I realized I was pregnant, thinking about the fact I was about to become a parent, I felt pretty foolish. But bringing you into the equation, so damn young, I didn't want to make a bigger mess of it."

"You didn't trust me."

"You were a kid. *A kid I seduced.*"

His mouth curved. "I like to think the seduction was mutual, Lena."

Lena frowned. "Don't do that."

"What?"

"Tease me. Like you can wrap me around your finger just by lowering your voice and looking at me like that."

"Like what?" he drawled.

"Like you could—" She pressed her lips together and shook her head.

"Eat you up?" he whispered. "I sure as hell want to. But we've got some problems to solve first."

Lena took a deep breath and turned away again. His words surprised her. She'd expected nothing but recriminations, but he was treating her like this was still about them, instead of all about Jake.

He acted like they actually had something to work out in their relationship. That thought gave her a burst of hope. But she couldn't trust that feeling.

Couldn't trust herself around him. Because more than anything, she wanted him to be real, for her feelings for him to be real. The fact he still wanted her sexually was clear. And she wasn't denying she wanted nothing more than to give both their libidos free rein. Sex with Gabe was as natural as breathing, as heady and intoxicating as the strongest tequila.

He tucked her hair behind her ear, and she shivered.

"What's his name?" he whispered.

"Jake. Jacob Anthony Twohig."

"Would you consider changing his last name to Triplehorn?"

"We have bigger things to think about."

"I want you both to come to the Triplehorn Ranch."

She aimed a bald stare his way. "You didn't want to ease into that?"

"What would be the point?"

"Want us to come for a visit? Because I have work, and then school will be startin' up in the fall." She lifted her shoulders. She needed time to get her head around this, to prepare Jake. "Maybe Christmas."

He shook his head slowly, and his gaze hardened. "Now. To stay. The both of you. With me."

Lena's chest constricted. "I barely know you. It's the truth. You know that."

"We know each other, Lena. We just haven't spent a lot of time together. *We work.*"

"So, we like to fuck. That's not reason enough for me to change my child's whole world so you can see whether you like playing daddy?"

"I won't be playing. I'll be his father. And you'll be my wife."

She shot off the bench and rounded on him. "You're not even going to ask me? You think because you're a high and mighty Triplehorn you can just make a pronouncement, wave your hand, and I'm supposed to just fall in line?"

Gabe rose and walked slowly toward her.

She wanted to back away but stiffened her spine. She wasn't afraid of him. But the closer he came, the more unsure she felt. Part of her wanted to run, the other part wanted him to force her to accept him, so she wouldn't have to make a logical choice.

He reached out his arms, slowly smoothed his hands down to settle at the small of her back, and pulled her against his chest. His cheek slid against her hair.

He held her until her fluttering heart slowed, and she could breathe again.

"Feel better?" he murmured.

Her next breath quivered. "Yes."

"I don't want to fight. I want to help. And more than anything, I want you and Jake in my life. I know I'm rushing you off your feet, darlin', but I have years to make up to you. Come for a visit. For now. No pressure."

Not looking at his face made it easier to think. "I have a campground to run."

"My brother's makin' arrangements for help, even as we speak."

"Jake's with grandpa."

"We can pick him up on our way to the ranch."

She shook her head, her cheek rubbing his chest. "This is crazy."

"Lena, only thing crazy is either of us walkin' away again." He tightened his arms around her.

She exhaled and sank against his chest. He dropped his head to the corner of her shoulder, and they stood like that, gently rocking as all the fight left her body. She was tired of going it alone. Of making every decision. Being the rock for her small family. "My grandpa? He's at my place. He's been in a wheelchair since he had a fall and broke his hip."

"Soon as Colt sees him, he'll have the hands buildin' a ramp. Your grandpa's welcome at the ranch. We have a couple of guest rooms. We'll make them both comfortable."

"There's so much to consider. And I'm not sayin' yes to marryin' you, just *maybe* to coming to stay for a while and seein' how things go."

"Sounds sensible," he growled.

"You sound like you don't like sensible."

"I like going with my instincts."

She snorted. "See where that got you?"

"Got me a son. And a woman who's as hot as a fuckin' firecracker."

She leaned back to study his face.

Wicked lust shone in his slate-gray eyes.

"I'll need my own room, too. My son doesn't need to see the intimate side of us just yet."

He nodded. "I agree. Just so we don't shock Jake or grandpa. But you'll be sleepin' with me."

She swallowed hard. "When will the help arrive?"

"I'll have to call Colt and see. When can we go pick up Jake and grandpa?"

"Guess we both have arrangements to make," she muttered, already ticking through a list of things she'd have to do.

He smoothed his hands over her butt. "Mind makin' those arrangements a little bit later?"

She didn't miss the sweet tension in his voice, or the stirring of his sex trapped against her belly.

Her breaths deepened. "I have dishes to do."

"I imagine Kayla won't mind takin' over."

She arched a brow. "She's a little disappointed in you."

"Then I'll have to redeem myself in her eyes."

She gripped the front of his shirt in her fist and rose on her toes. "How about you do a little redeeming with me first?"

Their lips met, and there was nothing tentative about the caress. They dove headlong into a steamy kiss that left both their bodies shaking.

"My bedroom?" she whispered.

"Too far." He stepped back, grabbed her hand

and pulled her down the path. The sun was dipping behind the trees, but it was still broad daylight.

"People will see," she whispered.

"They won't be lookin' unless you make too much noise." He led her to one side to the wooden pier with the gabled boathouse that housed her little paddle boat. He ducked inside and pushed her up against the planked wall. "I made you a promise."

A thrill shivered through her. Her pussy tightened.

Gabe began plucking at her clothes, tugging her tee over her head, unclasping her bra. When he knelt to remove her sandals and shorts, she gave a little moan. "Someone's gonna find us."

"Everyone's at dinner. Besides, we'll hear the poundin' on the boards. If we have to, we'll jump in the water to hide."

She glanced around the narrow confines of the covered dock with its planked walkway. "There's no room."

"I'll make do." When he had her nude, he held out his hand.

She gave it to him and let him settle her onto the wooden floor beside the boat slip. "What about you?" she said, lying back. "I'm the only one naked."

"Better I keep myself covered. Your pussy's too much temptation."

He lifted her feet one at a time, sliding them up and apart, and then splayed her knees with a firm press of his hands. In the shadow of the boathouse, he bent over her sex, his breath gusting hot against her exposed flesh. He thumbed up the top of her folds, exposing her clit.

Warm air brushed it, and she drew a hissing breath. "That's almost too much," she said in a little voice.

One side of his mouth crooked up. "Darlin', you're really gonna have to work harder on keepin' quiet."

"We could have had a bedroom, a soft mattress…"

His eyebrows waggled. "This is more fun."

She shook her head, fighting a grin. "Because I have to keep quiet, or we might be discovered? You're a wicked man, Gabe Triplehorn."

He smiled and leaned down to gently lick her clit.

She blew air between her pursed lips. Her heartbeat quickened. She dropped her knees open a few inches more, baring herself completely.

He parted her folds and swept his tongue along the outer folds then lavished her opening with wet swipes.

When he glanced up, he caught her fascinated stare. "It's okay to whisper sexy things. Tell me what you want."

"You're doin' fine," she said faintly.

Holding her glance, he stuck two fingers in his mouth, wetting the digits, then slowly inserted them inside her, fingers tucked facing upward as he tunneled.

When he found just the right spot, her body twitched. Her mouth gaped. "There. Dear God, right there."

"Good to know, he said, then slipped them out.

Fluid leaked out, and he coated his palm with it.

She shook her head, not understanding, until he cupped her sex with his palm and lifted his hand.

She tensed, knowing what he meant to do but still unprepared when he slapped her pussy.

Lena clutched a breast and squeezed it, more for comfort than to add to the sweet tension he built with three more well-aimed, juicy claps of his callused hand.

Her breath left in a harsh gust when he dove down and latched his mouth around her hooded clit. He suctioned his lips, pulling at the small, rapidly hardening bud. She dug her toes into the rough-plank floors.

He mouthed her clit, suckled it, flicked it with his tongue, ratcheting up the tension building in her core with a steady, spiraling heat.

She lifted her bottom, mashing herself against his mouth, tiny moans leaking between her bitten lips. Fingers dove into her cunt, teeth nibbled at her bud. She thrashed her head side to side and pinched both nipples, because suddenly the sensations he built below were too intense to stand.

"Gabe!" She gasped.

He inserted another finger and twisted the thick digits, encouraging a steady release of liquid lust that sounded so lushly erotic, so wonderfully dirty, she jerked her hips up high, holding them as still as her quivering ass and thighs would allow, because she never wanted him to stop.

And then he slid the hood up again, readjusted his lips to draw directly on her engorged clit, and electric darts of pleasure consumed her. He pulled it, lavishing it with the flat of tongue while thrusting his fingers deep.

She flew apart, shattering. Her moans slipping out, one after the other, soft murmurs from him vibrating through her, adding to the glorious release.

When at last she peaked and gradually slid back down, it was to find him rolling his finger and palms in the moisture he'd made.

She held her breasts, her breaths jagged, chopped pants, and watched as once more he began to spank her hot, reddened sex.

They weren't light taps. They pounded against her—quickening, sharp bursts then harder, thudding claps. She writhed and wriggled, trying to get away because her orgasm was cresting again, and she was coming undone.

"Jesus," she whispered. "Oh, fuck. Fuck. Fuck." She tried to close her thighs but couldn't resist the jolting pleasure.

Suddenly, he halted, ripped open his belt and tugged down his zipper, rooting inside his pants to pull his cock free. "On your knees," he rasped.

There wasn't much space, but she clambered up

and turned, sinking her back to raise her ass high because he was already nudging between her folds. When he thrust inside, she dropped her head to the floor, dug her fingers into the wood, shredding her nails.

He gripped her ass and parted her cheeks. Liquid dropped into her crease, and she groaned as he pushed a finger into her ass. When he began moving, fingers and cock burrowing deep, Lena wondered how she'd ever thought another man could satisfy her.

Gabe didn't have any inhibitions, didn't accept any demur from her. He molded her responses, her positions, with strong grips and fierce thrusts. Her body shook and shivered, her breaths broke apart, edged with quiet sobs. "It's too much."

Her admission only seemed to fuel his passion. He slammed against her, jackhammer thrusts that rocked her body. His groin slapped her flesh, making louder, lusher sounds, but by this time, she didn't give a damn who might hear. She was there again, rocketing upward.

Gabe reached around her and toggled her tender clit with a callused thumb. "Now, baby. Come for me. One more time."

She exploded, giving a garbled shout. He pounded his hips, slammed one last time and held.

Hot streams of come flooded her, a liquid burst that soothed ravaged walls. The stray thought passed that they hadn't bothered with protection. Maybe that had been deliberate on his part, but she was too consumed with pleasure to care. They jerked and writhed together, his hands clutching her bottom, holding her up because she would have melted to the floor without his strength supporting her.

When at last he pulled away, he pressed a kiss against one shoulder, sat back and gathered her into his arms. He held her, her back against his belly, his hands cupping her breasts.

"Think anyone heard?" she said in a small voice.

He laughed. One sharp gust that buffeted against her. "Do you really care?"

She shook her head and reached behind her to cup the back of his neck as he stroked her breasts again, pulling on the tips.

"I'm done," she muttered, sure the soreness between her legs would have her walking funny for days.

"No more arguments? Coming home with me?"

She turned her head to meet his lambent gaze. "All right. But let's give Jake a chance to know you all before we tell him."

His mouth tightened, but he gave a nod. "I'll let you decide when he's ready."

As her breaths deepened and slowed, she conceded she liked this. Being held in the embrace of a strong man.

He kissed her temple. "Think you could get to like this?"

She grunted, not surprised at all that his thoughts

had followed the same path. "Like's a really tame word. I think I might crave it. Like chocolate." She shook her head. "More than that. I'd hate it if I never felt this way again."

Gabe dug his fingers into her scalp. He turned her face a fraction more and sealed her mouth with a kiss filled with promises.

CHAPTER 6

When they returned to the lodge, two dinged-up pickups filled the spaces in front of the porch.

Gabe's steps slowed. He tightened his hand around Lena's. "Looks like Colt didn't waste any time."

His brother Tommy straightened from the rail he'd been leaning against. His gaze slipped from Gabe to land on Lena. His quiet expression remained neutral as he stared, but then his mouth stretched into a great big smile. "Must be Lena," he said, touching the brim of his hat in greeting. "You're prettier than I expected."

Gabe glanced down to find a blush coloring Lena's cheeks. She had to be embarrassed. Their clothes were wrinkled—hers were smudged with dirt. And anyone looking at her messy hair and swollen mouth had to know exactly what they'd been doing.

She reached up her free hand to touch her hair,

but then dropped it. "You're a Triplehorn. Just don't know which one."

"I'm Tommy."

She swiveled her head toward Gabe, eyes narrowed. "Didn't use much imagination," she muttered.

Gabe raised his eyebrows and flicked his gaze back to Tommy. "You bring a crew?"

"Yeah, Eddie Sandoval and Lane Whitley volunteered to spend the rest of the summer here. Said fishin' was a lot more appealin' than starin' at cows' butts." He hooked a finger over his shoulder and lifted his eyebrows. "They're busy chattin' up that pretty young thing at the counter."

Gabe suppressed a smile. Eddie and Lane would no doubt be shoving at each other trying to cozy up to Kayla.

Tommy kicked at a broken spoke in the porch rail. "They brought their tools, too. Looks like they can keep busy makin' some repairs." His gaze went to Lena. "They're good men. They'll pitch in. Kayla says she knows the ropes. Said not to worry about a thing."

Lena let out a long exhale and nodded. "I appreciate this. It's my grandpa's place. It's been a little too much for me to keep up with since he was forced to retire."

Tommy nodded. "Colt's on his way to Denton."

Gabe frowned, not understanding, but Lena's

hand gripped his so hard that he figured it out quickly. "Jake's in Denton?" he asked her.

"Yes. How the hell…" She shook her head, her lips twisting in a snarl. "Don't imagine it was that hard for your brother to find them. Not when you Triplehorns have money to throw around."

Tommy raised his brows and narrowed his eyes. "He's on his way, but only 'cause he wanted to have them at the ranch house so your mind'll be at ease," he said, speaking slowly. "He wants you to call them, to give them warning so they can pack. I know we're movin' fast, Lena, but we don't mean any harm. We take care of our own."

Lena didn't say anything. Gabe gave her hand another squeeze, telling her silently that everything would be all right. "Where's Zuri?"

"With Colt." Tommy smiled. "He figured she's less intimidatin'."

Gabe turned to Lena whose back was as stiff as a poker. He gripped her hips and forced her to turn her toward him. Then he bracketed her cheeks, lifting her chin because she wasn't meeting his gaze. "It's gonna be okay. Colt's a sheriff. He'll take good care of them."

Her lips tightened. "I better call and tell grandpa what's happening. Or they'll be on the doorstep, and he'll be greetin' them with a shotgun."

She pulled away, and he let her go, even though he could tell she wasn't happy with how fast things were moving.

When she'd entered the lodge, he turned to Tommy. "You could have waited another day."

Tommy shrugged. "Colt was determined. Said if he left it to you, you'd screw away the summer before you got the boy registered for school." He cleared his throat. "From the sounds comin' from the boathouse, I figure he was right."

Gabe's cheeks burned.

"Bro, I don't think he was exaggerating," Tommy said, dropping his voice. "The two of you look like you could use a hot shower."

"Not any of your business."

"Just sayin'. And, dude, damn she's hot. I can see why you fell like a ton of bricks."

Gabe gave him a hot glare. "I'm not sharin'."

"Didn't expect you would. Guess those days are over." He clipped Gabe's shoulder. "And you a family man..." He shook his head and chuckled. "Colt said you 'bout blew a gasket. Glad you simmered down. You have to do right by that boy."

"Did you think I wouldn't?"

Tommy's gaze narrowed as he studied Gabe's expression. "No, you'll be a great dad. But how nice is it for you that the mama's not hard on the eyes either?"

Gabe grumbled under his breath and swept past his brother whose chuckles grew louder the harder he stomped.

Inside, he glanced around.

Kayla leaned around the two cowboys hogging

the counter in front of her. "She's gone back to her room. Said she had calls to make."

Gabe gave her a nod and headed straight down the hallway. When he slipped inside the door, it was to find Lena sitting on the edge of her bed with her telephone cradled between her hands.

"Did you warn them?"

"I told him he couldn't shoot Jake's uncle," she said, not looking up.

"Did he agree to come with Colt?"

She nodded. "Said it was about damn time the boy met his father." Then she did glance up. A sheen of moisture glistened in her eyes. "I didn't know he felt that way. Like I'd made a mistake."

Gabe strode to her and sat next to her on the bed. He plucked the phone from her hands, tossed it on the bed, and cupped both of hers between his. "You didn't make a mistake. You did what you thought was best. Like you said, I was a kid. I needed to grow up first. Maybe I would have done it a lot faster if I'd had to man up sooner, but I'm here now. I want to help, not take over. I want to make things easier, not complicate your life."

She sniffed and rubbed her nose with the back of her hand. "The house, my job..."

"Details, Lena. And you don't have to take care of anything but our boy. Let me handle everything about the move for you. As for the job, if you want to keep teachin', I can put in a good word with the superintendent in Destiny. But you don't have to make any big decisions right away. Settle in. See what you want to do. If you decide you don't want to work, I'll support you. It's not like I can't afford it."

She sighed. "You make it so easy. It's another seduction, isn't it? Erase my problems with a wave of your hand."

"Am I a problem?"

She shook her head. "I didn't mean it that way. It's just happenin' so fast."

"My brothers and me, we don't know any speed but fast. If you need us to slow down, all you have to do is say so."

She leaned her head against his shoulder, and the tension in his chest eased. He bent and kissed her hair. Kissing her was already so natural. Comforting her came surprisingly easy. "Can I help you pack?"

"Not even sure what I need. I'm guessin' flip-flops and shorts aren't appropriate on a ranch. Most of my clothes are back at my house. I only bring casual things to the campground."

"You can wear whatever you want around the ranch, but you'll need jeans and boots when you ride."

Her shoulders shook. When she lifted her head, there was a smile quirking up her lips. "Didn't think I needed any clothes at all when I ride."

A grin tugged at his mouth. "I really like your dirty mind. You sore?"

Her eyes widened. "You did not just say that."

"Are you? If you need to take a hot bath to ease your..."

She pressed a finger against his mouth. "Any minute your brother might walk down the hall. He'll hear you talkin' about my pussy."

Gabe chuckled and bit her finger. Tommy'd be disappointed if I wasn't horny as hell every time I got near you."

She shook her head. "Our sex life's gonna be private. You better learn how to watch your mouth with Jake and grandpa always underfoot."

He waggled his eyebrows. "You're the one who said pussy."

Her mouth widened in a sheepish grin. "This is new to me, you know. Bein' this easy with a man."

"It's old, don't you mean? Our conversations always drifted to the gutter." He leaned toward her and kissed her mouth. "Get packed," he gritted out. "That is, if you want to christen my bed before the family descends."

He stood, gave her body a sweeping glance that left her no doubt about what he'd rather be doing, and then strode toward the door.

"Gabe?"

Hand on the door, he glanced back.

"We're doin' the right thing, aren't we?"

"Sweetheart, I've never felt surer of anything."

Her expression cleared, whether because he'd reassured her or she'd decided not to appear weak, he didn't know. He wanted more than anything to share what was in his heart, but he couldn't risk getting shot down now. Once he had her under his roof, at his mercy, he'd let everything take its natural course.

Gabe had no doubts she felt something for him, or she'd never have let slip about Jake. She'd placed the ball in his court. Now, it was up to him to prove he was worth the risk.

Lena had known the Triplehorn Ranch was big, but when he'd pointed to where their fence line started and then told her she could nap until they got to the house, she'd thought he was joking.

They drove miles past grassy meadows, tree-lined creeks, and huge herds of cattle. The sight of cowboys on horseback, lifting their hats in the distance to greet them, filled her with a sense of wonder that, just maybe, she might be a part of all this.

The size of the ranch made her feel insignificant, like she was an interloper among Texan royalty. No matter how long she might stay, she didn't think she'd ever grow inured to the grandness of it all.

And Gabe didn't see this ranch as all that special. To him, it was the place he grew up, a job he couldn't shirk, because he'd been born to it.

As they drove, he talked about his life, how the seasons affected the hours, the types of chores. The fact that it was a seven-day work week, and that he hoped she wouldn't mind, but that was what life on a ranch was like.

He worried she might find the pace a burden, then rushed to reassure her that with another woman in the house, they could divvy up the women's chores.

She didn't bother raising a brow at the phrase *women's chores*. What was the point? Work was divided according to strength and skill. She didn't even know how to ride a horse, but she did know how to be a mother and how to take care of a home.

If she hoped to make this work, she'd have to let him see she didn't resent the idea of her place among the Triplehorns—if only she found it, quickly.

The thought of intruding on Zuri's domain, her being the first woman in the house, left her feeling a little nervous.

"What if she doesn't like me?"

"Who, Zuri?" With his gaze on the highway, he gave a grunt. "She'll be glad to have a girl around to gossip with."

"Do you know just how chauvinist you sound?"

His chest rose around a deep inhalation. "Sorry. I'm not used to havin' women around. But I know guys like to gossip about girls. Figured you ladies would be the same. And Zuri's been doin' the bulk of the cookin' while supervisin' a cleaning lady who comes in a couple times a week. I know she'd like a break." He turned his head her way, his gaze snagging on her expression. "Are you really worried about Zuri? I know women can be territorial." He wrinkled his nose. "I did it again, didn't I?"

She laughed. "Let's agree never to talk gender politics. I'm just glad I had a boy."

"Smack me the next time I say something offensive. Like I said, other than Zuri and the cleaning lady, we don't have any other females on the ranch."

"I don't like to do the smackin'," she murmured, looking out her window and grinning.

He jerked his head toward her, "Don't say things like that when I'm drivin'."

"Road's flat. No bends. Wide shoulders. Haven't seen more than a couple of cars since we made that last turn." Lena fingered the top button of her pink, sleeveless shirt. She might not feel certain about how she was going to fit in at a working ranch, but there was one facet of her new life about which she felt no such ambivalence.

"We've still got twenty minutes," Gabe said, tightening his hand on the steering wheel. "I'll slow down." Without preamble, he reached down with one hand and unbuckled his belt, unsnapped his blue jeans, and tugged down his zipper.

Lena shrugged her arm past the shoulder harness of her seatbelt and loosened the band around her waist. Then she angled her body to face him. She reached into his pants and drew out his cock. It was soft but beginning to pulse. Steamy hot.

"What do you have in mind?" he asked, flicking her a hot glance.

"Just keep your hands on the wheel and your eyes on the road. I'm gonna return a favor."

She bent and opened wide, sucking as much of his quickly expanding cock into her mouth as she could manage. She groaned around him, loving the way he tasted and smelled, musky and purely male. She sucked, making slurping sounds that made him chuckle once, but then his thighs tensed, and he didn't utter another sound.

Lena ignored her own growing arousal, although her nipples grew hard and her pussy wet. She concentrated on his pleasure, happy to show him she could be an equal partner in at least this one way.

As his length straightened, she bobbed, pulling him with strong suctioning tugs, bobbing deep and then coming up, rubbing her tongue along his shaft as her lips sucked.

The salty taste of his pre-come exploded on her tongue, and she groaned, diving down to consume him, down again until the wide cap touched the back of her throat. And then she swallowed, giving his sensitive head a caress that had him cursing under his breath.

"Ten minutes," he whispered.

"Might not be enough," she said, coming up and fisting him. She liked the fact her fingers didn't meet, and she pumped him as she flicked his eyelet hole with the tip of her tongue.

The car veered to the side, tires kicking up gravel. He shoved the gear stick into park, unclipped his belt, unclipped hers, and scooted to the middle of the seat.

He ignored her blouse, made quick work of the button of her shorts, and shoved them off her legs.

With his hands guiding her over his lap, he forced her down on his cock.

Lena gave a glad shout as he filled her, ramming her hips down to take every hard inch. Then she gripped his shoulders and began to move, forward and back, up and down, letting the pronounced ridge around his cockhead stroke past her G-spot.

"Fuck, I want your tits in my mouth."

She shook her head. "No time. And someone might drive by."

"Think they won't know what we're doin'?"

"They can know, but I'd just as soon they don't see my tits bouncin' in your face."

His chuckle pulled a grin from her, and she jounced again.

"Your pants are gonna be wet."

"Don't give a fuck. I'll hold my cowboy hat in front of my dick."

"Lord, I love your sexy talk." She leaned close, wrapped her hands around the back of his head and kissed him as she gave him shorter strokes.

Then his hands were under her shirt. He slipped his fingers under the band of her bra. The moment he pinched her nipples, she bit her mouth to keep from screaming.

"That's it, baby, that's it," he said, kissing her neck. "God, I loved your mouth on me. Felt like you were tryin' to suck my come all the way from my toes."

She wrinkled her nose. "Sounds nasty."

"Tell you what I want to suck…"

"Later. We'll have time when we get there, right?"

"Only if God doesn't have a sense of humor." His head fell back, and he tightened his hands on her bottom. He pushed her up and down, faster and faster, until sweat trickled down her back, and she couldn't catch her breath.

Gabe licked her neck and the side of her cheek, catching salty streaks. Then he touched her asshole, and Lena screamed, cramming down his cock, bouncing up, rocking her body hard against his as her orgasm swept through her, tightening her core then rushing outward like a sonic wave.

She worried he wasn't there with her, but then he dug his fingers into her flesh, squeezing her globes so hard she knew she'd have bruises, and his hips jerked off the seat as he fucked into her, his stiff, straight cock hammering inside her.

When they both slowed their motions, she rested her forehead against his.

"That help with your nerves?" he asked.

"What nerves?" she gasped.

"Exactly."

She smiled and kissed him, opening her mouth to touch her tongue against his. When she pulled back, his half-closed eyes simmered. His mouth curved.

She lifted her eyebrows. "You look very satisfied with yourself."

"That's because I am." He cradled the back of her head. "I love you, Lena."

He waited. And she knew he wanted her to give him back those same words, but the part of her that was still scared this all happening too fast kept her mute.

"Better get dressed," he muttered.

Feeling as though she'd flunked a test, she eased off his cock and sat on the seat beside him while she pulled on her underwear and shorts. "I want this to work."

"Then don't think too hard. Don't doubt my intentions."

"It's hard. Good Lord, you just came back into my life yesterday."

"I've been in love with for years. Never loved anyone else."

She shot him a shocked glance. "But you never came back."

"I was a boy. And as I became a man I figured out you hadn't been near as serious about me."

She shook her head. "That wasn't true. But I was ashamed. Of getting knocked up by a boy not out of high school."

Gabe steady glare held her. "There were only two years separating us. You were in college but you were a kid too, Lena. I was still old enough to know how I felt." He grabbed her left hand. "Why did you keep that ring?"

Her fingers curled. She shook her head. Tears leaked from her eyes. "It made me feel...connected to you. Like it hadn't been just a dream or some tawdry episode. Every time I looked at it, I was reminded of your face when you told me goodbye."

"I said I loved you. That I'd wait." His voice was even, his words filled with conviction.

Lena uncurled her fingers and stared at the ring. Just a little silver band with a speck of a diamond in the center. "And you did," she whispered.

Gabe tucked a finger under her chin, he studied her face and a smile began to stretch.

Lena leapt forward and wrapped her arms around his shoulders, giving into the tears from a rush of happiness that swept through her. "I loved you, too. But I couldn't admit it. And seeing you again, some part of me knew it was you, because I've never ever been that way with another man. I swear it. I wanted you in an instant, and when you were inside me, I suddenly felt whole. It scared the heck out of me."

They held each other, Gabe dropping kisses on her cheek and squeezing her so tight she could barely breathe. When he let her go, she drew in a deep breath and laughed.

The ride to the ranch house took five minutes. All the way home, he held her hand, gliding his finger on the promise ring.

CHAPTER 7

Gabe sat on his horse, holding the reins of Jake's pinto as his son boarded the school bus.

At the top step, Jake turned and gave him a cheeky grin. "See you tonight, Dad."

Gabe smiled back, waving as the doors closed and his boy made his way to his seat. Rather than have his dad drive him in his pickup each morning, Jake preferred practicing his riding. The daily ritual was one they both enjoyed. Jake had taken to riding and life on the ranch like he'd been born to it. When he wasn't in school, he was in the barn, learning to muck stalls or riding with Gabe and his brothers when they moved the cattle from pasture to pasture.

Gabe remembered their first meeting. His son had taken a step toward him, looked into eyes that were the same slate gray as his own, and asked, "Are you my dad?"

There wasn't a dry eye among any of the people crowding the driveway to greet Jake and Mr. Twohig.

Gabe had gone down on one knee and opened his arms. The hug they'd shared as he'd gruffly said yes was the first of many.

Pulling the reins of his horse, he pointed him back to the house and the woman sitting on the top porch step. Lena had yet to join them on their morning rides, but it was going to be a while before he'd allow her to sit a horse. Not until she healed after the birth of their child, scheduled to arrive at the Triplehorn in early May.

A girl this time. And he couldn't be happier. Colt's little girl would need a playmate.

His smile stretched as he halted the horses and wrapped the reins around a porch rail.

"How many times I have to tell you the porch isn't a hitchin' rail," Colt grumbled as he opened the door.

"Maybe I'll remember if you repeat it a couple hundred more times," Gabe said, chuckling.

Colt patted his pockets then cursed. "Left the keys to the cruiser on the dresser." He opened the door. "Zuri, why'd you let me leave without my keys?"

Lena and Gabe waited until Colt's footsteps faded before they let loose with laughter.

"He does it every morning," Gabe said, as he lowered to sit beside Lena on the step. "He doesn't have anyone fooled. Just wants to sneak another kiss before he heads to work."

"And she stays in bed waitin' for it. Takes him an awful long time to find those keys."

Gabe drew in a deep breath as he watched the smile lighting up her face. "You look beautiful."

"If you say I'm glowing, I'll hit you. Never could figure out what that meant. If I'm glowing, it's because I'm always sweaty hot."

Gabe reached across and rubbed her rounded belly. "Breakfast staying down?"

"So far, so good. Don't think either of us is going to have to change our clothes today." She placed her hand over his and hugged it against her body. "Ready for another day?"

"Not getting bored yet?"

She rolled her eyes. "As if. Zuri and I will be busy baking all day."

"Don't overdo."

"Don't fuss. I'm not an invalid."

"How's grandpa?"

"Getting around nicely on his cane. Can't keep him down now. Says it's time to get rid of that damn ramp," she said, mimicking the gruff old codger's voice.

Gabe held her hand and looked out across the corral to the pasture beyond. "Is he happy here?"

"He hasn't said, but since he's got lots of ideas about how you should be runnin' this place, I'm guessin' yes."

Gabe laughed and turned to lock gazes with Lena. "Are you happy?"

Her eyes welled with tears, and she chuckled as she wiped a fingertip beneath one eye. "Worst part of pregnancy. Everything makes me cry." She sniffed, and her expression cleared. Her cornflower blue eyes held steady. "My son loves it here. Loves you."

"That's not what I asked."

Her gaze fell away, and she leaned against the rail beside her, still staring at him. "I've never felt this way. Like I've come home. Zuri's the sister I never had. Your brothers have been amazing, making sure we all feel welcome, and that we have a place here."

Gabe blew out an exasperated gust of air.

She laughed, a twinkle glinting in her eye. "And I have the most amazing husband. He can't keep his hands off me. Won't let me sleep at night. Whispers the sweetest, dirtiest little nothings in my ear. He makes me feel beautiful and desired. He rubs my feet when they swell. My belly when I'm nauseous." She shook her head. "I've never been so blessed."

Gabe dropped his gaze and smiled, winding his fingers with hers. "I'm a rancher," he sighed. "I should do some ranchin'."

She tugged on his hand, and he came closer. "Tommy said he had it covered," she whispered.

He arched a brow. "I owe that boy."

"He's not sleepin' so good. I think he's just glad to be out of the house. Says it's quieter."

Gabe's shoulders shook, and he tilted back his

head to laugh. "Soon as Colt and Zuri finish with their renovation, they'll be movin' into the new wing. Then he'll only have us keepin' him awake at night."

"We could try not to make so much noise." But her dubious frown said she wasn't sure she could manage it.

Gabe stood and pulled her up. "We can start practicin' now." He held the door for her, and then swatted her backside as she ducked beneath his arm.

"Ouch!" Her bottom swayed as she led the way down the hall to their bedroom.

Gabe canted his head, listening to the voices coming from the kitchen, of Zuri and grandpa arguing amiably over how many jalapenos to add to the chili. They'd be at it for a while. Would never notice if he and Lena got busy makin' hay.

He hurried behind his wife and waited until the door closed before pouncing.

She giggled as he swept her into his arms. "I'm too heavy for that," she said, swatting his chest.

Gabe ignored her, striding straight for the bed. He lowered her to the mattress, stripped off her pants and underwear and went to work opening her blouse and bra. He didn't bother removing his own clothing, just opened his belt, tugged down his zipper, and shoved down his jeans just enough to free his cock. He climbed onto the bed, rolled her on her side and settled behind her, lifting her thigh to ride the top of his, opening her to his thrust.

Only when he was eight inches deep did he slow

down and breathe. He wrapped his arms around her, cuddling her belly, and began to move. Gabe closed his eyes and breathed her in. He held his whole world inside his arms. "I love you, Lena."

"I love you, Gabe."

With the sounds of her soft moans echoing around the room and her warm body moving against his, Gabe gave silent thanks for all his blessings. He'd never felt so at peace with himself. He was at last comfortable with his place at the Triplehorn. He had a son he doted on and a woman who filled the empty places in his heart.

Lena moved his hands from her belly to her breasts. "They ache," she murmured.

Smiling against her hair, he filled his hands with her ever-ripening breasts and gave her gentle caresses until she groaned her discontent, and then he began to pinch and pull her sensitive nipples.

With their hips churning together, their breaths breaking apart, they loved each other, forgetting at the last to practice being quiet. No, lonely quiet was a thing of the past for at least two of the Triplehorn brothers.

∼

A LONG HOT SUMMER

THE TRIPLEHORN BRAND, BOOK 3

New York Times and *USA Today* Bestselling Author
Delilah Devlin

A LONG, HOT SUMMER

NEW YORK TIMES BESTSELLING AUTHOR
DELILAH DEVLIN

ABOUT THE BOOK

When two lonely hearts collide, age becomes just a number.

Sarah Colby's marriage was over long ago, but she's never shed the scars her abusive husband left behind. Add the one shameful indiscretion from her past, an affair with a much younger man, and she's haunted by that long ago summer.

Tommy Triplehorn is happy his brothers have settled down and started families of their own, but he's feeling a little smothered by all that domesticity. Carousing and drinking no longer holds a thrill, and he thinks he knows the reason why. He's waited long enough for Sarah Colby to get over being ashamed of their shared past. He's old enough to know what he wants, and he wants her.

Warning: A cowboy on a mission to seduce will do whatever it takes, including offering his woman a no-holds-barred weekend of sex, even a ménage with a friend, to prove he'll fulfill her every sexy need...

CHAPTER 1

Tommy Triplehorn sat back in his chair, drinking while trying to ignore the noise from the scratchy jukebox and the jarring laughter from the blonde at the bar, who couldn't seem to help glancing his way as she whispered with her girlfriend. After the annual Memorial Day picnic at the Triplehorn ranch, he was ready for a celebration of another sort. Looked like the blonde was going to be his date.

Candy Crowe. Tommy blew out a pent-up breath, relaxing as he gave himself permission to be disappointed. Looked like his partner this night was going to be a rarity for him—a repeat. But a quick glance around the room confirmed the only other women here were married or engaged or going out with friends of his, and he never crossed that line. So, Candy Crowe it would be.

He mustered up a smile and lifted his chin, inviting her to join him, and then cringed inwardly as she sauntered toward him, her wide hips swaying too deeply, a predatory gleam in her green eyes. Like a tiger on the prowl.

Or a cougar.

She topped him by ten years, but that didn't bother him. He'd had older. Age wasn't a deal breaker. Fact was, he liked women who knew their way around a man's body. Liked their confidence. Still, his chest hurt a little as she drew nearer, because even though she was blonde not brunette, and even though her figure was as full as a centerfold's rather than lean and trim, she reminded him of what he'd never have.

"Hey, cowboy," she said, sliding into the seat beside him. "Long time no see."

Tommy arched a brow. "Really wanna waste time with small talk?"

Her brows rose. "It's less rude then crawling right on top of me."

"Never complained before," he drawled.

Her lips crimped, and then her gaze swept down his frame, staying on his lap a moment longer than was polite. "And I won't start now. I'll get us a room."

And as quick as that, Tommy had his Friday-night hookup all lined up. He watched as she sashayed toward the door, knowing it would take her a few minutes more to cross the parking lot to the motel. He had time to finish his whiskey before she had a key in her hot, clever hand.

His glance went to the couples flirting, touching,

speaking quietly together, and something inside him tightened. Yeah, life was happening all around him, and he felt like it might be passing him by. Lord knew it was at home. He'd moved out of the ranch house to the bunkhouse to give his brothers and their wives space—and to escape the sounds of lovers enjoying themselves and babies crying.

Both baby girls, Colt's little Rose and Gabe's Violet, were charmers—when they were happy. And they'd already wrapped their daddies around their little fingers. Tommy had adjusted quickly to being an uncle, lending a hand when the women flapped around the kitchen serving up a meal. He drew the line at changing diapers. He wasn't that enamored.

As domestic as everything had become, he'd grown a little claustrophobic and made the move, despite his brothers' objections. Yes, he knew Colt's addition was only weeks from completion. And although Gabe was breaking ground on a cabin behind the big house, Tommy needed space to think. To shore up his resolve that being single and footloose was what he really wanted, because he'd damn sure never get the woman he wanted most. Like his brothers, he'd carried a torch a long time. Not that anyone but the woman in question had a clue.

And then he saw a familiar figure stride into the bar. *Well, hell.* His heart thudded hard and dull against his chest.

Even though she wasn't the prettiest woman he'd ever seen, she held herself like a queen. No ignoring her straight back, squared shoulders, or tall, lean frame that held a hint of swagger when she moved. She wore her trademark men's Wranglers over scuffed boots. Her tee hugged meager curves but emphasized the fact not an ounce of laxity hugged her waist. When she reached up to take off her brown cowboy hat, he held his breath. Russet brown and straight, her hair fell from the coil at the top of her head to trail down between her shoulders in a neat ponytail.

Her glance swept the room, landing on him for a moment before blinking and moving on. Barely a second's worth of recognition in that quick glance.

Tommy's stomach knotted. His chest tightened. She was the reason he pursued the Candy Crowes—women he'd never give more than a good tumble between the sheets.

He set his glass down with a thump and straightened in his chair. From the corner of his eye and through the plate-glass windows overlooking the parking lot, he saw Candy waving her arms from beneath the motel's awning to get his attention.

His cheeks burned. But he didn't dare look the brunette's way. He couldn't and not acknowledge that any betrayal of emotion in her expression, especially disgust, could still affect him.

He picked up his glass, downed the last sip of his drink, and slid off his chair. Without a glance toward the bar, he walked out the double doors and across the lot to the waiting blonde, his strides long and unhurried.

The kiss Tommy Triplehorn planted on Candy's mouth made Sarah Colby's mouth dry right up. She knew all too well how his kisses felt and couldn't help the jealousy stirring up inside her as the couple walked down the sidewalk to a motel room door in plain view of every person inside the saloon.

The man had no shame. The red in his cheeks as he'd exited the bar had likely just been from the liquor he'd consumed.

Sarah tamped down the disappointment that soured her stomach and summoned a smile for the man she was meeting this night.

Blake Morrow was thick-shouldered and tall. A burly man with a booming voice. His wealth and standing in the community made him a very suitable suitor. The fact he already had children from a previous wife was a relief to Sarah, who had resigned herself long ago to her barren state—something a reproductive specialist had confirmed years ago, and she'd come to accept as God's will. Blake didn't need any children from her. Blake liked her and desired her property even more. He was honest about that, gently respectful of her intelligence by not trying to romance the Rocking C from under her as so many men had.

His gaze noted her blue jeans, and he arched a brow. "I take it we're eating steaks here?"

She shrugged. "I ran into some problems before I could break away. No time to get dressed up." She made no apology. Blake knew her responsibilities as a ranch owner came first.

"You still look beautiful," he said, his tone gruff.

She appreciated the compliment and smiled, not wanting to read too deeply into anything he said. Surface congeniality, quiet respect. That was more than she was accustomed to. It would do.

Any stray thoughts of handsome cowboys like Tommy Triplehorn were consigned to her fantasy life, not her real life. The young rancher had been a mistake. One she'd regretted the instant she'd let him slip beneath her reserve. She'd felt alone, afraid for her future. She'd mistaken his rock-hard shoulder for maturity, his hot kisses for love. Eventually, she'd fallen from the clouds that had obscured her good sense and faced the cold hard truth. She was a plain woman, a natural woman. Twelve years older than Tommy Triplehorn and a barren, wealthy woman. The only things a man would ever want from her were what she owned and perhaps a bed partner. As sparsely populated as this section of Texas was, she had no illusions that sheer convenience was on her side.

No, she'd learned a hard lesson all those years ago about what men wanted from wives. One she'd never forget. Her destiny wasn't some fool's gold of a lover's promises.

Blake's strong hand settled at the small of her back to guide her toward a table, something she couldn't help flinching from. She didn't need to be led. Didn't need some big strong man showing her the way. But she kept silent. He was only doing what he'd been taught. He couldn't know that the last time she'd been led, she'd been forced to submit. The action that had left her cold, made her more reserved with men than other women might be.

Not that Blake seemed to notice as he smiled warmly across the table. "I'm surprised you accepted my invitation as many times as you've refused."

She blinked, surprised he was getting straight to the point without any polite preliminaries. "You've been asking me for a while. I thought we should get to know each other."

He nodded, his rugged face tightening just a little. "You know I want to court you."

"I appreciate your candor," she said softly. "I understand you have some expectations. I'm willing for us to explore a relationship."

Good Lord, they sounded like the oil men who'd come to her ranch a few years back asking to sink a test well on her property.

Blake reached across the table and cupped her hand. Just a brief squeeze before he withdrew and flipped open the menu.

The waitress arrived. Relieved by the distraction, Sarah ordered a steak and salad. Blake ordered the same, adding shrimp and potatoes. She supposed such a large man would need the calories. Hopefully, he didn't expect for her to let him finish her steak. She wasn't some deskbound rancher. She rode the fences, supervised the movement of the cattle to fresher pastures, and participated in the branding every spring. Every calorie she ate fueled her body, just like a man's.

She forced herself to uncurl her fingers. What was she doing? Looking for problems? For judgment? Was she simply hoping to find a compelling reason to send Blake on his way, like she'd done the past eight years with every other man who'd approached her since her husband's untimely death?

Sarah forced herself to uncurl her hands in her lap. In any other situation, she'd have been comfortable, in charge. But here, knowing Blake wanted to marry her, that he'd expect intimacies at some point, left her cold inside.

A damaged heroine in a romance novel, she certainly was not, but she had been tainted by a violent man. Left untrusting and wary. Glad for a long while for her self-imposed celibacy.

Pretending ease with the man sitting across from her seemed an insurmountable task. Who was she fooling? Sooner or later, he'd make a move, and she wasn't entirely sure how she'd react. Would she flinch or lean away? Or simply freeze in place?

The more she considered the idea of intimacy

with this man, the more the knot in her stomach hurt. The last thing Blake wanted was problems. He had his life mapped out. He hadn't looked any further than skin deep to determine she was his next move.

So, although he'd be disappointed in the short term, she knew she couldn't string him along with hopes she'd learn to deal with a husband in her life and bed. Before the salads arrived, Sarah made her apologies and quietly excused herself, leaving a befuddled Blake without a clue what he'd done wrong.

She headed straight to her car, hat in her hand, not looking around the dark parking lot. A scuff of gravel sounded, and she instantly regretted waving Blake back into his chair when he'd offered to walk her out. She cupped her keys, spreading her fingers around three to use as a weapon.

"You didn't stay for dinner," came a quiet voice behind her. Smooth as whiskey. Achingly sweet. *Tommy Triplehorn.*

She tossed back her hair and glanced over her shoulder. "You didn't stay for whatever..."

The corners of his mouth twitched. "My taste buds must be off. She was too sweet. What's your excuse?"

Sarah blew out a breath and turned, facing the young man who had plagued her thoughts since their long-ago affair—no intention whatsoever of answering his question. "You're looking good, Tommy." Lord, not the smart thing to say, but the plain unvarnished truth. Dark-brown hair worn short, thick shoulders and arms, thighs, heavily muscled... She darted her gaze back up before she exposed her fascination, only to linger on his handsome face. Age had carved maturity into his features, honed them to sharp-edged masculine lines. He presented an arresting picture, although she did miss the old softness in his now-piercing gaze.

A muscle along the edge of his jaw tightened. "When are you gonna face the truth, Sarah?"

She shook her head, swallowing down the hot lump that burned the back of her throat. "I have to go home," she said hoarsely, turning and jamming her key into the lock, but scraping the paint on her car instead.

He stepped closer, pressing his body against her back and reached around to gently cup her hand until she released the keys. Then, pushing long enough she felt the tension in his tall frame, he unlocked her door and dangled her key ring until she grabbed for it.

Tommy planted his hands on either side of her and nuzzled her hair. "Ever ask yourself why it is I can do this, move into your space, touch you, without you goin' cold as a block of ice?"

"No." She wasn't lying. The last thing she wanted was to remember. She kept the memory of how they'd been together closely guarded, even from herself.

"Didn't think so. Or you wouldn't have let all this

time pass, even though we both know you belong to me."

She shook her head. "I don't belong to you. There is no you and me. We're all wrong, Tommy."

His head nodded, rubbing her cheek. "Because I was too young. But sweetheart, age stopped bein' a good enough reason when I stopped bein' a teenager."

"We should never have—"

"Not then. I know it was a mistake. For you, anyway. I have no regrets. But there's no good reason now."

He nuzzled the corner of her neck, and her knees quivered. She had to be strong. Good Lord, what if someone saw them like this? "Look at me, Tommy," she said staring at their reflections in the window. "Look at us. That's why we don't belong together."

Tommy's brows lowered as he stared into his reflection. "I don't understand what it is you see that I don't. If it's age, that's not good enough, Sarah. Not anymore. I'm sick and tired of pretendin' I don't care."

She turned inside his arms and met his gaze with a steady one of her own. "You should respect my wishes. I told you no eight years ago. I haven't changed my mind."

Tommy leaned away, dropped his head, and stared at his clenched hands for a long moment. When he raised his head again, his gaze bored into hers.

The weight of that steady stare settled in her core, and she shivered beneath the raw intensity of his expression.

"Hear me now, Sarah Colby. I'm not givin' up on us. Everywhere you go, I'll be there. Waitin' for you to come to your senses."

She scoffed, while inside a traitorous part of her body rejoiced. "You sound like you intend to be my stalker."

"If that's what it takes to make you understand I'm serious..."

Sarah shivered, hearing the conviction in his deep voice, reading the icy resolve in his gray eyes. The tender cowboy she'd known years ago had been replaced by a man with dangerous edges.

She gripped the door handle behind her and tugged it open.

He caught the corner of the door, and swung it wider, gently handing her into the car. "You head straight home, Ms. Colby," he said, amusement in his voice. "I'll be right behind you."

She got in, slammed the door, and hit the locks. Fear hadn't triggered her reaction. *Oh, no.* It was the flutter of arousal awakening inside her, so strong her body clenched. She needed to get away. Drive to the sanctuary of her home to reinforce her resolve.

As she pulled out of the parking lot and onto the highway, she couldn't help darting glances at the rearview mirror. The lights of his truck were there.

But he was hanging back at a safe distance. Christ, he'd been serious.

She'd known one day she'd have to reckon with her past. Her one shameful indiscretion had cost her more than a little self-respect. Tommy wasn't to blame. She shouldered that burden all on her own. She'd been old enough to know better but hadn't wanted to resist because he'd been so earnest and heartbreakingly beautiful.

Stalled at the lowest ebb of her marriage, she'd been vulnerable, ready for a little tenderness, which he'd been so eager to provide. One touch, and she hadn't been able to resist another and another—until she'd cuckolded a dangerous man.

While that man was gone from her life for good, one fact hadn't changed. Tommy Triplehorn was all wrong for her.

He was too young. Too handsome. And from a family that was rapidly expanding. So many children were joining the ranks. Any woman who took him on would be expected to contribute to that expansion.

Her chest tightened, and she drew a deep breath to ease the tension making her fingers clench the steering wheel. She thought ahead, to the moment she pulled into her driveway and parked her car beside her house, knowing he wouldn't leave without trying to convince her to see him.

The last thing she wanted was a confrontation outside where her foreman and any hands might hear. She'd have to invite him inside her home. The thought both frightened and excited her.

But she could do this. Ask him in for coffee. Putter around the kitchen to keep him from trying to continue what he'd started back in Shooter's parking lot. There she'd been so intensely aware of him. So needful of his touch.

Damn, eight years and nothing had changed. She dashed a tear from her face with the back of her hand and cursed her own lustful nature. Not something her husband had ever been able to tap into, because he hadn't given a damn about what pleased her.

The tall gate post at the entrance to her private road loomed to the right. She slowed, signaled to turn, then drove onto the gravel drive, bumping over the cattle guard before heading straight to the house.

A glimpse in her mirror confirmed Tommy had been serious. His headlights bounced and then steadied, following her all the way up the hill.

Sarah breathed deep, calming breaths, and then let herself out of the car. She gave Tommy a wave and walked toward the porch, wanting to appear collected and needing a little distance and a few spare seconds to achieve that feat.

To her dismay, the quick clip of his boot heels matched the beat of her wayward heart. Seconds later, a hand cupped the small of her back, and he reached around her to hustle her inside the house and close the door.

At the thrill of his touch, Sarah had the fleeting

thought that Tommy Triplehorn might be all wrong for her, but her body was awfully happy he was here.

TOMMY SWALLOWED as he looked down at Sarah's averted face. Tension crimped her lips. A rapid pulse beat at her temple. She was like a cornered rabbit, and he'd done that. Made her afraid—perhaps not of violence but of intimacy.

Shame washed over him, and he sighed, taking a step back to give her space but unwilling to turn on his heel and leave. He was here. She needed to get used to his presence, because he was going to be part of her life from here on out. Whether she accepted his vision of the future right now or not.

Something that produced such a strong upwelling of emotion inside him had to be rooted in love. Anything else would make this whole attraction something ugly and desperate.

She stood so still he wondered if she'd ever make the first move to break the tension surrounding them. One of them had to speak first. But what to say?

"You look good, Sarah."

Her brows drew together.

So, she'd said pretty much the same thing to him when he'd cornered her in the parking lot.

"We need to talk."

She gave a sharp shake of her head. "I don't see the need. Not at all."

"I want to court you. Good and proper. I want to make you my wife."

Her breath left in a quick gust. "That's ridiculous. Sayin' it out loud is ridiculous. Who does that? We haven't even dated."

He ignored the snippiness of her voice. He had her rattled. "You won't let me start with a date. So, I thought I'd let you know up front what my intentions are."

She raised her chin. "I don't want to marry you."

"That may be true. And I can understand your fear. But I'm not Paul." Tommy pointed a finger and touched her with the tip, right above her heart. "You were with Blake Morrow tonight. That means you're ready to consider the possibility of marriage. I've waited a long time for you to reconsider. I just never thought it would take you so many years to figure out you don't have to be alone."

Her chest rose around a deep breath. "Tonight was a mistake. I realized it the moment I sat across the table from the man."

Tommy narrowed his eyes. "You realized you made a mistake the moment you saw me with Candy Crowe. That's when it started to fall apart, didn't it?"

She shook her head, but her whiskey-colored eyes had widened for just a second, and he knew he'd guessed right. "Thing is, I know that's true, because I couldn't work up a hard-on thinkin' about what Candy was ready to give me, not until I saw you walk through the door. Once I had her in the room, I couldn't touch her, Sarah, not when the woman I wanted was you."

Sarah's cheeks darkened with a blush. "You should go."

"Not until you agree to give me a chance."

Bright splotches of pink rode her cheeks. "I can't date you. When this doesn't work out—which it won't—everyone will think I'm a fool. I won't be left with my reputation in shreds."

"In shreds because you're steppin' out with me?" His lips twisted. "I guess I deserve that. I've been pretty fast and loose. Sarah, I'm willing to change for you." He lifted a hand, but she shied away. "Are you afraid of me?" he asked, his voice rasping.

Her eyes filled. "No," she whispered. "But I don't want this. I don't want you. Tommy, let go. Please, just let go."

He stood still for a long moment, staring into her eyes, trying to figure out if she really meant it or was trying to be noble for his sake. In the end, he drank in the sight of her dark eyes shining and her nostrils flaring slightly like she was ready to cry but wasn't willing to release her tears.

Tommy's shoulders slumped, and he glanced away, feeling his own eyes fill. He'd been so sure she felt the same as him. But he'd read her all wrong. Shaking his head at his own poor judgment, he met her solemn gaze. "You ever need anything, Sarah…"

She nodded quickly, perhaps sensing he was ready to release her. "Of course. We're neighbors."

"It could have been good between us," he said, his voice gruff. "Sorry I bothered you." He opened the door and let himself out, pausing on the edge of the porch until he heard the door shut firmly behind him.

Then, glancing up at the moon, he cursed the impulse that had led him follow her here. How desperate had he looked? She didn't want him in her life. She'd made that clear so many times over the years. He hadn't paid her any mind, hadn't believed her because he hadn't been willing to accept that this longing was all one-sided.

Feeling like a lead weight had settled in his gut, Tommy headed to his truck. He was done pining for Sarah Colby. But he was also done chasing tail. It was time to get serious about the rest of his life.

CHAPTER 2

The late morning temperature was so hot it shimmered on the horizon. Moisture pooled in Sarah's boots, and trickles of sweat slid between her breasts beneath her thin, long-sleeved T-shirt. But the hot mid-July sun was only partially responsible for the fact she was sweating.

After many stern conversations with herself, Sarah had hoped Tommy Triplehorn was out of her system for good. However, one glance of his shirtless torso as he worked a horse on a rope in a corral, and she knew she suffered a permanent malady. One that kept her awake late into the night all too often, twisting the sheets and exhausting her batteries.

More than a month had passed since she'd rejected him, but time hadn't eased the empty ache inside her one little bit. But then she'd carried this ache since she'd been smitten the first time she'd noticed he was maturing into a handsome young man eight years ago.

Lord, he'd been a beautiful boy—dark hair, long lashes framing an earnest, open gaze. He'd been so willing to please her every time their paths crossed. He'd hired on for a summer to see how other operations ran and to escape his brother Gabe's constant harping. She'd taken advantage of his eagerness and seduced him, knowing what they did was dangerous but driven by a desperate need for affection.

Staring at him now, she admitted he'd far exceeded her expectations of what he'd be like when he finished growing up. He was one of the most deliciously well-made men she'd ever seen in the flesh. And so beyond her reach. He deserved much better than some dried-up widow. Not that she believed for a minute he still held a torch for her. Not after the way she'd shooed him away. He'd had more than a month to lick his bruised feelings and find himself another Candy Crowe. After all, she hadn't given him any hope that waiting would ever change her mind.

No, he had to have moved on. And that was a good thing. She wanted Tommy happy.

Footsteps scraped, and she dragged her gaze from Tommy, meeting Gabe's curious expression as he glanced from her to Tommy and back, before pasting on a polite smile and offering his large, callused hand. "Ms. Colby, what can I do for you today?"

Gabe was good looking too, and more relaxed

then she'd ever seen him. Happiness became him. She'd seen him and his wife, Lena, in town a time or two with their baby girl. An adorable little thing with golden curls. At first glance, he and Lena appeared a little mismatched as he was so much more handsome than she was beautiful. That is, until you noted the happiness that leant a lovely glow to the blonde woman's tanned face.

Now, there was a well-loved woman. That fact alone made her stunning.

Every time she'd seen them together, Sarah had tamped down the biting jealousy. She had only herself to blame for her solitary state.

Sarah shook Gabe's hand then let it quickly drop. Touching hands seemed a more intimate act when she shared it with a Triplehorn. These men were blessed with good genetics and all had a charisma that drew a woman's attention.

Cursing the impulse that had brought her here, she got straight to the point. "I'm going to the auction in Abilene and will be leaving on Sunday for Tuesday's auction. I have about twenty feeder cattle and calves to unload before the drought sets in. My foreman is laid low. He broke his leg a couple of days ago, or he'd be the one goin'. I have to take one of my more experienced hands to help me with the rig."

"What is it you need, Sarah?"

"Someone to check in and make sure things are runnin' well while I'm away."

"Why not leave your experienced hand behind?"

"Like I said, I need help with the rig." She wrinkled her nose. "I've never been comfortable drivin' with a big trailer behind me."

"I can send someone along with you to drive and to help with loadin' and unloadin' the trailer."

Her breath left in a long whoosh. She'd hoped he'd say that. Leaving her own man in charge of her place would give her peace of mind. "I'll pay your hand's expenses. Put him up in the same hotel."

Gabe smiled. "I know you'll treat him right. When do you need help with loadin' the cattle?"

"Oh, I'm sure we can handle that part."

Gabe shook his head. "I'll send him over. When do you want him?"

"Since you insist, Sunday morning before dawn. We've already cut out the cattle for the sale. It'll be an easy thing to run them through a chute and onto the ramp. We'll leave as soon as we're done. I want to be at the auction house to get them off the truck before the worst heat of the day."

"Not a problem. Glad to help." His smile was easy and his gaze steady.

As she left, she kept her gaze off the corral and Tommy, not wanting to let anyone see where her attention wanted to linger, or for Tommy to get the wrong idea. They'd been over before they'd ever truly begun.

She and Tommy ought to be able to move on to being friendly neighbors. When things got rough, it was nice to know folks cared and were willing to pitch in to help. Just like they had after Paul's death.

She shoved the memory aside and stepped up into the cab of her truck. At last, she glanced forward and instantly locked gazes with Tommy, who stood still in the corral with his rope clenched in one hand. His expression was impossible to read, but her heartbeat quickened. She looked away, started the truck, and pulled out of the drive. Only when she entered the highway did she let out the breath she'd been holding.

First time she'd set foot on the Triplehorn in eight years, and she'd survived it. That had to count for something.

Gabe leaned against the fence, staring after Sarah's truck kicking up dust as it drove away.

Tommy put the coiled rope over a post and climbed the fence to drop down beside his brother. "What did she want?"

Gabe's mouth twisted in a wry smile. "You, by the look on her face."

Tommy's mouth tightened. He didn't have a sense of humor where Sarah was concerned. "Must have been important to bring her here."

"Not so much. She wants a man to ride with her to the auction next week."

Tommy nodded. His gut churned. His first

impulse was to blurt out he'd do it, but then he'd be setting himself up for all kinds of hurt.

Not that Gabe would give it a rest. "Needs someone to drive a truck with a trailer," he murmured, "and help with delivering the cattle to the auction house. Said she'd put him up in her hotel."

Tommy heard the teasing note in his brother's voice and wished he'd cut it out. Tommy had confided about Sarah. Told Gabe all about their long-ago affair, and how she'd turned him down flat again. Gabe had encouraged him to forget her and move on. So why was he hinting he wanted him to take the job?

Gabe's lips pursed, and then twitched into a smile. "You could get her out of your system. Once and for all. The way she looked at you, she's ready to let loose. When you both come back, you can get on with your lives. Way I see it, right now, you're both held back by your past and too many regrets."

Tommy angled his head toward his brother. "What if I do it, and all I want is more?"

Gabe's mouth curved into a softer, nostalgic smile. "If it's good after all those years, it ought to tell you both somethin'."

Tommy met his gaze. "You don't think I'm crazy?"

Gabe shook his head. "I'd be the last person on the planet to say you shouldn't go there, Tommy. Look at me. I didn't know I had a son. Wouldn't have mattered how I felt about Lena, because I wasn't gonna let any kid of mine grow up without his daddy. But the first time I had her in my arms again, she just felt right."

"You goin' to the river this weekend?" Tommy asked, referring to Red Hawk Landing, the small summer-camping destination Lena's grandfather owned.

"Yeah, in the morning."

"You're gonna be short-handed here what with Eddie Sandoval and Lane Whitley pitchin' in this summer to help Lena's grandpa at the campground."

"We'll be fine. You go sow some wild oats. You haven't had that kind of fun in a while."

Tommy hadn't been with another woman since the night Sarah turned him down. Hadn't been able to stomach the idea of going back to his wild ways, and he had never found a woman who held his interest for longer than a minute. "I better go pack."

Gabe chuckled. "You've got two days before you leave."

"Need to make sure I have clean clothes so I can take her out to dinner."

His brother's chuckles followed him all the way to the front porch of the house. Although in a hurry, he brushed off his boots on the boot cleaner beside the door before entering. Lena would have his ass if he trailed dirt all over her clean floor.

Inside, the aromas of baked bread and hearty chili made his mouth water.

After Colt had moved into the new addition with

Zuri and little Rose, there'd been more room and a lot less noise. Tommy had moved back into the main house. There was plenty of space, even with the traffic of blended families and shared meals. He'd grown accustomed to being fussed over by the women and had finally let go of the resentment he'd harbored for years against Zuri, Colt's wife.

Lena's grandpa stayed through the winters but was always eager once spring came to get back to the river and prepare for the season. Not that the Triplehorn brothers would let him go alone.

Even after the old man's leg had healed, Gabe sent along two young hands the past two summers to help him with the upkeep of the camping ground. The same two hands, Lane and Eddie, were eager to head back to the river. Everyone knew the real attraction was the pretty office manager, Kayla. The two men had both tried to court her the last three summers, but she had resisted both men's attempts at flirting.

Lena kept house and watched over Jake and the newest Triplehorn, Violet. The women had chosen names of flowers for their girls to honor the brothers' mother, Iris Triplehorn. Something that had made all the men tear up, because their mother would have loved it.

The sound of Violet yammering from her playpen made Tommy soften his footsteps as he passed the living room. No doubt Lena had laid her daughter down for a nap. If she saw him, there was no way little Vi would let him pass.

A floorboard creaked beneath his feet. Vi rolled in her playpen, and her little blonde head perked up. The moment she caught sight of him, her cornflower-blue eyes widened. "Da-da-da-da." She hadn't learned to be specific. All the brothers were *da-da*.

Tommy pressed a finger over her his mouth, glanced toward the kitchen door, and then crept softly toward the playpen. Her chubby arms reached, and he bent to scoop her up. The moment he held her against his chest, she began another round of da-das, this time louder.

"Shhhh, sweetheart," he whispered. "Lena'll have my ass if she knows I didn't let you nap."

"Lena'll have your ass if her daughter learns to *say* ass."

Tommy wrinkled his nose at Vi before glancing sheepishly over his shoulder. "She insisted."

Lena stood with her arms crossed over her bountiful chest. "What is it with you Triplehorns? You can't resist a pretty girl's smile?" But she was grinning and leaned toward Vi's face to shake her head and make baby noises to the happily gurgling infant. She sighed. "Doesn't look tired, does she?"

"'Fraid not."

Her gaze went from her daughter to his face. Her eyebrows drew together as she studied him. "I saw Sarah Colby through the window."

"She stopped to ask for help gettin' cattle to the auction in Abilene."

Lena quirked an eyebrow. "She ask you?"

"No, Gabe told her he'd send someone."

Her eyebrow rose higher. "Gonna spring it on her at the last minute so she can't shut you down?"

Tommy wrinkled his nose. Did everyone know his business? "Something like that. Think it might work?"

"Wear a light-blue shirt and that scrolled leather belt with the big brass buckle. She'll be so befuddled, you'll be halfway to Abilene before she unglues her tongue from the roof of her mouth."

Tommy's eyebrows shot up.

His sister-in-law laughed. "I'm married. Not blind." She held out her arms, and the baby leaned toward her.

Tommy relinquished the infant. He wasn't sure how much Gabe had told Lena, but he really needed a woman's point of view. "Do you think her askin' for help was just an excuse?"

"I'm sure she really does need help, or she wouldn't have gotten off her ass to come over here." Lena waggled her eyebrows. "Bet she's talked herself out of it a dozen times. But I saw through the window the way she tried *not* to look at you. Sarah's interested."

Tommy let out a long breath. "I don't think I can take it if all she wants is one night."

"Have to start somewhere, Tommy," she said,

patting his arm. "Have to get her used to havin' you around, of feelin' your touch. By the time she gets to Abilene, she'll already be wonderin' how she'll stand it when you two come home and part ways."

"Should I romance her?"

Her eyes narrowed as she considered her answer. "She's a hard nut to crack. She might resist if you try somethin' ordinary like plyin' her with flowers. Think happy accidents. Catch her off-guard. If her breath catches, pause. Move closer. See how she reacts." She laughed. "Like I need to give you pointers. I know you and Gabe were both big ol' man-whores."

Tommy tsked. "What are folks gonna say if Vi's first distinct words are ass and man-whore?"

"That she's been spendin' way too much time with the Triplehorn boys."

Tommy tweaked Violet's nose, winked at Lena, and then headed to his bedroom. Not to look at his wardrobe as he'd told Gabe, but to have a few minutes alone to think about Sunday and seeing Sarah up close again.

The last month and a half had been hell. He'd pulled away from his old carousing ways. Spent more time on the ranch, pouring himself into every aspect of the operation. While Colt found his time divided between being sheriff and a rancher, Tommy and Gabe took up the slack. Gabe had rededicated himself to the brand after he'd married Lena, perhaps because he finally had a child to pass his legacy to.

Tommy had always loved the ranch, loved the

hard work. He'd always thought he'd been born in the wrong time, because he couldn't imagine anything more exciting or fulfilling than running a ranch. That Sarah owned a ranch made sense in his life. He'd want a woman who understood the workload. The fact she wasn't any chair-bound rancher herself was something else they had in common.

But she might never see how well-suited they really were, because she couldn't let go of the thought that he was too young. And then there was the memory of what they'd done all those years ago that continued to embarrass her. He understood. She had a strong streak of honor, and the fact she'd strayed right under her husband's nose had to have left her angry and disappointed with herself. And while Tommy had a code he lived by too, he didn't consider what had happened between him and Sarah wrong. Paul hadn't deserved her.

Tommy settled into the chair beside the bedroom window and gazed out at the paddocks and the barn. He heard the voices of the hands and Gabe shouting in the distance, but he didn't really pay them any attention.

In his mind, he was eighteen again and was mad as hell at Gabe. That long-ago summer, Gabe had been coming down hard on him, trying to be the boss after their big brother had signed up for a stint in the Army. Tommy'd had enough of Gabe and had gone to Paul Colby to see if he needed any help.

Paul had hired him for the summer, and Tommy

had moved into the ranch house as opposed to bunking with the hands since they were neighbors. Living there, inside the limestone and cedar house, the first thing Tommy noticed was that Paul was a hard task master with everyone, including his wife. It was one thing for a man to berate a hand for a mistake, but quite another to cuss his wife without a care for who might hear.

Tommy had felt sorry for Sarah Colby but had quickly grown to admire her, because she didn't lose her stride when Paul set into her. She didn't raise her voice but gave him chilly stares and disappeared for long periods, until Paul was spitting nails. No, she didn't hide from him. She ignored him, even knowing there'd be consequences when he got her alone.

Tommy's admiration had grown into something else the more time they spent together, because there wasn't anything about her he didn't like. Her hair was just the right shade of brown blended with fiery strands of copper. Her eyes were a soft, warm whiskey. Her skin was pale, and the few freckles that dotted her nose only made her seem younger. And her body was long and lean and muscled, something he fantasized over when he lay in his bunk at night. No, there wasn't a thing he didn't like about Sarah Colby.

But Tommy had detested Paul. If it hadn't been for Sarah, he'd have quit inside a week. But he'd discovered her bolt hole, the place she liked to escape to when Paul was on a tear. A rocky ledge overlooking the ranch from an escarpment that ran through the northern part of the ranch.

The first time he'd seen her, sitting with her legs dangling over the edge, she hadn't heard him. The wind was up, blowing away the noise he and his horse made. He'd tied his horse off on the branch of a tree and crept quietly up on the boss's wife. There, he'd let himself take a good long look. Something he'd been careful not to do where anyone might see, but he had the luxury that time to admire her long, lean frame and angular jaw. She wore long sleeve T-shirts despite the heat, but he understood the need. She was pale, her skin tending toward freckles, so she was careful to always wear gloves and a hat. She didn't accept any shortcoming in herself, didn't accept any excuses.

"All you gonna do is stare?" she'd asked without turning around.

His face had gotten hot as he'd stepped forward, lowering beside her to glance outward. From this vantage point, he could see all the way to the Triple-horn. "Didn't mean to disturb you, ma'am."

"Sarah. Everyone calls me Sarah."

"Yes, ma'am. Sarah."

Her lips twitched, and she looked his way, her gaze skimming his features. "Well Tommy, you're as handsome as your brothers."

"Thank you, ma'am…Sarah." He blew out a breath. "You're pretty, too."

"You think so, Tommy?" she'd asked softly, and then she shook her head. "Doesn't matter."

They'd sat silently for a long moment, until he felt the need to say something. "I don't like the way he talks to you."

Her back stiffened. "It's not your business."

"I apologize if I'm making you uncomfortable, but a man ought not treat a woman that way."

"I prefer it when he uses words," she said softly.

He'd been young, but he understood in an instant what she meant. "You can't leave him?"

Her mouth stretched. "My folks didn't give me a choice. We're related. Distant relative. We both own equal shares of the ranch. So, neither of us really had a choice. Family always expected us to marry to keep the property from being parceled out."

"Maybe you need to find someone who can take care of you. Someone who could support you if you walked away."

A smile stretched her mouth. "Now, where would I find someone like that?"

"You're a pretty woman. I bet a dozen men would love to call you theirs. Hell, I'd take care of you."

Her smile had slipped, her gaze had bored into his, and she must have seen the truth in his eyes. She'd quickly risen and brushed off the bottom of her jeans. "Now, Tommy, I know you're a good young man, from a good family, and you mean well—"

"I'm not some kid who doesn't know what he wants." The thought had never fully formed in his head, but the moment he'd spoken the words, he'd known they were true. "I want you, Sarah Colby."

Her mouth had dropped open, and he'd been tempted to draw her close and press his mouth against her soft, pillowy lower lip, but she was backing away from him, looking a little alarmed.

"Don't be afraid of me," he'd said and risen. "I just wanted you to know."

She'd nodded and mounted her horse. Without giving him another glance, she'd nudged her horse, and they were away.

His feelings for her had never dimmed. The illicit flirtation they'd entered, though forbidden, was the sweetest thing he'd ever known.

Tommy sat, looking out the window, his body growing tight, his dick and balls growing heavier by the minute, and he gave into the feeling rather than tamping it down.

He leaned back, opened his buckle, and unbuttoned his jeans, lifting to shove them down his hips. Then, with sunlight filtering through the curtains, he took himself in hand, remembering a time when she'd been as hot for him as he was for her. Something that strong couldn't have simply dried up.

Come Sunday, he'd have one last chance to make his case. One last opportunity to lead the widow into temptation.

With his dick hard and warm, he lifted his hand and spit into his palm, then he quickly finished, gasping her name as come striped his shirt and legs.

He'd had enough of jerking off in the shower. Enough of waking up every morning hard and cranky. Sarah would either come to terms with the fact he still wanted her, would always want her, and give him a chance, or he'd have to leave Texas to find any peace of mind.

CHAPTER 3

With a sinking sense of inevitability, Sarah watched the dented brown pickup pull to a halt beside the barn. Hadn't she known all along that he'd be the one to come? She gave her hand a smile and walked over to Tommy who was pulling a duffel from the bed of his truck.

His gaze when he spotted her was steady. Not a hint of what he thought was revealed in his face, but there was a little wariness in his eyes.

He was right to be wary. Part of her wanted to screech at him for being this damn stupid. The other part was...confused. And getting hot. Her core was winding tighter than a spring. Good Lord, they were going to spend three days together—too much temptation for a woman who hadn't had sex in years.

"You sure this isn't a horrible inconvenience?" she asked, her words inane, but she had to say something as her gaze locked reluctantly with his.

"I'm glad I can be of help," he said, his voice as soft as velvet.

She could imagine all kinds of ways he could help. Most of them involved acts illegal in most Southern states. Sweet Jesus, she was already wet. "The boys are lining up the panels. Shouldn't take long to get the cattle loaded."

He placed his hat on his head and lifted his duffle bag. "I'll stow this in the truck and go lend a hand. Leave it to us...ma'am."

Although she was perfectly capable of helping, she was glad to stand aside and watch. Standing away from the ruckus, she felt as though time slowed as Tommy pitched in naturally with her hands, while they lined up panels, dropped the ramp of the truck, and quickly herded the cattle inside.

She blamed the heat for the perspiration dotting her forehead and upper lip. *Doesn't have a thing to do with him*, she thought, lying to herself. Every stretch and flex of muscle turned her on. "I can't do this," she whispered to herself. "I can't. I can't." But she mustered a smile when they finished, allowed Tommy to hand her up into the cab of the truck, and off they went.

Once they passed through the gate and turned onto the highway, she breathed a sigh, having just realized how long she'd held her breath.

"We'll be there before noon," he said. "It'll seem like no time at all."

"I'm not worried about that."

"You're tense. What has you worried?"

She was too tense to make up a story. They might as well talk about the gorilla in the truck cab. She rolled her eyes. "As if you couldn't guess."

His gaze remained on the road ahead of them, but a smile curved up the side of his mouth. "Do I bother you…ma'am?"

"Stop that."

"Stop what?"

"Calling me that."

"Why?"

"You know why." No way was she going to say she remembered how he'd continued to address her like that all those years ago when they'd found themselves in her bed.

"I like calling you ma'am. Like I'm your servant, ready for you to command."

"Tommy…you can't talk that way."

"Why's that?"

"Because this can't go anywhere."

"This?"

She shook her head. "Don't be an ass and pretend you don't understand. This…*attraction*…can't go anywhere."

"So, you admit something's there? Between us?"

"Of course, I do. You know it's true. If I didn't feel it, I wouldn't have hesitated cutting you off cold over a month ago."

"Thought so." He sighed. "Too bad we've got such a long drive."

"Minute ago, you said we'd be there in no time," she muttered.

He aimed a hard glance her way. "That, sweetheart, was before I realized you were horny."

Sarah gasped. "What?"

"I'm not eighteen, ma'am. I'll call it like I see it no matter if it embarrasses you."

"I'm not embarrassed. I'm also not...horny." But her thighs tightened. She hoped like hell he didn't notice.

"And you're lying. If I snuck a hand between your legs right now, I bet I'd find your pussy's wet."

"That's crude."

"I feel crude. Feel damn raw." His hand tightened on the steering wheel. "Truth is, ma'am, I jerked off in the shower this morning just so I could stand bein' in a cab with you all morning, but it's not good enough."

Her jaw fell, something she didn't notice until they hit a pothole, and she bit her tongue. No one had ever said anything like that to her before. Not ever.

And strangely, she wasn't disgusted or enraged. Her imagination took her straight to that shower where this big, raw-boned cowboy had taken his cock into his own hand and masturbated. She knew just the expression he would wear, too.

Realizing her mouth was suddenly dry, she swallowed. "If it's so hard bein' in the same truck with me, why'd you come?"

He tightened his jaw. "I figure I won't get another

shot at this. To show you how it could be with us. I'm offerin' you a no-expectations clause. If things go well this weekend, you'll just have to get over bein' embarrassed about wantin' me. If at the end of it you can honestly tell me you're ready to move on, I promise you, I'll let you go for good."

"One last weekend?"

"Or the start of something real for us."

Out of habit, or perhaps self-preservation, she shook her head, although there was no denying the fact her breaths had just been cut in half. "You're crazy."

"Tell me you haven't been thinkin' about the fact we have the rest of today and all day tomorrow to spend time together alone?"

She pressed her lips together. No way was she going to admit it. Didn't matter she was already jumping ahead to all the nasty things she hoped they'd be doing the minute the hotel room door closed behind them. Putting it into words was just too much stimulation. And he didn't need any more encouragement.

Lord, neither did she. She shifted on her seat and crossed her legs, squeezing her thighs together to calm the throbbing of her sex. When his glance shot down to her swinging foot, he chuckled.

Heat filled her cheeks at her telltale action. She lifted her chin. "You should keep your eyes on the road."

"I have 'em on the road. But it's not quite fair, ma'am. You have the freedom to look your fill o' me. I understand I have to keep a hand on the wheel and my gaze straight ahead to keep you safe, but you could touch me...however you like. Or...I could touch you."

Again, she felt her mouth ease open, but she quickly snapped it shut and angled her body to stare out the passenger-side window rather than catch even a peripheral glimpse of his masculine frame.

But looking away didn't lessen the tension that kept her foot swinging and her pussy hot and swelling. Her nipples prickled, the tips beading and scraping against her lacy bra. She should have worn a sports bra, like she did most every day. Something to keep her nipples mashed and her reactions hidden from knowing gazes.

Who was she fooling? The thought of what he'd suggested—one weekend of hedonistic excess—might just be what she needed to get her fill of lust and perhaps find reminders of why they'd never work. Because the longer she sat in this cab beside him, the harder it got to muster up a good argument against his plan.

"So...you're saying..." she said softly, trying to find words that didn't commit her and didn't cause her to feel too uncomfortably exposed, "if I say we're done at the end of this weekend, you'll honor my wishes?"

His chest billowed around an indrawn breath.

He shot her a gaze, and then faced forward again, readjusting his hold on the steering wheel. "Yes, ma'am."

"Then…" she closed her eyes and took a deep breath, "…I accept the terms."

"Unbuckle your belt and scoot closer."

He hadn't even taken a breath before issuing that command. And she was glad he didn't give her time to think. She unbuckled, slid across the bench seat, and clipped the center belt around her hips.

"Loosen it a little," he rasped.

She pulled on the belt, easing the fit.

"Now, open your pants and ease them down just a little. We're up high. No one's gonna see, but I want to feel. Will you let me?"

Since she hadn't known how she was going to pass the hours in the truck now that they'd struck their devil's bargain, she was eager to comply. Her breaths were shortening, the crotch of her underwear damp.

With shaking hands, she unlatched her belt, then unbuttoned and slid down her zipper. Then she eased down her pants, just far enough there was room, should he want it, to fit his hand between her legs.

She waited as he checked his mirrors, his mouth tipping up at the corners. Slowing the truck a little, he set the cruise control. "Afraid I might gun it if I get too excited," he said, his voice husky.

But he didn't immediately dive into her pants. Instead, he reached around her, laying his hand on her far shoulder and encouraging her with nudges to angle her body so that she leaned into him.

He cupped the base of her neck, his callused fingers touching her pulse then sliding up to cup her jaw and trace her lips.

She eased open her mouth and let him tuck a finger inside, greeting it with a tentative lick. She liked the salty flavor so much she closed her mouth around it and sucked.

His feet shifted on the floorboard, pushing. "Damn, I'll want that mouth on me, ma'am."

She bit his finger then waited until he pulled free. "I'll expect quid pro quo," she said, although she didn't know where the confidence came from to say it. It wasn't like she'd had oral often. In fact, she'd only had it once before. With him. Her pussy gushed at the memory of how she'd pushed his face between her legs, and how eagerly he'd plied her with his tongue and lips.

He gave a terse nod. "Done. It'll be my pleasure."

He dropped his hand to her lap and eased under her shirt, gliding up her tummy and leaving gooseflesh rising in its wake. He cupped her left breast through the lace. "Take care of the clasp."

She unbuttoned the top two buttons of her shirt and unclipped her bra. His hand swept the cups to the side, and he quickly palmed a breast, giving her a gentle squeeze. "Damn, Sarah. I wanna see it." He pinched the tip. "I wanna chew on this, suck it hard. See if I can make you come with just my mouth here."

He twisted the tip and released it, and her breast hardened. She arched her back to press more fully against his hand, encouraging him silently to continue his caresses.

Under her shirt, he pulled his hand away and lightly slapped her nipple.

She gasped. "Why'd you do that?"

"What do you feel?"

"Like I want to slap you right back."

"Where?"

She pictured it, kneeling in front of him, slapping his nipples then clamping her hands over them and squeezing his chest before leaning forward to nibble with her mouth.

"Tell me the truth. It turned you on—the thought of smacking me the same way."

She didn't want to say it. The tips of her breasts were painfully tight. She placed her hand over his still massaging her breast and tugged it lower, sinking her belly and making space, shoving it toward the opening of her pants. "That's where I need to be touched."

"No please?" But he didn't make her wait. He pressed his hand against her lower abdomen and moved to cup her mound and then her folds, his thick middle digit sliding between and thrusting into her wetness.

She wriggled, making a little mewling sound as she settled deeper against his shoulder and tightly closed her eyes. Her mouth fell open as she panted, so excited by his stroking, probing finger she was quivering.

He sighed. "Damn, Sarah."

She clasped his wrist in both hands and curled her hips, taking him deeper.

"I can't wait to fuck you. Wanna come now? Can you fuck my finger, Sarah? You're so wet. Shit." His finger sank, immersed in her juices.

"More," she said. "Another finger, please."

"Want 'em all?"

Her eyelids drifted open to find his gaze on her in the rear mirror. "Don't think I can take that much. Not like this."

"Let's see what we can do. Shove those pants down past your knees, I want you spread."

"This is crazy. We'll both be arrested."

"Only if you make me pull over and do you right now. Give me what I want...ma'am."

Her breath huffed in a choked laugh, but she did as he asked, shoving down her pants, eager for his questing hand to return to her pussy.

When he cupped her between her legs, he tsked. "Shouldn't have waited so long. Bet you wet your jeans right through."

Sarah didn't care if he teased her. She was too desperate for him to enter her again. She parted her legs, leaned hard against his side and opened another button so she could lay open her blouse. If he glanced down, he'd see her breasts and what she was going to do to them.

While he fingered her, his gaze darted to her hands. She cupped her breasts and pulled on the nipples, stretching them and then twisting them. She'd discovered long ago in her own self-play that she liked a painful pinch and tug. There, anyway.

Her eyelids dipped again, and she rolled her head on his shoulder. "Please, Tommy."

"I aim to please," he growled, then thrust three fingers inside her, cupped together, and so thick, they satisfied her need to be filled.

Easing her belt just a little more, she dug her feet into the floorboard and began to pump shallowly, rocking as he swirled and thrust, his clever thumb rasping her burgeoning clit.

"You like that?"

"Don't talk."

He pulled his fingers free and slapped her pussy.

Her eyes shot open. "Do that again," she said urgently.

She opened her legs wider, and he smacked her, fingers cupped to deliver a dull pop. She whimpered and lifted her legs, jeans still clinging to her knees, but she needed to curl herself, get him to thrust his fingers deep inside her, mimic the way it would feel when he crawled on top of her and fucked her with her wrapped around his body. "Now, dammit. I fucking want to come now."

He thrust three inside, reaching deep while she held her breath and strained, feeling the escalating tension and not wanting to let it break.

At last, with his thumb scraping her hard knot, and his fingers making shallow pumping thuds, she came, the sound she uttered not pretty—a tearing, painful yowl that shocked her into stillness.

With his hand patting her pussy, his strong shoulder under her cheek, she rocked herself, thighs closing to hold him.

Her nose ran, and she sniffed. Her tongue swept her upper lip to catch a tear. Glancing up to the mirror she found him watching her.

"Feel better now?" he asked, his voice gentle and soft. "Less cranky?"

Her lips twitched. "I feel...like I want more. But I can wait."

"Better cover up, or I'll be tempted to find the first rest stop and have you right here on the seat."

She blew out a deep breath and eased up to sit beside him, her hands making quick work of her clothing. When she was decent again, she gave him a stare. "I've never been that way with anyone."

"What way is that, sweetheart?"

"Desperate." She let her gaze drop. "I've only ever been that way with you. Like some hot-blooded floozy. I'm just not like that."

"You are with me. That not tell you somethin'?"

She drew her brows together to give him a little scowl. "It tells me you've got skills."

"And I've had years to get better at it, Sarah."

She wrinkled her nose. "I don't want to hear about your women. Heard enough of the gossip over the years."

Tommy grimaced. "Yeah, I wasn't too choosy. Fucked any girl who wagged her tail at me. But all I wanted was you."

"You got a strange way of showin' it."

"I'm a man. I was mad and hurt. Only way I could feel better about the fact I was lonely as hell was by fuckin' someone. A lot of someones. Didn't last longer than it took to roll off the condom, but it was something. I needed arms around me. A soft body under me."

"I get it," she said, a little too loudly. Now, she felt foolish, having let him see the fact she'd been jealous as word of every one of his conquests made its way back to her. She'd heard the sly whispers from the ladies at church.

She unclipped her belt and scooted down the bench.

"Don't." He raised his arm. "Come closer. I promise I'll keep quiet. You can take a nap. Bet you need it."

Her eyes did feel heavy and itchy, and, yes, the invitation to rest against his sturdy body was a delicious gift. If she closed her eyes and pretended to sleep, they wouldn't have to talk.

Pressing her lips together so she didn't shout at him again, she clipped her belt and leaned back, letting him move his hand, belly to breast, in soft, soothing glides.

CHAPTER 4

At the hotel, she surprised him, not bothering with the ruse of two rooms, but getting keys for a single with a king-sized bed. Spots of warm color rode her cheeks, but she handled the arrangement with crisp professionalism.

It had been hours since she'd come apart riding his hand. She'd slept another two, her soft snores making him smile. He'd wondered whether she'd had a hard time sleeping the night before because she'd guessed he would be the one who accompanied her.

At the auction house, they'd unloaded the animals and handled the paperwork. Now they were back at their real destination, the hotel—the afternoon and evening looming.

"Are you hungry? Want lunch?" he asked. "We could hit a restaurant. Get a steak."

"Fortification?"

He raised an eyebrow. "I do plan to expend some calories."

"Might need two steaks," she murmured.

He laughed, surprised she'd made a joke. "Room service then?"

Her warm, brown eyes were luminous and large. She gave him a slow nod, and he felt his cock jerk.

He'd been hard for hours. He just hoped he'd last long enough to bury himself inside her before he came. She'd have to get over the disappointment. He'd do his damndest to make it up to her.

Off the elevator, they walked swiftly, side-by-side to their door, not looking at each other. He held their bags. She fumbled with the magnetic card, sliding it in the lock.

The soft snick made his cock jump again, and Tommy gritted his teeth against his arousal, walking stiffly into the room behind her.

He tossed the bags to the floor. "Get your clothes off," he said, his voice rough.

She didn't face him, but he caught her curt nod. Her hands were already flipping open her belt.

They undressed in seconds, and then stood still for several seconds more as they stared, gazes devouring the other's body.

"Let your hair down," he said, his voice gruff, and his cock lifting between his legs.

She reached back, tugged the band from her hair, and then shook her hair around her shoulders. Thick, dark locks shivered around her head.

"Damn, Sarah. You're so fuckin' hot." He groaned inwardly, wishing he could manage to think of something romantic to say, but his body was hard, and his brain was seizing up right along with it. "Get on the bed. Hurry it up."

"And you're a sweet talker."

"Want pretty words? Gonna have to wait until I come."

"Hurting a little?"

"Been hard for hours."

"I know," she said, one corner of her mouth curling up.

"Witch." He took a step toward her, and her eyes widened, her chest lifting on a gasp.

The moment held as he recognized the hesitation for what it was. He grew still inside. "Stay there." He walked to the bed, flipped the bedspread to the floor, arranged the pillows, and then climbed onto the mattress. He stretched out his body, crossing his hands under his head. He could do this. Give her what she needed most. "I'm all yours. Whatever you want…ma'am."

SARAH'S EYES FILLED. He'd done it so easily. Recognized her fear, even divining what she needed most from him at this crucial moment. Control. Not tie-me-down-and-spank-me control, but freedom to choose how this encounter would flow.

Staring down, she knew it wasn't easy for him to

hold still, to let her be the aggressor. His cock was red and full, rising from his groin. So straight and lovely, she felt her pussy contract as she imagined sliding right down his thick hard rod.

"Hold it up for me," she said, kneeling on the edge of the mattress, sliding up one knee then the other and then crawling right between his spread legs.

He wrapped his large hand around his straining erection. The cap took on a purplish hue.

She halted the moment the backs of her wrists touched his inner thighs. "Pump it."

He growled but complied, moving his hand slowly up and down his shaft, while his jaw hardened and his nostrils flared.

There was a wildness in his eyes, a watchful clarity that made her entire body warm. Like a feral call to mate. Something so elemental she was helpless to resist.

She cupped her breasts and squeezed them, whimpering a little because the tips were engorged and sensitive to the touch. "I've imagined being here. In a bed. With you. I never imagined my mind would get stuck on the picture of you and not know what to do next."

"You know."

"I want it to be good for you."

"Don't think about the other women I've had, Sarah. You aren't gonna disappoint me. It's not possible. The fact you're even here—"

"I want you to fuck me," she blurted, cheeks heating. "But I don't want to feel...trapped. I'm sure I'll get...easier with this, but right now, I need..."

His palm continued to slowly stroke his cock. "To not to feel trapped. I get it. Trust me?" he asked, tenderness in his voice.

She nodded. "I always did."

"I'm not so different now. I'm all grown up—a little bigger—and that has to cause you some alarm. But I'm the same man inside, Sarah. You'll see. Come lie beside me."

She climbed from between his legs and waited while he rolled to his side. Then she eased down beside him, facing him. His cock brushed her belly, and she briefly closed her eyes, liking the warm, soft touch, but her nerves were jangling with alarm.

"Look at me?"

She opened her eyes, her breath catching at his expression. Splotches of bright red rode the blades of his sharp-boned cheeks. His nostrils flared, no doubt catching a waft of her arousal. His pupils nearly devoured his slate-colored irises.

Inside her, the tension transformed from something wary and tight to something lush and sensual. She dipped her knee, which stretched her hip and deepened the indent of her waist, presenting a sexier picture, she was sure, when his gaze swept her curves.

Unwilling to wait for him to make the first move, she plumped her breast, rubbing her thumb over the beaded tip, her eyelids dipping for a second at the sweet curling heat her own touch aroused.

Everything slowed. Her breaths, which grew loud in her ears. Her heartbeats, which thudded against her temples and chest wall. Her pussy clenched, making a lewd, slippery sound, which he didn't miss.

His mouth curved. "You said you wanted to fuck."

"I do. But could we start, face-to-face, like this?"

Smiling softly, Tommy scooted closer until the air between them warmed. He curled his hand over the one still caressing her breast. "Mine," he whispered. And then he scooted down, cupping her hip while his mouth rooted at her nipple.

Sarah gripped his hair with both hands and forced him closer. The lips latching around her were sucking so hard she felt the strong pulls all the way to her pussy.

He slipped a hand between her thighs, and she raised one, slowly sliding it over his torso to open herself to his touch. Fingers sought her entrance, swirled around the opening, and then sank inside. Two. Not enough to stretch her, but enough to coax more fluid down her rippling channel.

His mouth released her nipple, and he slicked his tongue between her breasts, up over her collarbone and under her chin. She bent her head to meet his kiss, sealing her mouth over his, suctioning softly as he slipped his tongue inside to push against the tip of hers. Suddenly desperate, she sucked his tongue inside, pulling hard, wrapping her thigh around him to bring him closer.

Tommy drew back and kissed the front of her shoulder, encircling an arm around her waist to enfold her. "You're as hot as a firecracker, Sarah Colby."

She liked the rasping quality of his voice. Liked the heat of his skin against hers. His fingers continued to play inside her vagina, thrusting and circling, his thumb brushing her clit now and then—a tease that had her toes curling. "If I ask, will you give me what I want?" she asked, her voice deepening with emotion.

"Anything."

Her hands cupped the sides of his face. "Come inside me," she whispered. "*Now.*"

He scooted up her body, a hand on her hip, an arm slipping beneath her to wrap around her back. They lay side-by-side, and she was content inside his embrace, sheltered, protected. So much more intimate an act than she'd ever experienced lying beneath her husband with him rutting and pounding inside her.

Tommy's hand slipped to her thigh, and he urged it over his hip, bringing her closer until his cock was right there, his length pressed between her labia and riding the crest of her mound. He was so large, so heavy...

"Please, Tommy," she groaned.

He drew a short, sharp breath. "Dammit."

Her gaze sharpened on him. "Problem?"

"You're so fucking hot I almost forgot protection." He slid a hand beneath a pillow and pulled out a plastic packet.

"Are you a magician?" she teased, watching as he leaned away to roll the condom down his shaft.

"Put it under there when I flipped back the coverlet. Didn't wanna kill the moment by making a big production. And I wanted to feel you, skin-to-skin before I cloaked."

"If you weren't such a ladies' man, I'd tell you not to bother."

"I'll keep you safe, Sarah. Always." He smoothed the latex down and raised his gaze to hers. "Now, come here."

She drew a deep breath. "Where did we leave off?"

The barest of smiles tipped up the corners of his lips. "You were beggin' me."

"Was I?" she said, touching her tongue to her upper lip.

He picked up the hand she'd laid on his chest and pushed it down between their bodies until he wrapped her fingers around his cock. "It's yours—if you want it bad enough."

Sarah skimmed his length through the latex, wishing she was directly feeling his skin. Her hands weren't small, but her fingertips didn't meet when she enclosed him. Good Lord, he was going to fill her up. "You're a big boy," she murmured.

Tommy grunted, another small smile curving his mouth. "You've told me that before."

Startled, she blinked and met his smoldering gaze. "I did, didn't I? You were hosing off behind the barn after you'd cleaned out the stalls."

"I knew you were watchin'."

"You shoved down your jeans, stripped yourself raw, and then faced me, your eyes closed while all that water streamed down your chest." She gave his cock a pump. "My mouth filled with drool. I'd never seen anyone so well made. Every part of you." She released his cock and slipped her hand lower, cupping his balls. "I don't know how you stuff these into snug jeans." And she wasn't joking. His balls were large, heavy. She could already imagine how they'd feel banging against her once she got the nerve up to let him take her from behind.

"When I opened my eyes, you ran back into the barn."

"Because I shouldn't have been watching. Anyone might have caught us. It was wrong."

"Didn't feel like it. Hottest thing that had ever happened to me, up to that point."

Sarah gripped his shoulders and tightened the thigh she had slung over his hip, coming closer, higher, letting his cock slide from her mound to between her legs. With a pulse of her hips, she rubbed her folds against the broad cap. "Come inside," she said, nuzzling her cheek against his and whispering in his ear.

Tommy slipped a hand between their bodies, found her slit with his fingers and parted her. With a flex of his hips, he pushed his blunt cockhead against her and thrust inside.

Air left her in a whoosh. She was wet but unprepared for the thickness shoving inside her. Still, she leaned her chest against his, clamped her hand on his arm and tensed, waiting for him to sink deeper.

"This really would be easier if you were on top," he murmured in her ear. "You could take your sweet time sinkin' down on me."

"I don't want easy. And I need you to take me, Tommy. I know I get bossy, but it's only because..." She bit her lip to keep from a full confession. She was bossy with him in bed, because it kept her from feeling as though she was submitting. Even if, in fact, she really was.

He slid his fingers into her hair, soothing her scalp and tilting her head to press her cheek against his shoulder. She snuggled as he pumped his hips, pushing on her buttocks and rocking his cock inside her, giving her shallow pulses that got her wet but didn't soothe the ache. "You can take over any time you like," he said, his voice tight.

This was what she'd loved. The fact he let her work her way up to things, earning her trust while getting her so hot she forgot to worry about the fact he was a man and stronger. If she pushed him, he'd give way. Give her room to breathe, always.

Sarah gripped his shoulder, tightened her thigh

around him and rolled backward, tugging on his body until he slowly followed, coming up on his arms to give her space, letting her position herself before he settled his knees between her legs. Still embedded, he wasn't any deeper than he had been.

Sarah knew her eyes were large, her skin a little pale, but he waited, not speaking, letting her call the shots. As hard as he was, and the fact he'd been that way—painfully aroused all afternoon—she appreciated him even more.

She swept her hands over his chest, toggling his spiked little nipples with her fingertips. Then she dove downward, one hand wrapping around the part of him still exposed, ringing him and giving him a squeeze while her other hand slipped beneath his cock, fingers cupping his balls. "You're so big, so powerful, and yet you hold yourself so still when you could easily take me."

"I won't ever hurt you."

"I know that. Not unless I want you to," she said with a brief smile.

"I'm not Paul."

She shook her head. "I don't think about him anymore."

"I still remember. I saw how he was with you."

She closed her eyes. "He wanted you to see. He suspected I was attracted to you. He waited until he was sure you were near. Stripped me naked in the barn, and then held me down while he took me."

"He was rough with you. I could hear it in your

cries. I was ready to kill him," he said, a quiver in his voice. "Had the shovel in my hands."

"I didn't want you to. And it was over quick enough anyway."

"He backed off you, rubbing himself, calling you names. And all I could do was watch from the dark. I never felt less like a man."

Sarah cupped his cheek and rubbed her thumb on his bottom lip. "I wasn't afraid of him. Just didn't like him touching me. But I submitted, knowing if I held still he'd quickly get it over with. I didn't know sex could be anything but distasteful. That I didn't have to feel demeaned."

"He was a jackass," he growled. "After that, I didn't worry about the fact I was messin' around with a married lady. He didn't deserve you. If I could have convinced you to run away with me, I'd have done it for you and never looked back."

She gave him a little smile, remembering the aftermath of that violent episode when her husband stormed out and headed to town to drink. "You were sweet. Helped me find my clothes."

"I gave you my shirt because he tore yours off." He shifted his hips, and his cock sank another inch or two deeper.

She was pinned but not worried about it. "When he went to pick up hay in Oklahoma, I couldn't wait to be with you. All you did was touch me; you used your fingers while we watched each other, and you got me off. It was magical."

"Your expression, the shock that shivered right through you—I felt it all around my fingers."

"My first climax. It was kind of embarrassing, bein' thirty and havin' a boy show me how to touch myself to make me come."

"Didn't realize just what a jerk he'd been until I rubbed your clit. You looked so surprised."

She smiled. "You asked me to let you show me pleasure."

"You scoffed when I offered to pleasure you. Like you thought it was a fairytale."

She ducked her head, but he nudged her with his nose until she met his gaze again.

"No hidin'," he murmured.

Her eyes were wide as she met his gaze. "When we're like this, I forget everything else. Forget why we shouldn't."

"You forget, because this is where we're stripped raw. Honest with each other. I can't hide the fact I want you." His eyes narrowed. "You can't hide the fact you're dyin' for me to fuck you."

"What gave me away?" she asked, liking that he'd given her a chance to get back to teasing, that they could leave the shadow of her husband behind.

His eyebrows waggled. "Your pussy just gave me a squeeze."

She giggled, and then gasped because the action tightened her muscles around him again. "It's okay to come closer now. Swear, I'm ready."

Tommy lowered his hips until they rested against

her. He came down on his elbows, his chest mashing her breasts, but not enough she couldn't breathe.

"I like the way this feels. You're so warm an' heavy. Makes me feel feminine. I don't often feel like a woman."

"You need a man around to remind you how much woman you are, Sarah."

It was true. She did. But could she really allow Tommy to be that man? Didn't he deserve better?

"You're thinkin' too much," he growled. "And now that I'm here, right where I've been dyin' to be, sunk inches deep in your silky pussy, I don't want you thinkin' about anything at all except the orgasm I'm gonna coax out of you."

"I'm ready. Do your worst."

"Worst?" He grunted and arched a brow. Then he bent and nuzzled her ear, while his fingers tugged her hair. He bit her lobe, wresting a gasp from her. His mouth glided over her cheek until he found her mouth. Again, he kissed her, this time taking command, circling, forcing her to follow, thrusting his tongue into her just like she hoped his cock would start doing soon.

And then, at last, he was moving his hips—rocking, driving his cock forward, tunneling through her tender channel.

Sarah bit her lip to keep from crying out, but Tommy leaned down and sucked her lower lip, nipping her as he pulled back again. "Stop it. Don't you dare cheat me. I want everything, Sarah."

So did she. If this was all they had, these few days together, she was going to make the most of it. Her feet were still planted in the mattress, her knees slightly bent, but she wanted to curl again, give him an angle that would allow him to penetrate more deeply. She lifted her legs, hugging the sides of his hips, raising them until she locked her ankles behind him, high on his back.

He drove deeper, more of his length sinking into her. His cock thrust and thrust, pushing through her engorged tissues, building a heated friction, torturing her because the glides were too gentle. She gave his shoulder a glancing bite. "I need more. Harder."

"Tell me."

"I just did."

"Uh-uh. Tell me, ma'am."

Sarah curved her hands around his shoulders and dug her nails into his skin. She bared her teeth, lifting her head to lock gazes with him. "Cowboy, I want your cock so deep I feel the thud of your pubic bone against my clit. I want you poundin' against my pussy, smackin' into me, bouncin me on this bed."

"Like this?" he said, jerking his hips.

Yes, the thrusts were sharper, but she wanted more power. She shook her head. "I want you hammerin' me, Tommy. Like a fuckin' man. Hammer me."

He flashed her a smile, and then pushed up to kneel. He pulled her legs from around his waist and shoved his arms beneath her knees, pulling her hard against him, bouncing her in his rough embrace.

With her hips higher than her head, she lost leverage, able only to watch as he used his arms to pull her into him while his cock thrust toward her core. Over and over, he gave her hard, centered strokes.

She curled her wrists, lifting like a gymnast to arch her back, pushing her chest into the air, then lowering, trying to change the angle her vagina presented, trying to get it just right, because she was getting more and more excited and wanted to rush to the end.

Straightening her legs, she spread them wider, stiffening her knees and curling her toes, straining and gasping, because he was sharpening his thrusts, the lush sounds he made as he hammered her wet pussy as lewd as she imagined a porn flick might be.

She closed her eyes, letting the heat build inside her, the motions of his pistoning hips rocking her forward and back, the impact of his groin against hers, the hottest, sexiest thing she'd felt in....*forever*.

Opening her eyes, she found him staring down, heat smoldering in his glance, sweat dripping from his hair line.

He was young, buff, every muscle pumped and flexing as he worked her body, coaxing her toward a finish she began to fear, because she knew she was going to lose complete control. And then it was there, and her back arched, her head digging into the mattress as he continued to pound her, delivering hard, shortened strokes that quickened like a jackhammer, shaking her body, causing the bed to squeak and her breaths to come in harsh grunts.

But she didn't care. She exploded, a scream ripping from her throat.

She was aware of his shout, and then a ragged, "Fuck, fuck…oh fuck."

She smiled, clasped her breasts for comfort and drew deep, cleansing breaths as the coiling pressure in her belly released completely.

His hips slowed their raucous churning. His cock quivered and pulsed inside her. His breaths moved his shoulders up and down.

They could only stare, caught in the moment. Sharing something so elemental, so deeply wonderful, they both felt it.

What *it* was, she wasn't entirely sure. Maybe love. Maybe relief.

All she knew was she needed to be held against his chest. She lifted her arms, inviting him in, and he lowered her hips and legs, not pulling free but settling onto her with his thighs clamping hers together, trapping his cock inside her pussy and closed thighs. Slowly, he settled again, onto his elbows, but with his face snuggled into the corner of her neck.

Sarah could breathe, but every inhalation brought the scent of sex and his lovely musk. She felt surrounded but secure. Cherished. She glided her hands up and down his back, her fingertips lightly scratching him. At last, his breaths slowed and deepened. Sarah yawned.

His head drew back sharply. "Tired or bored?"

She raised a brow. "You really think I could be bored right this minute?"

"Want to order in some food or take a bath and go out?"

"Would you mind if we went out?"

"Need a little space?"

"Maybe." She shrugged. "A little fresh air." She bumped his ass with her heels. "A chance to stretch my legs."

"I might find it hard to keep my distance."

Sarah scratched a nail down his cheek. "I don't want distance, Tommy. I think I'd like you to hold my hand."

CHAPTER 5

Tommy took her at her word, not letting her put much space between them. Arm's length was too much. They'd showered together, managing to not let lust overtake them again. They'd dressed in the room, watching each other out of the corners of their eyes.

He'd wondered if she was as fascinated with his every move as he was with hers. Watching her don a bra had been the sexiest sight ever. It was a lacy thing with the clasp between her breasts. She slid it onto her arms like he donned his shirt, and then quickly pulled the cups over her small round mounds and clipped it closed. But then she'd slid a hand into one cup, moving her breast to fill it, and then repeated the process with the other breast, until both cups swelled. He hoped she'd let him put her bra on for her just once this weekend.

When she'd glanced up, a question in her eyes,

he'd adjusted himself, cupping his burgeoning erection and grimacing because his pants were too tight.

They left the hotel to drive to a place they both knew well, an upscale steakhouse with a pricey menu but a spacious dining room that allowed for quiet, private conversation. It was early evening, but the hot sun was still punishing.

Sarah wore a black sleeveless dress that hugged her lithe curves. He wore a dress shirt and slacks and dark, highly polished boots. He'd left his cowboy hat behind. Beneath her approving stare, he was glad he'd made the effort to look like he belonged beside her. They'd unpinned the trailer, and he was driving the truck, giving her sideways glances, because he simply couldn't stop looking.

Sarah Colby was going on a date with him. The world would look at them and know they were together, because they both wore very well-satisfied expressions, had relaxed bodies, and shared soft intimate smiles.

He'd love to have this every day, knowing other men looked at her and coveted the tall, strong woman beside him. So, she had a few wrinkles beside her eyes and lining her forehead. So fucking what.

"You keep staring," she said, tucking a strand of brown hair behind her ear.

Her makeup was light, barely there, enhancing rather than covering her pale skin. Strawberry gloss was on her lips. At his insistence, she'd worn her hair down. She'd styled it, complaining she never took the time. But she'd packed a blow-dryer and a flat iron, so she must have planned to primp.

The thought made his smile stretch.

She glared from beneath her dark lashes. "Stop looking like that or everyone will know what we've been doing."

Tommy snagged her hand from her lap and squeezed it. "Sugar, it won't be my smile that telegraphs that fact. You have the look."

"What look?"

"The look of a thoroughly ravished woman."

She chuckled. "Ravished, huh? Not sure what that looks like."

Tommy laughed while he pulled into the restaurant parking lot. "Don't jump down the moment we stop. Let me be a gentleman."

"Tommy Triplehorn, that's exactly what you are."

He liked the soft inflection of her voice, the Texas lilt that sang along the words, emphasized perhaps because, for once, she was relaxed and comfortable with him. Most often, she spoke in short sentences. Her words clipped and her mouth crimped. He liked that he'd given her this night. A chance to be a woman, not a rancher.

He parked the truck and hurried around the vehicle to open her door. Then he gave her a hand, loving the way she gracefully stepped down, her pale nude legs ending in strappy sandals that climbed onto the rail then stepped to the ground.

The heels raised her until the top of her head was level with his mouth. He liked that she was tall. Liked that he only had to bend his head to lay a kiss on her cheek, which he did right at that moment. *Build memories*, he thought, aching a little but still too excited to heed any advice about protecting himself from the devil on his shoulder.

She didn't jerk away, simply pursed her lips and shook her head. But the sparkle in her eyes said she'd liked it.

Inside the restaurant, they were led to a booth in a corner. Maybe the waitress guessed they'd like to sit side-by-side, a chance for their thighs to touch or his hand to rest on her bare leg. The blonde's smiling eyes teased as she took their order.

"Not so hard, was it?" he said under his breath as he unfolded the linen napkin on Sarah's place setting and laid it in her lap.

"What?" she asked a little breathily because his fingers trailed too slowly away.

"It's not so hard bein' seen in public with your boy toy, now is it?"

She gave a soft feminine snort. Her gaze swept the room. "No one even raised an eyebrow. I'm thirty-eight to your twenty-six. I expected at least a 'you go, girl'."

"Know why they aren't wonderin' what I'm doin' with you?" he said, tipping her chin toward him.

She shook her head.

He leaned close. "It's because all they see is a beautiful woman with a man who knows he's lucky to be by her side."

"I shouldn't care what people think," she said, curling her hand around the napkin in her lap. "I don't about most things."

"You're sensitive because of the way we first hooked up. You've been carryin' around a lot of guilt. Misplaced guilt."

"I seduced a high-school boy."

He grimaced. "I was eighteen, not twelve. And I'd already had my share of sexual partners. You seem to forget who did the seducin'."

"Well, maybe that was mutual." She pressed her lips together and glanced up at him from beneath her lashes. "I left the bathroom door ajar on purpose."

His lips twitched. "Really? And there I thought I was just damn lucky."

"Uh-uh," she said, leaning against him to whisper. "I wanted you to see me naked. I used my vibrator after that, thinkin' about how fast your breaths had come as you watched from the shadows."

"And here I thought you didn't know I was there. Of course, everything slowed. I felt frozen in place, and my cock got so hard it was stranglin' in my jeans." He leaned close to her ear. "I've jerked off to that memory for years."

Her hand brushed his leg and slid in between,

touching the length held by his trousers against his thigh.

His cock twitched and swelled. "Careful," he whispered.

"No one can see."

He liked the fact she felt easy enough with him to tease. "I'll have to walk out of this place," he muttered.

"You can always grab a menu."

"We could always hit the restroom...together," he growled.

Her eyes widened, and Tommy grinned.

"I'm not going to win this one, am I?" she said, arching a dark brow.

"Not when I'm ready and willin' to call any bluff."

A throat cleared. The waitress was back. They both ordered steaks, although his was much larger and smothered in mushrooms. She ordered a side salad. He had potatoes and a side of green beans. They ordered red wine and sat enjoying the quiet and each other's company. When their food came, they both groaned over the flavors.

"Sex always makes food taste so much better," he said.

"I'll take your word for it," she murmured.

Tommy cleared his throat and set down his fork. He thought she might be ready to play. "I have something for you."

She lowered her fork. "A gift?"

"I hope you'll think of it that way."

Her eyes narrowed. "What is it?"

He reached into his pants pocket and brought out a small velvet pouch, which he slipped into her hand. "Take it into the restroom with you. Go now."

Her hand clenched around it, and she must have guessed what it was by the shape because her jaw sagged. "You expect—"

"I expect nothing. If it pleases you, put it inside you. I have the remote."

"You want me to use this, here?" Her eyebrows lowered, but excitement shone in her eyes.

"It's our secret. No one will know."

"And when my pussy hums?" she whispered, her eyes glaring.

"No one will hear it. Promise. It's got a quiet motor." He waggled his eyebrows. "Go."

Tommy watched the expressions crossing her face, shock and then grudging curiosity. When her cheeks filled with color, he knew he had her.

She scooted out of the curved bench and walked sedately toward the corridor, a little more sway to her hips than usual.

Tommy chuckled, wondering how quickly they could finish their meals, or whether he would let her *finish* right here in the restaurant, with no one the wiser.

The thought swelled his cock, and he adjusted himself. Yeah, he was gonna need a big damn menu.

SITTING IN A STALL, her lacy panties around her ankles, Sarah shook the small oval vibrator from the velvet drawstring bag. It was metal and cool to the touch. The thought of slipping it inside herself when the inner walls of her pussy were still hot from their earlier play made her shiver.

She knew what it was—and how good it could feel. Heat filled her cheeks when she thought about the fact she'd walked around with one inside her several times back home, when she'd thought about sex and been frustrated over the fact she was always doing it alone. Some of that frustration had been assuaged by the act of pleasuring herself while she went about her daily chores in the company of men she knew and liked. The thought that one of them might discover what she was doing had only added to the excitement.

Which meant she understood exactly what Tommy was up to. He wanted her climbing the walls, ready to come at his command, whenever he decided.

She wondered if he intended for her to come while they sat at their table. The thought had her pussy clenching, and she quickly inserted device into her vagina.

When she stood, she bent to pull up her panties, but decided she'd add another element of naughtiness. Now, she'd have to pay full attention to the metal egg and hold it inside herself with the grip of her inner muscles. If she didn't, it would drop straight to the floor.

Then she decided to take it a step farther and reached under her dress, pulling her arms inside and quickly stripping off her bra. Would he notice?

Crumpling up her bra and panties, she stuffed both into her clutch. She exited the stall, washed her hands, and then left the restroom to walk slowly toward Tommy, who sat leaning back against the leather squabs, his stormy gaze giving her a long sweep, locking on the movement of her hips, and then the bounce of her unfettered breasts.

She couldn't help the extra sway. With the vibrator snug inside her channel, she felt sexier. Slutty, even. Not that she minded. With Tommy, she felt free to explore her naughty instincts. Sliding into the booth required extra attention, and she didn't breathe easy until she leaned against his side.

"Ready?" he said, nuzzling into her hair and whispering right into her ear.

She gave a little nod, and then gasped as the vibrator erupted immediately, sending shivers throughout her lower body. She dug her fingers into his thigh.

"Shall I take it down a notch?"

She nodded a little wildly then closed her eyes when the egg's raucous rattle slowed, settling into a smoother groove, one that aroused a pleasant, subtle heat inside her.

He sucked on her ear lobe and gave her a spicy bite. "Raise your skirt so your bottom's right on the leather. Don't want you leaving a wet spot on that pretty dress."

"But—"

"You took off your panties, right?"

Her cheek bumped his as she pulled away to stare. "How'd you know?"

His mouth twitched. "I knew you couldn't help raisin' the bar."

Sarah blinked. Not in a million years before today would she have imagined she'd act on that impulse. Did he know her better than she did herself? "You're a bad influence. You make me want to be scandalous."

"And I'm eager to lead you into sin."

They finished their meals, or at least Tommy did. After several bites of hers, she gave up, enjoying the warmth the wine and her new toy spread throughout her body. Luxuriant arousal kept her nipples tight and pressing against her dress. Time and again, she moved her arms to graze the tips, plumping them, presenting them to Tommy in a sultry, subtle tease.

"Your tits are pretty, Sarah," he murmured. "So pretty there's not a man here who hasn't noticed them."

She glanced down, indeed the nubs were prominent, even the outlines of her areolas showed through the thin fabric.

"Know what I really want?" he whispered.

She shook her head.

"I wanna sit you on the table in front of me and suck on your puffy nipples. Then I want to eat you out."

And she'd have let him. Even saying it, the picture was there in her mind, of her with her skirt hiked up to her waist, the straps of her dress down her arms, and her nipples exposed. And she wouldn't have cared who watched so long as his mouth got busy.

Heat pooled right between her legs, and a gush of fluid wet the seat beneath her. "We'll need another napkin," she murmured.

"You can have mine," he said, sliding his napkin across his lap to hers, then tucking it between her legs. "Seeing as you're finished with your meal, do you want to move on to dessert?"

"I couldn't eat another bite."

"Not talkin' about food, sweetheart."

The gentle vibrations increased in speed and strength. Sarah mewed and leaned back against her seat, opening her legs beneath the table, the air wafting against her hot flesh providing added stimulation.

"Keep that up, and I'm gonna come," she said, her eyelids drifting downward.

"I'll keep eating. Let me watch."

"I don't know if I can keep quiet," she said, gritting out the words as the vibrator hummed, seeming to roll side-to-side inside her. Was the squeeze of her inner muscles making it rock?

"Don't keep quiet. I don't care who hears you."

Her eyes widened, and she cast a desperate glance around the room. Other patrons seemed not to notice—except for one man who sat at a table not far from theirs. She thought he glanced her way but wasn't sure. And now she suspected he watched from the corner of his eye.

"Do you mind?" Tommy asked quietly.

"Mind what?" she said, gasping and squirming.

"Havin' him watch you come?"

She didn't answer, because her response would be damning. The thought of a stranger watching her orgasm ratcheted up the excitement building between her legs.

Tommy cut a piece of steak and forked it into his mouth before setting down his knife. Then he dropped his hand to her thigh. Fingers stroked her wet cunt. "Come for me, Sarah. Let him see."

Her breasts were hardening, the tips lewdly exposed beneath the sleek black fabric, but she didn't care, arching her back and pushing them out, and then grinding down on the fingers cleverly delving between her folds.

The egg pulsed hard, rattling right through her. Her breaths were jagged, rasping, she put her hands down on the seat and lifted her bottom to rock ever so slightly, raising the thigh next to his so she could hook it over his knee and open herself wider.

"Thank God for the tablecloth," she gasped.

His chuckle was husky. "Look at him, sweetheart."

She glanced toward the man who was looking straight at her now and dropping his hand to his lap.

Their gazes locked. He was handsome. Blond, with a scar that bit into his mouth. He wore a fancy plaid cowboy shirt with snap buttons. Arousal darkened his cheeks, and his gaze slipped to Tommy, a brow arching.

She didn't dare look at her date, waiting for the other man's gaze to return, and then the vibrator erupted, and Tommy's fingers plunged. Right there, where anyone might see, she let her head fall back and issued a groan as she came.

When she slowly blinked open her eyes, Tommy tucked her into his side and continued to eat, acting as though it was the most natural thing in the world to get his girl off, and then resume his meal.

She cast a glance toward the other man. He was rising from his chair. He gave her a nod, and touched the brim of his imaginary cowboy hat as he met Tommy's gaze and left.

Tommy patted her thigh. "Was that good for you?" he asked around a bite of pink meat, not looking her way.

"Did you know that man?"

"If I did?"

"Did you plan this?"

He glanced toward her, eyebrows raised. "How could I?"

"Do you know him?" she asked more insistently, because shock was settling in.

Tommy chewed another bite of steak and, then glanced down his gaze sweeping her expression. "I do. We've shared women."

Her breath caught as she realized the rumors had been true. "And you didn't mind bein' in the same bed with another man?"

"The woman was between us. Her pleasure was why we shared."

"Oh." She glanced away, because her cheeks were flaming hot.

A finger dug under her chin and lifted her face. "Sarah?"

She pressed her lips together. Good Lord, she hoped he couldn't read her mind.

He traced her bottom lip with his finger. "Would you like to know what that's like? Bein' shared?"

"I'm not sure," she said truthfully. "I trust you, but I don't know whether I could extend that same trust to a stranger."

He bent until his mouth hovered just above hers. "Does it make you wet—thinkin' about it?"

Sarah swallowed, staring at his lips, then reluctantly raising her gaze. She nodded.

A smile stretched. "I'll be right back. Have to talk to a friend about a favor."

Her eyes widened. "*Tommy*. Are you gonna chase him down in the parking lot?"

"He's likely waiting right outside to see if I'll invite him."

"You two have this all worked out—signals or something?"

Tommy clicked his tongue. "You let him watch you come. He figures you're into threesomes."

When Tommy left, adjusting himself, she sat back in her chair, careful not to meet anyone's gaze as she let it sink in that she was going to allow Tommy Triplehorn to arrange one of his naughty ménages.

Oh, she'd heard about him and Gabe. And now there was this other mystery man. Thank God he wasn't from Destiny, or she'd die of embarrassment. So many years of celibacy, and she was really a slut at heart.

Not that she was ashamed. But it was surprising —this state of euphoric arousal that engulfed her whenever she was in Tommy Triplehorn's presence. Things she'd never have considered before, watching him jerk off behind the barn, letting him watch her bathe, bending over a counter without any underwear on so he could view her femininity... She'd done all that.

Never before. Never again since. Only with him.

Tommy came back inside the dining room, stopping their waitress and handing her a wad of cash. Then he strode toward Sarah, reaching down to grab her clutch purse and help her up.

He bent toward her. "Remember, don't drop the vibrator."

Concentrating, she clamped her pussy around it and let him lead her out the door.

Thankfully, the gentleman wasn't waiting outside. Who else might have guessed what they were up to if he had been? By Tommy's tight jaw and heightened color, she knew the game was on.

CHAPTER 6

There was freedom in letting go. Letting a partner plan her adventure. She'd trust Tommy to let his friend know about the things that would stop her cold. She trusted the other man was safe and discreet.

Precisely a minute after she and Tommy let themselves into their room, a soft rap sounded on the door, and Tommy let the man inside.

She stood mute. Like a doll. The vibrator still snuggly held inside her. Arousal dripped down her thighs.

"Good to see you, Tommy," he said, his voice pleasantly deep.

"Nice to see you again, Karl. Here for the auction?"

They talked like they might have in the restaurant, politely, but all the while they were stripping. Methodically. Neatly folding their clothes and placing them atop the dresser, while she stood and stared, comparing their physiques.

She'd only seen one other man naked, her husband Paul, and he'd been tall and burly. Frightening really. Tommy was a large man but lean. His friend Karl was a little shorter, perhaps only an inch taller than she was, but his frame was nicely muscled and buff.

When he dropped his trousers, she must have made a sound because he glanced over at her and grinned. "It's got a bit of a kink."

Indeed, it did. His cock curved gently upward like a spoon. How he'd managed to keep an erection that size hidden in his pants was a mystery.

She dragged her gaze reluctantly to Tommy who stood nude with his arms crossed over his chest. "Should I be worried?" he asked.

She shook her head, and then laughed. "I, um, this is..." She waved a hand. "Sorry, this is new to me."

"So, Tommy said..." Karl began, humor glinting in his blue eyes. "No restraints. No crowding, he said. Anything else you'd like me to know?"

Since he'd been so blunt, she nodded. "Only he gets to fuck this pussy."

Karl's mouth stretched wide. "I can see why you're so hot for her." His gaze trailed down her body. "Don't suppose since this will be our one and only time that you'll let me do the honors..."

Sarah gave Tommy a glance. He gave her a nod

and a little smile. With his permission, she turned her back and held up her hair, giving Karl access to her zipper. And then she remembered the fact she wasn't wearing a stitch of underwear underneath, and her breath caught.

Silk slid downward, snagged briefly on the flare of her hips then pooled at her feet.

She held still. Karl circled her, his gaze raking her body. When he slowly lifted a hand, she didn't flinch or jerk away, accepting his touch. He slid his fingers under a breast and lifted it, and then bent and drew her nipple into his mouth.

Without so much as a warning, they'd begun.

Turning her head, she met Tommy's smoldering gaze. His hand was on his cock, stroking himself. He looked content to watch, interest burning in his eyes with perhaps a hint of challenge.

Taking her cue from him, she cupped Karl's head and pulled him closer, inviting him to deepen the caress of his lips and tongue. She could be wanton. Tommy wouldn't mind a bit.

When a hand trailed in the moisture leaking down her thighs, she widened her stance, giving Karl access. She tossed back her hair and opened her mouth to drag in deep breaths as he skimmed upward, sliding his fingers into her folds where he swirled and stroked.

"It's okay to finger fuck her," Tommy said, nearer than before.

She jerked. She hadn't noticed he'd come up beside her.

"First, this has to go." Holding her gaze, Karl thrust his fingers inside her and snagged the vibrator. When he pulled it out, he held it up for Tommy to take. "Nice, very little noise."

Sarah's lips were pursed, and she was breathing in short, ragged streams. The moment his fingers had entered her, she'd risen on her toes.

"You okay?" he asked, cuddling her sex.

Karl was so relaxed about it, his eyes brimming with amusement, he left her bemused. She gave a quick nod.

He smiled. "Where were we?"

With a breathy laugh, she said, "I think, Tommy gave you permission to finger fuck me."

"Right." He chuckled and slowly went down to his knees.

Tommy slid in behind her, his cock riding the cleft between her cheeks and his hands cuddling her breasts.

"Got her?" Karl asked.

Tommy snaked his arm around her middle and held her against his chest, while Karl lifted one of her legs and draped it over his shoulder.

"Better," Karl growled.

Sarah stared straight ahead until the black of her sandal caught her eye. She was nude, standing between two men, and she still wore her black heels.

How thoroughly decadent. How unlike the Sarah Colby she thought she knew.

She wasn't shocked, wasn't dismayed or ashamed. Her body was on fire. Her mind riding a high. She'd never felt this free. This alive. She turned her head to rub her cheek against Tommy's shoulder. "Thank you."

"No thanks required. I expect to be rewarded for being this generous."

"I'll let you do anything you want. Give you anything."

"Don't say it if you don't mean it, Sarah."

Rather than rushing to affirm her promise, she bit her lip. What if he wanted forever?

Karl followed a trail of sticky arousal up her thigh with his tongue, and then licked along the seam between her thigh and her engorged labia.

She was done with the teasing. She forked her fingers and drew up her folds, exposing her clit.

Karl leaned back. "Do you want something, sweetheart?"

"Do you need diagrams?"

"No, sugar, just direction."

His wicked arching brows made her laugh. "I want you to suck it."

"My pleasure." He bent toward her, latching his lips around her clit to draw hard.

Again, she rose on her toes, the leg she stood on quivering while she dug her fingers into his shoulders.

Tommy pinched her nipples.

"I'll come like this," she warned.

"Is that the way you want it?"

She shook her head. "No. I want..." She bit her bottom lip. She'd been bold up to this point but to ask for *that*...

"Show us," Tommy whispered.

Hands dropped away. The men stood back. Maybe they were surprised when she didn't crawl immediately onto the bed, but they didn't make a sound when she bent to reach for a pillow on the bed and dropped it in front of her. She knelt then pointed at two spots on the floor. "I want you here."

She watched as both men dragged in deep breaths that swelled their broad chests. They stood close, their sides nearly touching as she glanced from one rigid cock to the other. Then she gripped both shafts, pointed the heads at her cheeks and glazed her skin with dribbles of pre-ejaculate, turning her head to give openmouthed caresses to each blunt, fat head.

Both men were wonderfully made, generously endowed. Her grip couldn't encompass either's girth. She let go, spit into both palms, then wrapped her hands around them again, beginning to pump her hands, squeezing firmly as she'd been taught by her husband, twisting slightly. Unlike her experiences giving her husband blowjobs, she wanted this and had all the control. No hands forced her head over a straining cock. No fingers pulled her hair when she failed to do what they desired.

With choices to make and instinct to follow, she turned toward Tommy's cock first and locked her lips around him, letting the moisture in her mouth wet him thoroughly, and sinking over him to take him deep. The ridge surrounding his satiny cap grazed her tongue. The blunt mushroom cap butted against the back of her throat. Taking a breath and easing open her jaw, she took him deeper still, pushing forward to take him right down her throat.

His tortured groan drew fierce satisfaction. When he tangled his fingers in her hair, they didn't pull her into position, they petted, showing her his pleasure.

But she had another man waiting, so while she pumped her hand on Tommy's slick cock, she turned to Karl and took him deep, bobbing and suctioning, unlocking her jaw and inviting his shallow thrusts, gurgling a little as he filled her. She continued working them, turning side-to-side, moaning to herself over the delicious treat.

"Sarah," Tommy cupped his hand over the one she used to stroke him, stopping her. "Not like this. I want to be inside you when I come. And you're not nearly ready."

"Ready for what?" she asked, then glided her open mouth down one side of his dick.

"For us."

She hadn't thought about what this was going to be like. She hadn't thought beyond this moment. If she had, she might have envisioned each man taking his turn with her. But when both men drew her up, Karl bending to kiss her mouth and saying a polite thank you, and then both leading her between them to the bed—only then did she realize she'd be having sex with them both. At the same time.

"How does this even work?" she asked, her voice oddly throaty.

"Don't you worry," Tommy said. "We'll do all the thinking. You just enjoy."

"I don't want to just lie there and let you both pleasure me. I want to be involved."

"So you keep some control?"

She nodded, lifting her chin.

"All right," Tommy said, approval glinting in his eyes. "Kneel at the edge of the bed."

How awkward would that be? Both men would be able to look right up her pussy, see her ass.

Tommy narrowed his eyes. "Don't you trust me?"

"This is embarrassing."

Tommy grunted. "You're naked. You came in the middle of a restaurant, and now you're embarrassed because Karl is going to stare at your lovely ass?"

"I have a little cellulite," she muttered, stalling.

Karl grinned. "Where? You're just about the most fit woman I've ever seen. Must spend lots of time in the saddle."

"Well, hell. Can I take off the shoes?" Both men's expressions fell, so shaking her head, she crawled onto the mattress, gripping the coverlet for balance.

Her knees were on the mattress, but her feet were not. Her ass was high, her shoulders low.

Behind her, she heard the stretch and snap of latex. Then hands, she wasn't sure whose, widened her stance.

Another cupped her sex. "Very nice," Karl said, nearly purring. "When will you shave her?"

She gasped. She'd never considered such a thing. That was for movie stars and strippers.

Another hand smoothed over her bottom, a thumb dragging down the center, pausing alarmingly on her tiny rosette.

"Also not something you can fuck," Tommy murmured.

Karl laughed. "Leaves only one thing." A caress glided over her behind followed by a light slap. "I've never seen Tommy so territorial. He likes you."

At his tone, at once teasing and questioning, she smiled. That was one thing she didn't doubt. Tommy liked her. Probably loved her. How did she feel about him?

"Guys..." she whined and then grimaced as they chuckled.

Lips lapped at her pussy, and she couldn't stop the involuntary clenching. A face nuzzled into her sex—nose, mouth, and chin gliding in her moisture. She didn't know whether to be grossed out or aroused, but the finger tapping her clit had her attention narrowing to the tiny bud. It swelled, hardening, and she felt the tightening in her core. They could do whatever they wanted. So long as they touched her there. Her knees were widened again.

"Just the right height now," Tommy said. Fingers spread her labia and a hot blunt cock pushed between her folds, sinking only an inch or two. "Your turn, Karl."

Karl walked around the bed and sat on the mattress. He swung up his legs and crawled toward her on his knees. When he was right in front of her, he raised his brows. "I'm going to fuck your mouth until I come. You okay with that?"

She licked her lips.

"Guess you are. I'll have to hold your head in place while I stroke. You gonna be okay with that?"

She nodded, and he pulled her hair to the side, bunching it in one hand, and then cupping her skull and gently bringing her closer. She opened her mouth, taking him inside, then waited as he pumped, adjusting his stance to center himself. As her jaw eased, he stroked deeper, and she angled her head to accommodate his girth, breathing through her nose.

The moment he began to pump in earnest, so did Tommy.

"Do you like this, Sarah, being fucked in front and from behind?" Tommy asked, his voice deep and raspy. "I won't allow this often. Don't think my heart could stand it. But I'll give you anything you want. Whatever pleasures you. So long as you're mine."

She heard what he said but couldn't think, not stuffed with big pulsing cocks.

Her pussy was soaked. Each time Tommy drove deep, she felt the squelch, heard the lewd moist sounds they made. Spit was leaking from her mouth as Karl continued shafting her.

On her knees, her hands fisted in the covers, all she could do was take what both men gave—and then it hit her.

She was being restrained, pinned in place—but she didn't care. She couldn't work up a good gasp or quiver of horror. Tommy was the reason. She'd always trusted him with her pleasure, had always known he wouldn't hurt or demean her.

Even letting his friend fuck her mouth somehow didn't feel tawdry. She felt gifted, lucky beyond belief. And then there wasn't time to think at all.

Tommy slammed against her buttocks, his big cock cramming inside and his heavy balls thudding against her clit with each hard, straight thrust.

The cock in her mouth was pulsing, expanding. Karl's breaths were getting shorter.

She couldn't resist the urge—she peeled off his condom. She had to feel his hot skin against her lips, lick him up and down, nothing between them. His fingers pulled her hair, holding her back. Tommy paused his strokes behind her.

"You safe?" she asked, her voice thick.

"Yeah, baby." His gaze shot up and past her. Tommy must have nodded, because Karl thumbed open her jaw and stroked back inside her mouth. "I'm gonna come in your mouth," he said, his voice tight. "You okay with that?"

She nodded her head around his cock, suctioning harder, letting him know she was okay.

A groan sounded, and then thick scalding spurts squirted down her throat. She swallowed down his come, and then used her lips and tongue to clean him up, groaning as she swallowed down the sticky, salty fluid.

Tommy's fingers bit into her ass, holding her still while he hammered faster, his huge cock taking up all her space, crowding her walls, heating her up with luscious friction.

Sucking softly at Karl's cock, she moaned around him as another thrust from Tommy pushed her over the edge. She gasped then closed her lips again, arched her back and clenched her pussy around the cock reaming her from behind. Glorious waves of ecstasy washed over. She'd never had anything approaching this before, this free-falling delight.

When the motions slowed behind her, she let go of Karl's cock, glancing up and then laughing at Karl's admiring expression.

"I've never had a woman suck me quite like that. Like I was a pacifier or something."

She grinned and wiped her mouth with the back of one hand, balancing because Tommy was draped over her, still embedded inside her while his penis pulsed, flooding his condom.

"I've never come with a man in my mouth and

another in my pussy," she said huskily. "So, we're even, I think."

Karl bent toward her face, kissed her mouth with a lusty slant of lips, and then quickly left the bed. She didn't watch him dress because Tommy was climbing up behind her, shoving her knees forward, keeping his cock inside her as he climbed onto the bed and fell over her body.

"Anytime, bro," Karl called out, chuckling as he let himself out of the room because neither of them could muster a reply.

Tommy nuzzled his face into the corner of her neck. "Did you like that?"

"You killed me. And I think I'll be blushing for a week."

"Blushing because you're humiliated or because you liked it too much?"

"You make me crazy, you do know that? I should be all kinds of ashamed."

His arms surrounded her, hugging her against his belly. "But you're not."

"No, I'm satisfied like I've never been before. Not because I had another man, Tommy, but because you trust me. You have to or you wouldn't let another man near me." She drew a shaky breath. "You know, don't you?"

"That I'm your one and only, where it matters, in your heart?"

He said it so hopefully, she couldn't deny him an answer. She nodded. "Yeah, something like that."

He gave her another squeeze. A kiss pressed against the top of her shoulder. "Let's sleep."

"You're twelve years younger than me," she said, smiling. "I should be the one ready to fall into a coma."

"You exhaust me. You'd damn near kill a man your own age."

She chuckled and let him move again, turning them on their sides and spooning her, his slackening cock still warm inside her. She could get used to this. Not the threesomes. That would be just plain greedy. But she could get used to falling asleep in Tommy's arms.

CHAPTER 7

The time in Abilene had been so perfect that it was shocking to Tommy when Sarah never called him.

August stretched, hotter than hell. Everywhere trees and grass were brown, burned. Tempers flared. None more than his. And he knew the cause.

Disappointment was a bitter pill. He ached inside, wondering what he'd done wrong. In the end, he finally figured out that she'd always intended the weekend to be a chance to work him out of her system for good.

"I'm gonna leave," he said at the dinner table one night.

Silence followed his pronouncement. Zuri scowled at Colt, likely wanting him to fix the problem.

Lena's expression was solemn, her eyes moist.

Gabe cussed and tossed his napkin on the table. "Enough. Just go to her. Tell her how you feel."

"She knows how I feel."

"You tell her you love her?"

"I don't know. Maybe not in so many words, but there's no way she can't know."

Lena reached out and placed her hand over his. "She's a woman who doesn't trust in men. The longer you failed to pick up the phone and call her, the more time she had to worry about all the reasons she thinks you won't ever work."

Tommy rubbed his hands over his face. "Well, maybe she's right."

Lena frowned. "Don't be an idiot. How'd it feel when you had her to yourself? When she was in your arms?"

Tommy glanced away, because his eyes burned. He'd felt like he'd come home. She was everything he'd ever wanted, and he'd been sure, bone-deep certain, that she'd felt exactly the same way.

Colt cleared his throat, drawing all eyes. "You deserve an explanation. Face-to-face. Don't wait for her to come to you." His face was shuttered, hard to read.

Tommy wondered what he really thought about all this. "She's worried about the difference in our ages."

"She might be worried about something else, too."

Tommy frowned. "What are you talking about?"

Colt sighed. "Something Paul mentioned before he died. Part of his excuse for always gettin' drunk. She can't bear children."

Tommy's stomach dropped. His breath left in a long whoosh. He'd always thought he'd be a dad.

Colt's jaw tightened, and his glance fell to his little girl, happily chasing peas around the tray of her high chair. "Be sure. If you approach her, you be sure that's something you won't blame her for on down the road."

Tommy nodded, and then shoved up from the table. "Sorry, Zuri. Guess I'm not so hungry."

He strode out of the room, slamming his hands against the door harder than he'd intended, but the loud crash and the sting of his palms felt good. He'd been stewing for weeks, hoping for a fight, but no one had accommodated him, instead steering clear of him altogether. He'd been in his truck half a dozen times, pointing toward her ranch, only to pull to the side of the road and beat up his steering wheel because he was so damn frustrated and confused.

Outside on the porch, he played with his keys, flipping them around a finger as he watched the sun dip behind live oaks, glowing orange through the dark branches.

"He's right, you know," Gabe said behind him. "You can't leave it like this, bro. If you still love her, you need to try."

"What about children?" Tommy said, squeezing his eyes shut as the pain flooded him.

"I can't imagine not havin' mine in my life. But just 'cause she can't carry them, doesn't mean there aren't other ways."

"If I adopt, a child that isn't Triplehorn blood will inherit my part of the ranch."

"Any child you bring here will be family. Don't think for a minute we won't accept him or her. Question is, did Colt just give you a good enough excuse to let her go?"

Tommy bent his head. "I've loved her since that summer. Every woman I ever spent time with couldn't measure up. The fact she can't have kids—it hurts, but only 'cause I know it causes her pain."

Gabe grunted. "Yeah, sounds like a Triplehorn. I don't think it's in our genes to love more than once." He clapped a hand on Tommy's shoulder. "What's it gonna be, Tommy? You gonna keep gettin' more surly and mean, or are you gonna take a chance? See whether you've been wastin' time moonin' around here?"

The breath Tommy blew out billowed his cheeks. He closed his fist around his keys. "I won't be back tonight. I'll either be with her or gettin' shit-faced in Destiny."

"I won't keep the lights on."

Sarah heard the slamming of a vehicle door in the distance and wondered who it might be coming this late at night.

When she opened her front door and stepped out onto the porch, her eyes widened on the figure stomping through her grass. "Tommy?"

He didn't answer. Didn't even appear to be looking at her. His head was down, the brim of his hat hiding his face, but the clenched fists were telling.

Her heart stopped, and then sluggishly began thudding in her chest. She backed up toward her door, reaching behind her for the knob.

Tommy stomped up the steps, his boots slamming against the wood, until he stood in front of her, gazing down with his storm-cloud eyes. "You didn't call," he said, his voice gruff.

Tommy angry was different from Paul Colby in a snit. Something she shouldn't have to remind herself about. She let go of the knob and leaned back against the wood, staring up into the face she'd dreamed about every night when she'd laid in her bed alone. "You didn't call," she said softly, repeating his words.

Moisture filled his eyes, and he glanced away blinking. "It was your choice. It was always your choice. Either you accepted me, or you used that weekend to get me out of your system. I waited for your call."

Sarah dropped her head, wanting to hide her face so he couldn't see her expression, couldn't guess what a coward she'd been. He'd been so proud of her that weekend, loving the fact she'd let go of her fears and inhibitions. But the moment she'd come back home, she'd been assailed with doubts.

Destiny wasn't Abilene. People knew them both. And there was the fact she hadn't been completely honest with him about the baggage she'd bring into their marriage. The fact she was barren.

"I was afraid," she whispered. "Afraid that I wouldn't be strong enough to tell you, or if I told you that you would brush away the truth like it didn't matter, when I know it will."

Tommy stepped closer, so close his boots touched hers and his chest crowded against her breasts. When he looked down, the intensity of his stare nearly shredded her resolve. She wanted nothing more than to melt against him, cling to him. She wanted him to carry her inside and tear the clothes from her body. She wanted him deep inside her, her body wrapped around him while he plunged toward her center, baring her heart.

"I can't give you children," she said, tears blinding her. "I can't get pregnant—not without a lot of medical intervention, and even then…"

"Doesn't matter," he said gruffly, pressing closer, his hands landing on the sandstone wall behind her.

She smacked his shoulders and shoved against him. "Of course, it matters!" she cried brokenly. "It matters," she whispered, then slid down, only to be propped up by the thigh he pushed between her legs.

"You're out of excuses," he whispered.

"Excuses?" She dashed away her tears with the back of a hand.

"Yeah, never heard such whinin'—too old, barren—you make it sound like all you have to offer a man is your cunt and your womb."

She gasped. "What did you just say?"

"You heard me, Sarah Colby. I'm not buyin' it. Your little pity party has cost me nearly a month of lost sleep. My dick's raw from me rubbin' on it, because I can't get you out of my head."

Sarah could hardly breathe. Her stomach felt cramped, her chest ached. And there, right between her legs, she felt the telltale pulse of her heartbeat. She stared up at Tommy, at the ruddy splotches of color on his cheeks, at the deep emotion clouding up his eyes, and she couldn't bear it another second. Something inside her snapped, and then eased. Everything became clear. Crystal clear.

"I love you, Tommy Triplehorn," she whispered. She scrunched the front of his shirt in her fist and tapped his chest. "And I don't care about the fact some folks might give us a second look because you're so damn perfect and I'm…not. But I'm not lettin' you go. You're mine."

His brows drew together, and his chest heaved as he sucked in the deepest breath.

"How long you been holding that?" she teased.

"Since you looked at me like I'd run over your cat. Like I was gonna throw you away because you can't get pregnant. Seriously, Sarah? Did you think so little of me?"

She gave him a watery smile. "Paul was gonna. It's why he was in such a tear to get drunk. He was givin' up his dream of ownin' all the ranch, because he just had to spread his damn seed. He was gonna divorce me. Only he died drivin' home before he could."

Tommy bent his head, and the brim of his hat slid over the top of her head. "That's the last time you mention his name. The last time you measure my responses against him. The man was a bastard. I'm not."

"I know you're not. I wouldn't love you if you were."

His eyes closed. "Say it again."

"I love you."

His forehead melted against hers, and his hat slid to the side and fell to the porch. "We're marryin'."

"Yes."

"I didn't ask."

She bit the inside of her mouth to keep from smiling, because she didn't want to stop him from talking. The way he growled at her, and the way he was shaking, she knew he was still mad as hell. For the first time in her adult life, she reveled in the fact she could make a man that damn mad.

"I'm gonna spank your ass, Sarah. I'm gonna have to lay hands on you."

"I deserve it."

"And after I do, I might just have to fuck you for a month because that's how long I've been hurtin'."

She jutted her hips, rubbing the large, hardening knot at the front of his jeans. "Guess I'll have to resign myself to walkin' funny for a while, seein' as how I owe you."

His eyes narrowed, and his gaze fell to her lips.

She couldn't help the fact a smile was tugging at her mouth.

"You laughin' at me?" he growled.

"I wouldn't dare."

"You let me do you here against the wall?"

Her eyes widened. The porch light was burning. Any of her hands might see if they stepped out of the bunkhouse or the barn. "I'll let you do me here. Now. I'll give you anything."

He slammed his mouth over hers and grabbed her ass, lifting her.

She wrapped her legs around his waist, her arms around his shoulders, and surrendered herself to his kiss. He ground his mouth against hers, teeth clicking together until he gentled, tilting his head to align his nose with hers, then suctioning to seal their mouths. Their tongues probed and danced, much like she guessed their bodies would be doing in a very short while.

When he lifted his mouth, she nipped his chin. "You really want to fuck me in front of God and everyone?"

He shook his head. "I don't want to let you go."

"You're gonna have to if you wanna get my pants off."

A growl rumbled through him. "Reach behind you and open that door."

She grinned, twisting the knob and waiting as he clumsily used his foot to widen the door far enough for them to get through. And then he left the door wide open as he stomped through her house. They made it as far as the living room. There he let go of her ass and let her slide her legs down to stand.

Then he was bending, lifting her feet to tug off her boots, which he sent flying, his hands undoing her belt and jeans and jerking them down her hips so fast she didn't have a chance to step out of them before he whipped her around and pushed her to drape over the back of the couch.

He smoothed a hand over her rump and then pulled away. A sharp slap landed, the sound startling, the sting invigorating.

But she needed to protest. It was her feminine duty. "That hurt!" she said, mustering a pale anger to infuse into her voice.

Another slap landed, and he bent and pulled her jeans the rest of the way off. Another slap and another followed, and now she was squirming, her ass on fire and fluid trickling down one thigh. "Tommy, please."

"Don't know if I can stop," he said gliding his hand over her bottom. "Your skin's on fire."

"I deserve it, I do," she said. Without glancing back, she bent farther over the couch and widened the space between her thighs. "I need spankin', bad."

Laughter gusted behind her. Not soft chuckles but loud gusting chortles.

She gave him a scowl over her shoulder. So

maybe her plea had sounded a little cheesy. "It's not nice to laugh."

"Baby," he said, still laughing. He bent and kissed her bottom. "If you want your pussy slapped, I'll oblige."

"I don't want my pussy slapped," she grumbled, her cheeks hot because she'd really tried for sexy, not side-splitting.

He cupped her sex, and then drew his fingers away. She held her breath. When it came, the slap was delicious. Painful and sharp. And oh so wet.

"Again," she said, her voice straining.

He popped her, and she wriggled. He cupped her again, but then something else, not his hand, butted against her. When had he gotten his pants down?

His cock pushed between her folds, sinking deep.

"I'm not through givin' you smacks, baby."

"And I'm not sorry. You're just gonna have to bang me 'til I am." She said it with a smile on her face, knowing that if she looked in a mirror at that precise moment, she'd see a woman whose eyes were just a little wild and whose face was blushing with happiness.

Young, strong Tommy gripped her hips and pulled her back, guiding her onto his cock, leaving her unbalanced and dependent on his grip while he thrust into her again and again. His hips jarred her, his groin slapping her butt, his heavy balls thudding against her clit. Eventually, Sarah shouted and begged, cussed and cried, telling him how much she loved him and how badly she'd missed him with every ragged, gusting complaint.

Only when she came did she go silent. Quivering shoulders to toes, so weak she'd have fallen if he didn't hold her tight, which he did at the end when he pumped hard, erupting inside her with a shout that had to have been heard all the way to the bunkhouse.

"Think they'll come running to see if I killed you?" he said, kissing her neck.

"They can come running. They can damn well sell tickets. You're not movin'," she said, reaching back to rub his cheek.

Tommy kissed her palm. "Not married yet, and you're already bossy."

Sarah turned her head. His mouth was there, slanting across hers. "I love you," she said when he drew away.

"I know." His grin was wide and very self-satisfied, but she'd let him have his little moment. He'd earned it.

EPILOGUE

Sarah awoke with the sunlight streaming across the bed. She held her hand up to shield her eyes then glanced quickly to the clock on the nightstand.

Eight o'clock. She'd overslept again. She tossed back the covers and swung her legs over the side of the bed, swaying slightly because, suddenly, she felt a little dizzy and nausea threatened to overcome her.

The bedroom door opened, and she pulled up the covers to hide her nudity until she saw it was Tommy who strode inside and closed the door behind him.

Lord, she didn't think she'd ever get used to how handsome he was, or how quickly just the sight of him made her tingle inside.

But his expression this morning was a little disturbing, and she wasn't sure why. A frown drew his eyebrows together, but his gaze was raking her. He looked wary, but there was something else.

"You should have woken me," she said, frowning at him. "It's the third time this week you've snuck out without bothering to get me up. Your family's gonna think marriage made me lazy."

"I didn't sneak out. You were sleepin' like the dead." He flashed her a smile. "Must have worn you out last night."

She blushed. "You are not the cause of this. I must be sick. Or maybe my age is catchin' up to me."

Tommy blew out a breath. "Or maybe it's something else. Will you humor me?"

"What is it?"

Tommy settled on the edge of the mattress next to her. His gaze studied her expression. "I talked to Lena. She gave me something. Said you have all the signs."

"Is it bad?"

Tommy sighed and reached into his back pocket then brought forward a white and blue stick.

She glanced down at the wand and grew still. Her eyes filled. "You know that's not possible."

"Not probable. I know. You're not very fertile. But let's just rule this out."

She was afraid to take the wand. Afraid she'd hope too much. "I don't want to do this."

Tommy leaned toward her and cupped her face between his hands. "You know I love you, right? No matter what?"

She nodded. She no longer had any doubts about

that. Not after Tommy had planned and paid for one of the biggest weddings the town had ever seen. She'd been mortified by the expense and fuss, but understood in her heart just how important it had been to Tommy to make a big splash the moment she walked down the church aisle.

He'd been showing her just how much she meant to him. Just how perfect he believed she was. He had wanted a fairytale wedding for his queen. He'd even had her wear a tiara.

"All right," she said, her gaze locking with his. "But after you see I'm not pregnant, I really do think I need to see a doctor."

"Okay." He helped her up and led her to the bathroom.

At the door, she glanced up. "I can handle this alone."

"Why should you?"

So, despite the embarrassment, she sat on the toilet, held the wand between her legs and let loose a stream. When she finished, he handed her a wad of tissue and reached for the wand.

They traded. She took care of herself, washed her hands, then closed the toilet seat lid and took a seat on top of it while he set the wand on the counter, checking his watch and sitting on the edge of the tub.

"How long do we have to wait?" she asked, her stomach beginning to knot with nerves.

"Three minutes."

"How will we know?"

"If there's only one line you're not pregnant. If there's two, we'll still make that appointment."

She didn't know why she was so nervous. Her knee bumped up and down. "I should get dressed," she said when his gaze swept her frame.

"Don't bother. Whichever way it goes, I'm makin' love to you."

Her eyes filled. "Don't know what's makin' me such a baby," she said, wiping her eyes with her fingertips.

Tommy reached across the space between them. She placed her hand inside his, grateful he knew she needed reassurance.

After another long pause, he turned her wrists to glance at his watch. "It's time." He pulled her up and kissed her forehead. "Ready?"

Sarah held her breath and closed her eyes, steeling herself for disappointment. Her life was as near to perfect as it could be. Even though she had a house on her own ranch that they could have moved into, his family wouldn't hear of it, insisting they take the main house at the Triplehorn ranch. Gabe's cabin had been finished just before the wedding. Everyone had pitched in to help her move.

She'd never known what she'd been missing until she was welcomed into the Triplehorn clan with open arms.

A kiss pressed against her mouth. "I can look for you," he said softly.

She opened her eyes and shook her head. "I may

be whiny, but I'm not a coward." Together, they bent over the wand lying on the shiny counter.

Her heart stopped. She sucked in a breath. "All right, but these things can be wrong, right?"

"It's more likely to get a false negative than a false positive, or so Lena says."

Her eyes grew wide, and she straightened. The room swirled around her.

TOMMY CAUGHT her before she hit the counter or the floor.

He picked her up, carried her to the bed, and tucked in the covers. Then he chafed her wrists, because he didn't know what else to do. At last, her eyes blinked open.

"Well?" came a muffled voice from the hallway.

Tommy rolled his eyes. Had Lena been listening with her ear pressed against the door the whole time? He walked softly to the door and swung it open.

Two, not one, sisters-in-law straightened from where they'd crouched with their ears against the door. "Do your husbands know you're snoops?"

"Come on, Tommy," Zuri said. "Tell us."

"I think I'll let her do the honors," he said, glancing toward the bed where Sarah was shrugging into her nightgown behind the sheet she held against her chest. When she was finished, she bounced out of the bed and ran straight to Zuri and Lena.

The look on her face gave them their answer.

Zuri and Lena shrieked, and the three women jumped up and down, laughing and crying.

Somehow, he didn't think he'd get a chance to make good on his promise to make love to her. Two more figures appeared in the doorway—Colt, who frowned at the noise the women were making, and Gabe whose smile stretched wide.

Gabe slung his arm across his shoulders. "Knew you had it in you, bro."

"It's a damn miracle," Tommy said, still shaken inside.

Colt cleared his throat. "It's gonna get damn noisy around here."

"We can start our own zip code," Gabe said, his gaze on the women who were now giving each other tearful hugs.

Colt clapped a hand on Tommy's shoulder then another on Gabe's. He drew both brothers in for a hug.

Tommy's eyes burned as the three shared a rare embrace. He'd never imagined his life would be this perfect. That he and his brothers would find happiness with the women who'd stolen their hearts when they'd all been so young.

Across the room, despite the happy chatter from Lena and Zuri promising to share baby clothes and bassinets, Sarah's gaze met his. There was so much joy in her face, his heart ached. He'd have moved heaven and earth for her. He was grateful to his bones that he'd given her the one thing she wanted most.

I love you, he mouthed.

I love you more.

No, there would never be a more perfect moment.

∽

ALSO BY DELILAH DEVLIN

Montana Bounty Hunters: Dead Horse, MT

Cage (#1)

In the Wild (short story)

Preacher (#2)

Hardman (#3)

Chase (#4)

Cowboy (#5)

Eli (#6)

Gabriel (#7)

Mica (#8)

Jackson (#9)

Montana Bounty Hunters

Reaper (#1)

Dagger (#2)

Reaper's Ride (#3)

Cochise (#4)

Hook (#5)

Wolf (#6)

Animal (#7)

S*x on the Beach (related)

Big Sky Wedding

Quincy (#8)

Brian (#9)

We Are Dead Horse, MT

Cold Hard Cash (#1)

Hard Knox (#2)

New Orleans Nights

Hot SEAL, New Orleans Nights (Prequel)

One Hot Night (#1)

Uncharted SEALs

Watch Over Me (#1)

Her Next Breath (#2)

Through Her Eyes (#3)

Dream of Me (#4)

Baby, It's You (#5)

Before We Kiss (#6)

Between a SEAL and a Hard Place (#7)

Heart of a SEAL (#8)

Hard SEAL to Love (#9)

Big Sky SEAL (#10)

Head Over SEAL (#11)

SEAL Escort (#12)

Texas Cowboys

Wearing His Brand (#1)

The Cowboys and the Widow (#2)

Soldier Boy (#3)

Bound & Determined (#4)

Slow Rider (#5)

Night Watch (#6)

Cowboys on the Edge

Wet Down

Controlled Burn

Cain's Law

Flashpoint

Lawless

Triplehorn Brand

Laying Down the Law (#1)

In Too Deep (#2)

A Long, Hot Summer (#3)

Night Fall

Sm{B}itten (#1)

Truly, Madly...Deadly (#2)

Knight in Transition (#3)

Wolf in Plain Sight (#4)

Knight Edition (#5)
Night Fall on Dark Mountain (#6)
Frannie and the Private Dick (#7)
Sweet Succubus (#8)
Truly, Madly…Werely (#9)
Bad to the Bone (#10)
Long Howl Good Night (#11)
First Knight (#12)
Big Bad Wolf (#13)

Texas Billionaires Club

Tarzan & Janine (#1)
Something To Talk About (#2)
Who's Your Daddy (#3)
Love & War (#4)

∽

Some Standalone Stories

Brotherhood Protectors: Gunn's Mission
Brotherhood Protectors: Guarding Hannah
Brotherhood Protectors: Victoria's Six
Brotherhood Protectors: Defending Evangeline
Hot SEAL, In His Memory
Hot SEAL, Decoy Bride

Begging For It

Hot Blooded

Raw Silk

Warrior's Conquest

Rogues

Enslaved by the Viking Short Story

Conquests

Smokin' Hot Firemen

ABOUT DELILAH DEVLIN

Delilah Devlin is a *New York Times* and *USA TODAY* bestselling author with a reputation for writing deliciously edgy stories with complex characters. She has published over two hundred stories in multiple genres and lengths, and she has been published by Atria/Strebor, Avon, Berkley, Black Lace, Cleis Press, Ellora's Cave, Entangled, Grand Central, Harlequin Spice, HarperCollins: Mischief, Kensington, Mountlake Romance, Running Press, and Samhain Publishing.

You can find Delilah all over the web:
WEBSITE
BLOG
TWITTER
FACEBOOK FAN PAGE
PINTEREST

Subscribe to her newsletter **so you don't miss a thing!**
Or email her at: delilah@delilahdevlin.com

Printed in Great Britain
by Amazon